Jake kept his hand firmly over Nora's mouth as he half-dragged, half-carried her down the hall, then down the stairs toward the front door.

He was quite certain she aimed one or two most unladylike kicks at his shins as he hustled her away and he was equally sure the words being spat against his palm were nowhere near fit for a drawing room tea.

"If you raise your voice I'll haul you right out to the woods and leave you there," he warned when he finally got her, squirming and writhing, out onto the relative safety of the porch.

She struggled against him as he debated whether to release her fully or just allow her the use of her mouth. Enticingly round parts of her decidedly female anatomy moved against him in a manner he was quite certain she would not have continued had she any awareness of the seductive havoc she was wreaking on his body and his patience.

He gritted his teeth and smothered a groan. The faint scent of honeysuckle swam in the night air. It was definitely time to either let go of her or suggest they find a more secluded spot. Before his inclinations got the better of him, he released her.

"I hate you, Jake Warren," she said with her pent-up fury.

THE
DARLING

Elizabeth Keys

ZEBRA BOOKS
Kensington Publishing Corp.
http://www.kensingtonbooks.com

Prologue

Boston, Massachusetts
Spring, 1859

"We're agreed, then?"

"We'll not cower before their demands."

"We'll support one another as we face the future on our terms."

The whispered affirmations slid along All Saints rectory's soft cream walls and polished floors. Determination echoed back from the confines of the all but empty parlor, far more serious than the laughing acceptance of an hour before. Then the full complement of Boston's prized young misses had sounded their agreement to the unorthodox defiance and promptly burst into giggles.

Now it was just three of them, each acknowledging their individual need for the revolution about to sweep them away from the accepted course for young women of their stations.

Their hands gripped together, slender and white, as their wide-eyed gazes met and held. Aquamarine, ice blue, and smoked amber filled with hope and sparked with uncertainty as to just what they were undertaking.

The cream of Boston society: Two of them patterned on the very finest and governed by parents determined to have them marry equally as well as the generations before them. And the third possessed a likewise determined parent, propelled for different reasons along the same course.

The vow, spoken first amidst the remnants of their weekly meeting, echoed for these last three. A boisterous challenge, a battle cry for the unlikeliest of warriors, the Brookline Daughters of Grace, known more for their elite ranks than for the actual charitable work they sponsored. The vow was spoken when yet another of their number tearfully fell victim to dread expectations.

We shall no longer bow to the dictates of others, but seize our destinies with our own hands.

"But where do we start?" Lenore's tentative question opened the gates of doubt for all three of them as a shiver traced first one back and then the others. Tall and slender, a golden-haired vision, she was the youngest, the one who had struggled the hardest to mold herself to the expectations of her family.

"Where indeed?" Amelia's sleek dark curls bobbed ever so slightly as she spoke in a dry tone. "It is all well and good to wish to save ourselves from the foibles of our parents, but without a serious idea of where to start, a journey can never begin."

"We must begin at the beginning. One step at a time." Tori said the obvious with more force and conviction than she generally showed in their weekly company. As the rector's daughter, she was normally quiet and reserved, acting as their hostess, but speaking only when spoken to.

Amelia arched an elegant eyebrow. Despite the recent tarnishing of her family's Mayflower reputation,

Amelia wore her imposing poise and refinement like a favorite set of gloves.

"We must change our surroundings. Our circumstances. New habits in new places." Amelia rose from the settee. Muted pink linen skirts swirled in gracious circles around her ankles as she walked across the room. Her move to the parlor windows allowed the sunlight to glisten on her ebony hair as she pulled back the lace curtains.

"The auction is in two weeks. I shall detest seeking shelter at my aunt's in the Berkshires like some poor relation." Her chin rose a degree as Amelia turned to pace back to the others. "When Helena's new fiancé offered to rescue me with an alliance a fortnight ago I, turned him down flat. I could never marry a man of his advanced age."

Lenore shuddered her agreement. "He wheezes just walking from the front door to his coach."

Amelia quelled any further encroachments on her discourse with a raised eyebrow. "I cannot imagine what persuaded the silly goose to bow to her parents wishes when she knows full well his affections are not even engaged and she is terrified of him."

"He is quite wealthy and respected in the community. I can only imagine that her parents believe this is what's best for her." Tori offered the cold comfort of conventional rationale.

"Then her parents are blind." Amelia was not about to reveal that the alliance Charles Fitzsimmons had offered her the day after news of her brother's financial scandal broke was that of his mistress, not his bride.

"How can we begin a journey if we do not know where we are heading?" A defeated sigh edged the simple truth behind Lenore's question and brought them all back to the matters at hand.

"You could answer an advertisement in *The Herald*." Tori offered. Humor laced her tone, but certainty underlaid it. "No one would expect such a course from any of us."

Lenore gasped. "An advertisement?"

One couldn't get much more common than that. But indeed it would be unexpected. A step fully in the opposite direction of everything the three of them had done in their lives up to this point.

That was the foundation of their newborn decision, after all.

Amelia shot Tori a glance. "You are full of surprises this afternoon, Victoria. You should display backbone more often. I like you better this way."

"Thank you." Tori's lips rose in a wry smile, her sea blue eyes sparkling with heady mix of mischief and decision.

"An advertisement." Amelia's voice was firm as she sat once more on the settee. "Any idea to free me from my current predicament is worth investigating."

Lenore swallowed audibly.

"And what of you, Victoria?" Amelia examined Tori's animated features beneath their auburn crown with an interest she'd never before displayed.

"I have a few ideas of my own. There are any number of opportunities that cross a rector's desk." Tori answered with enough aplomb to stop any further questions from Amelia.

"What do you think, Nora?" Tori turned a compassionate gaze on the obviously overwhelmed younger woman.

Lenore all but jumped at the shortening of her name. She cast Tori the cold glance that had for so long effectively stopped others from using the old pet name.

"Very well. *Lenore.*" Tori stopped just short of rolling her eyes. "What will you do?"

"Go somewhere else." Lenore offered, trying hard to imitate Amelia's coolness. "It hardly makes sense to start a journey if one has no plans to travel beyond the city's confines. Things worked out well for my sister when she went to Maine, perhaps I can convince Mama and Papa that it is time for me to visit Grandmother."

Tori eyed her for a moment longer before accepting the answer. "Very well. But I think we should stay in touch. By letter. That way if one of us is in trouble. . . ."

She left the sentence dangling.

"Agreed." Amelia spoke quickly, as if unwilling to let the thought go any further.

"Agreed." Lenore echoed.

Their hands met again, just as the parlor doors burst open.

"Come along, Lenore, don't dawdle." Alberta Brownley barked the command with no regard to who might hear her. She had definitely been out of sorts this past month or more.

"Good luck." Tori squeezed Lenore's hand and Lenore squeezed back.

"Same to you."

"Don't forget to write." Amelia winked, standing at Tori's side.

"And you." Lenore answered as she hurried out the door in her mother's wake, wondering just how she was going to perform the impossible task she had just agreed to.

We shall no longer bow to the dictates of others, but seize our destinies with our own hands.

If only she could.

One

Ancient pine and oak boughs creaked overhead, their leaves cackling mockery even over the jingles and groans of the coach as it jostled the last few miles toward the Maine coast.

Lenore Eugenia Brownley caught herself patting the sleek twists of her chignon to make certain no hair was out of place and sighed. Like so much else familiar to her, the empty gesture belonged to another life. Fleeting images of pastel and lace teagowns and the distant chink of fine silver teaspoons on even finer saucers in the rectory parlor at Brookline's All Saints Church whipped through her thoughts, seeming so much farther away than the actual physical distance of this journey.

She laced her primly gloved fingers together to prevent further useless fussing and banish the wave of homesickness that threatened to overtake her.

"As if anyone in the wilds of Maine really cares about appearances." She spoke her thoughts aloud.

"Beg your pardon, Miss Lenore." Her maid, Jenna Watson sitting on the opposite side of the coach, answered her without turning her head from the passing view. "I was so busy admiring the scenery I did not quite hear you. It's been so long since the family journeyed to your grandmama's I'd nearly forgotten how impressive the trees are and how fresh the air smells so far from the city."

She took a chest-swelling breath as if to emphasize her feelings and closed her eyes before letting the air out on a long, satisfied sigh.

The further they got from Boston the less formal and more talkative the maid became, Lenore had noted more than once without displeasure. She'd been glad of Jenna's company when the maid left her perch atop the coach after their stop for lunch to join her in the Brownley coach's elegantly appointed interior. She'd taken on this trip as a means to seek a new direction for her life, only to discover that being left alone with her own scattered thoughts and indecision was tedious beyond belief.

Lenore allowed her own glance to wander the towering forest surrounding them. Jenna was right. There was something indefinable here. Ageless existence? Primordial wisdom? Something that brooked little of the modern age's transitory artifice, the very illusions she veiled herself with in an effort to be exactly what her parents wanted. Somehow all the effort she exerted along that path seemed inconsequential in the midst of these ancient evergreens and tall-standing oaks. Surely they spurned the fears and uncertainties of one young refugee from Boston society.

"Miss Lenore?" Jenna fixed Lenore with an appraising look. "Are you feeling quite well? You seem a trifle out of sorts and have been ever so quiet all day. We're nearly there, as I recall."

They were indeed.

The cold rock of nervous dread, growing steadily larger as the miles passed, settled harder in Lenore's stomach. They had crossed the Piscataqua River some time ago, surely Grandmother Worth's cottage would come into view at any moment.

She shrugged aside her doubts about coming face to face with a past that seemed even further away than Boston. "You could hand me my bonnet from the case, please, Jenna. The one with the gold-shot ribbon. I want to look my best when I greet Grandmother Worth."

No one in Maine might care about appearances, but she did. At least she cared about her grandmother's first sight of her in nearly six years. She wanted to begin this visit on a new footing with Grandmother Worth. To show her she'd grown from a gangly spotted adolescent into a sophisticated and well-bred young woman. She struggled to ignore the inner voice insisting that was all she was.

Well-dressed and well-bred. A hollow doll.

She gripped her hands tighter together in her lap.

"Perhaps she will not spend the entire visit this time frowning at me and telling me to straighten my shoulders."

"You were so self-conscious about your height when you shot past Miss Margaret that spring." Jenna shook her head and unlocked the case on the seat beside her. "What was that, five years ago?"

"Six." Six long years since her grandmother had last invited her for a visit. With a pang, Lenore remembered every single invitation that had not included her. Maggie had come every summer in between, but Lenore had not been on a visit after the last disastrous time.

She had told herself every summer she didn't care when Maggie departed Boston and she had been left to the exclusive attention of their parents. She assured

herself it didn't matter because she was benefitting
from things Maggie would never understand: singular
focus from her mother and her father, as well as de-
tailed and protracted advancements in society. But the
painful twinge inside her had stamped each statement
a lie every year without fail. This year Grandmother's
ready consent to her proposed visit had surprised her
and warmed her straight to her toes. And even better,
it had delighted her parents, as they now saw a clear
path to regaining her grandmother's affections.

So why was she so desperately nervous now?

"Six. That's right. Miss Margaret stayed the whole
summer that year, recuperating from the measles."
Jenna pulled out a rice straw confection trimmed with
silk green ivy and pale yellow artificial roses. "I'm certain Mrs. Worth will see how well you have grown into
your stature. You are quite the picture, as always, Miss
Lenore. It's a pity Miss Margaret's off to Ireland visiting her new family and all. I'm sure she'd agree."

Not for the first time Lenore wished her elder sister would be there when she arrived. She'd missed
her more than she anticipated when Maggie ran
away last year to marry their temporary coachman
and settle in Maine with Grandmother. But Maggie's
absence had made Mama and Papa much more willing to let their younger daughter try to win back
Grandmother's favor. Perhaps if this visit went well
she would be able to arrange to come back when the
new Mr. and Mrs. Reilly returned from their trip.

Lenore tied the bonnet ribbon in a jaunty bow
and smoothed the topmost flounce of her pale
green traveling dress. With its gold velvet trim and
fashionably wide pagoda sleeves, she hoped to make
a good enough impression on her grandmother to
at least buy her some uncensured breathing room to

contemplate her future and how best she could undo the mess she had made of her life so far. She could only hope she would please her grandmother somehow. Despite her wishes to change what she was, her appearance had proved her best accomplishment as she made her way through society's shallows at her mother's elbow. It was all she had to offer at the moment.

We shall no longer bow to the dictates of others, but seize our destinies with our own hands. Wasn't that part of the pledge they'd all taken only a few weeks ago in the safety of the Carlton's front room? The Brookline Daughters of Grace, issuing a challenge to the whims of fate and vowing to accept only a future of their own choosing. She'd snickered at first with Amelia in the corner of the rectory parlor, then joined in the rebellion a few moments later in the smaller group, little realizing how deeply the second repetition of their pledge would affect her.

The cry of a gull in the distance pulled Lenore back from a the despair threatening to consume her thoughts. The road brightened just ahead. They were close indeed. Her heart beat faster with a jolt of anticipation as the trees came to an end and a meadow spread before them, bright green with a sprinkling of wild flowers.

She craned her neck out the window in a decidedly improper fashion to catch sight of Grandmother Worth's cottage on the rise at the far end of the clearing. Rough hewn and stalwart as the massive trees the coach left behind, the house stood on a natural pedestal of rolling hills, providing an excellent view of the ocean beyond Belle Cove, which was just out of sight on the other side.

Everyone indulged Grandmother's habit of calling

the imposing structure a cottage, but it was a grand mansion. Two stories high with glistening windows and enough rooms to comfortably house a family of a dozen members, with rooms to spare for guests. Lenore hadn't realized just how much she'd missed coming here until a wave of nostalgia swept through her, tightening her throat as she clutched the coach window.

A few minutes more and she was up the steps and across the wide porch that wrapped the house, leaving Jenna and her husband, Marcus, to tend the baggage and horses.

"Grandmother," she called, eagerness lilting her voice despite her attempt at calm as she pushed the door open and stepped into the open foyer. "Grandmother, are you here?"

There was nary a sound beyond the ticking of a mantel clock in the distance and the lingering echoes of her shouted greeting in an empty hall. Grandmother Worth did not appear to be home.

"Grandmother?" Lenore couldn't halt the forlorn-little-girl feeling sweeping through her. Nor the small flare of hope that either Grandmother Worth had not heard her arrival or had merely stepped out for a moment.

Had she really expected the grand dame to be standing by the door waiting to greet her with open arms? What with Grandmother running the lumber yard full time again, Lenore doubted she'd see much of her at all during this visit. Isn't that why she'd come in the first place? To seek a quiet place to contemplate her future course?

She closed the door behind her with a snap and paced to the center of the foyer past the open doorway to the formal reception room and the closed pocket doors of the dining room opposite the grand staircase. Should she await grandmother in her study or in the parlor that faced the ocean?

"So much for making a grand entrance." She pulled off her new bonnet and gloves and tossed them on the hall table, trying to avoid the tall mirror on the wall above the polished mahogany surface and thereby avoid seeing the havoc her wary emotions had surely played on her complexion.

A cream colored envelope tucked into the gilt edge of the mirror drew her closer than she had intended. *Lenore* scrawled across the front in Grandmother's handwriting. Obviously Grandmother had not intended greeting her younger granddaughter in person.

As Lenore took the note from the mirror, she couldn't help seeing the stain of color on her cheeks and the shimmer of disappointment at the corner of her eyes. How childish. She could hardly expect to govern her life if she couldn't even govern her reactions to trifling frustrations. Surely Amelia and Tori were not letting small disappointments interfere with their own quests for independence.

"At least Grandmother did not forget I was arriving today," she lectured the image in the mirror, then pulled out the folded note to read.

I had hoped to be home when you arrived, but there are pressing matters at Worth Lumber that require immediate attention. If Kate is not back from her trip to the market, pray make yourself comfortable in the room you used in years past. Mr. Warren and I will look forward to seeing you at dinner this evening.

Fondly,
Sylvia Worth

It was as if she were signing an impersonal business letter rather than a greeting to her granddaughter. Had she really believed Grandmother might have been looking forward to a visit from *her?* Grandmother had always far preferred Maggie over Lenore. Lenore stuffed the note back into the envelope, tempted to spin on her heels and announce to Marcus and Jenna that they were leaving immediately for Boston.

Only there was nothing for her in Boston either. Nothing save speculative glances and a stifling life of superficial smiles and empty chatter. She hadn't come all this way to let Grandmother's lack of interest turn her away.

"Miss Lenore?" Marcus Watson stood in the doorway. "Have you any idea where I'm to put your trunks? Mrs. Butler does not appear to be in the kitchen."

"Tell Jenna I'm to stay in the same room I used as a child, please Marcus. And would you ask her to put out the gold plaid taffeta dinner dress? Mrs. Worth is expecting company for dinner tonight."

"Very good, Miss." Marcus disappeared from the door.

Lenore had always liked Jacob Warren, a kindly man with a twinkle in his eye and lemon drops in his pockets. Much to Papa's chagrin, Grandmother treated Mr. Warren as more stalwart family friend than employee for all the years he'd worked as the lumber mill's manager.

His son Jake had practically run tame here during the summers. Not that Jake ever paid much attention to Lenore. He'd been more Maggie's friend, merely tolerating her own presence on berry-picking or fishing expeditions or when they scrambled over the Belle Cove rocks below Grandmother's cottage. She'd tagged along anyway, entranced by the rumble of his voice and the glint of humor in his hazel eyes. And the tickle the combination seemed to make in her belly whenever he had deigned to acknowledge her.

An irresistible need to see the cove overtook Lenore. She'd always loved the sunlight sparkling on the waters and the tang of salt in the air. Jake used to tease her that she must have been a pirate in an earlier life with all the time she spent gazing at the sea.

She crossed the central foyer and opened the heavy oak door to the front porch. Blinking at the brightness of the sun on the water, she stepped over to the rail. Everything was just as she remembered.

Better than she remembered.

Pine trees and scrub-brush clung to the rocky bluffs surrounding the cove. Gentle waves soothed the edges of sand at the base of the small cliffs. Gulls dipped and swirled on the air currents rising over the water, which nipped her cheeks and nose.

Evergreen, salt and fresh air filled her as she counted the bright yellow and white corks bobbing near the far point, marking Job Pruitt's lobster pots, which lurked on the bottom for the unwary sea treats. They looked tiny from here, but up close they'd be bigger than both her hands fisted together. How she and Maggie had squealed when Jake taunted them with his living haul as he tended Job's pots, and how they had enjoyed the sweetness of the lobsters served steaming hot for a Saturday supper when even Grandmother ate the succulent meat with her fingers. Remembering the long ago days sent a pang straight through her.

She missed Maggie.

Missed her with an intensity she'd smothered for the year that had passed since her sister ran away to help Grandmother with the mill and marry the man of her own choosing. They hadn't been close since Lenore had left Maine and Maggie behind to return to Boston with Mama and Papa so long ago.

"I wish you were here, Maggie. I wish I had your courage to know what I want and go after it," she whispered. "I wish you could help me figure out what I am to do."

But in truth if Maggie and her husband, Devin, had been in residence, Papa would never have allowed this visit to take place. The newlywed Reillys had sailed to Ireland to acquaint Maggie with her husband's family and homeland, and William Brownley, Sr. had deemed this the perfect time to send their darling Lenore to attempt to seal the breach with his mother-in-law that occurred after the disaster of the previous summer's encounter.

"*What with the Lawrence scandal tempering her chances of a match at the moment and our own financial difficulties, it might serve us well to get back into Mother's good graces,*" Lenore's mother had pointed out when Lenore had first broached the idea of a visit to Maine. She'd been so relieved when she'd gained their consent she remembered how her chest had hurt from holding her breath.

"Here you be, Miss Lenore. Just where I thought to find you." Jenna slipped a silk paisley shawl around Lenore's shoulders.

How long had she been lost in the memories of her summer visits from so long ago? She could not say, but she was grateful for the shawl's protection from the breeze. "Thank you. How ever did you guess I'd be out here?"

Jenna moved to stand beside Lenore at the rail, shading her eyes as she too surveyed the view and clutched a wool shawl tight to the bodice of her serviceable black traveling dress.

"Mrs. Butler remembered whenever you went missing as a girl, this was the most likely spot to find you. Unless of course your sister or that Jake Warren had pulled you away on some adventure."

Jenna turned her gaze to the line of caned rockers that stood along the wall. "More times than not you were out here reading something your mother thought inappropriate for a young girl, usually something from the pile your grandmama had set aside for Jake's studies. Mrs. Butler tells me he's a doctor now and quite well respected. Hard to believe how some folks will turn out once they set their minds to something."

"I suppose you're right."

Jake was a doctor and Maggie ran Worth Lumber with Grandmother, just like they'd talked of doing all those years ago. As for the younger of the Brownley sisters, she'd certainly turned out to be exactly what she'd set her mind on also. An ornament for Boston's finest salons and drawing rooms. A bit of fluff whose greatest worry was what color gown to wear and if she had caught the right gentleman's eye. Her parents' *darling daughter,* hardly fit for anything beyond gossip and organizing a social event. She'd almost forgotten she'd been so lost in memories of happier days.

She shivered, despite the shawl.

"You'll catch your death out here, cold as it is with this wind. Mrs. Butler set a pot of tea to steep for you as soon as she rode in from the market." Jenna fussed. "Would you like it served in the parlor or would you prefer to have a rest in your room after our long journey?"

Lenore couldn't face the isolation of a bedchamber or the echoing silence of an empty parlor. Too much opportunity for thought. She'd had enough of that for right now. "I think I'd prefer to have a cup in the kitchen like we used to. The kitchen here always smelled so warm and welcoming. What of you and Marcus? Have you had anything since we arrived?"

Jenna shook her head. "It's very kind of you to inquire, Miss Lenore. It has been a long day already. But I've got the rest of your boxes to unpack while Marcus sees to our few things and brushes the horses. We'll both have a bite when we're through."

Lenore nodded and headed down the porch past the rockers to make the turn and use the side entrance into the kitchen. She stretched out her hand and touched each caned seatback in turn, setting them in motion as she had loved to do as a girl. Satisfaction warmed her as she turned and watched them all rocking as if she'd left an unseen band of sentries behind to guard the view in her absence.

Walking into the kitchen she took a deep breath of the sweet cinnamon and herb scents that marked Kate Butler's domain. She'd always loved spending time in this warm sanctuary with its brick floor and scrubbed work tables. Many a happy afternoon had been spent cutting out gingerbread men or having a warm mug of tea or milk with her sister and Grandmother's cook and housekeeper who was more times than not left in charge of them while Grandmother attended to business at Worth Lumber or the Somerset docks.

"Ah, Miss Lenore." A diminutive Irishwoman with a broad smile bustled out of the pantry at that moment and crossed the room to take Lenore's hands in her own and give her a quick glance up and down.

"Aren't ye all grown up and just as pretty as St. Brigid's Cross, and that's a fact." The housekeeper nodded in satisfaction, her round cheeks still spread wide with her smile. "Herself will be very glad to see that ye've learned to carry yer height with such a grand air."

They both smiled at the memories of Grandmother's admonitions for Lenore to cease stooping, which started when she grew taller than her sister. Lenore had been miserable, but Kate, who stood no taller than her former charge's shoulders now, had been the one who comforted her with the wisdom that the world was such a grand place, the height from which you viewed it changed very little. Her words had made all the difference to an awkward girl.

"It's good to see you too, Mrs. Butler." With the exception of deeper creases around her eyes and more silver in the hair gathered in a knot at the top of her head, Grandmother's cook and housekeeper looked just as Lenore remembered. "You haven't changed a bit."

"I certainly haven't changed into Mrs. Butler while ye've been away. I'm still just plain Kate to ye. And that's the way I like it." She chuckled and looked up with a twinkle in her blue eyes. "But ye've changed, and that's a fact. It's hard to believe ye're the same little mite that liked to stand on a stool and help me cut biscuits. Turn around and let me get a proper look at ye."

Lenore dutifully turned in a small circle, drinking in the delight of being in the sun-dappled kitchen. Save for the unpleasantness of her last visit, some of her happiest memories had taken place within these spacious four walls with the view of the meadow and trees behind the cottage.

"Ye've grown into a fine looking lady, Miss Lenore. The cut of yer dress and that shade of green suits ye. If Miss Margaret were here ye'd make a dazzling pair." Kate nodded her satisfaction when Lenore faced her once more.

"How is Maggie, Kate?" The longing to see Maggie swept through her again with surprising strength. She thought she'd put missing her sister behind her months ago.

"She's always busy, coming and going to the mill with Mr. Reilly or Mrs. Worth. Busy, but living the life she wanted and as happy as can be, as surely ye know."

"I have no idea how she is." Lenore shook her head. "Mama and Papa refuse to speak of her. I garner what news I can from the letters she sends to her friends."

Upon their return from Maine last year, her parents had all but ignored the fact that they had an elder daughter, let alone that she was married to the son of an Irish shipbuilder and helping her grandmother run the family business.

Kate gasped. "Surely ye don't mean ye haven't gotten her letters! Miss Margaret writes to ye near every week. Sometimes she asks me to post her letters if I'm going to the market, or Dr. Warren sends them if he's off to Kittery. Mostly, I think she sends a letter to ye and one to yer parents, along with her correspondence on behalf of the lumber yard every week."

The revelation stunned Lenore. Maggie hadn't forgotten her.

She'd written every week. Mama and Papa must have intercepted those letters. Lenore wished she could take back all the mean, spiteful thoughts she'd directed at Maggie for deserting her this past year. And she'd been so jealous of the regular letters Tori had received, acting for all the world as if she either already knew or cared little about the snippets of news Tori sometimes shared at teatime.

The suspicion that Mama and Papa had confiscated more than just her mail *from* Maine sank through Lenore. She gripped her hands in front of her, agonized that she'd never thought of this before. She'd been too proud and hurt to even ask Tori to send a message to Maggie on her behalf when the first couple of letters she'd written herself last summer had gone unanswered. And she'd rebuffed Tori the times she'd approached her to speak privately about Maggie.

She'd given up on her sister, but it seemed Maggie hadn't given up on her.

"Are ye well, Miss Lenore? Ye've gone a bit pale. Perhaps ye should sit for a spell or go and have a little lie down. Travel can take a lot out of a body." Kate touched her arm and then directed her gaze to one of the tall stools by the table.

"I wish I'd tried harder, . . ." She sank onto the stool and examined the tips of her soft traveling shoes, ashamed to meet Kate's possible disapproval. ". . . I wish I could let her know. . . ."

"Now, don't fret." The housekeeper put her hand over Lenore's and squeezed. "I doubt she's holding anything against ye. She mentioned she was afraid ye were not getting yer letters or that yers were not getting to her. She always brightens a bit when Miss Carlton's letters include some mention of what ye'd been up to or how ye'd looked or fared at some event or another."

Lenore finally raised her eyes to lock with the compassion in Kate's bright blue gaze. "Besides, if ye extend yer stay by a week or two, mayhap ye'll have a chance to talk it over with her yerself. The Reillys plan to return by late July."

Lenore nodded.

We shall seize our destinies with our own hands.

Maggie had done very well for herself in doing just that. Perhaps she could pattern herself after her sister's example.

"Would ye like me to fetch ye a cuppa tea and some of those raisin cookies ye were so fond of? I told yer Jenna Watson I could bring a tray to yer room or to the parlor if ye'd like."

"I'd just as soon sit here, if you don't mind."

Kate beamed. "Just as ye used to. Ye're one of the few people I never minded in my kitchen. I'll have ye all set up in a trice."

Kate bustled to the stove and the steaming cast iron kettle was set to one side. After deftly preparing the tea in a brown pottery teapot, she took a matching plate from the shelf and dipped into a large blue tin to fill the plate with the cookies Lenore liked best of the delights she used to make for *her girls* as she had called Maggie and Lenore when they were small.

All the while Lenore sat watching the little Irishwoman who hummed a vaguely familiar ditty, she felt foreign and out of place, whereas years ago she had felt completely at home. So little had changed here and yet everything was different. She was different. What had happened to the little girl who counted her sister as her best friend in all the world, especially during their summer holidays with Grandmother? How could she have allowed herself to get so wrapped up in becoming the darling daughter her parents envisioned that she seemed to have lost touch with what she was before? How was she going to recognize her destiny if she barely recognized herself?

"Tell me, now, if ye don't mind me asking . . ." Kate carried a tray laden with tea and all the trimmings. "With all yer finery and the grand parties ye must attend, is there a special young man that has caught yer fancy down there in Boston?"

The pallid image of Jonathan Adams Lawrence, III, Amelia's elder brother, rose for a moment. There had been a time after Maggie eloped, when Lenore had been very flattered that Maggie's former suitor Jonathan had turned his attentions toward her. Mama and Papa had been delighted. Lenore shuddered to think of his paunch and his meaty hands. She'd come here to escape Jonathan, not dwell on what might have been between them.

"No," she said a little too strongly and winced. "At least no one in particular."

"There, there, Miss Lenore. Don't fret yerself. Drink yer tea and forget all about the prying clucking of this old hen." Kate took a sip from her own mug after watching Lenore do so. "More than likely he was not worth the heartbreak, anyway."

Before she could correct Kate's misconception over her reaction, a distant clock struck four times and Kate fairly leaped to her feet. "Well, by St. Peter's sword, think of the time! I've dinner to fix yet and all this still to get settled away. You sit here, Miss Lenore, and enjoy yer tea. I must get busy or dinner will be late, and ye know how Mrs. Worth is about punctuality."

"I'd love to help you," Lenore could hardly believe her ears as the suggestion tumbled out of her mouth. Proper young ladies such as she knew more about preparing a menu than they did about preparing the actual dishes on them. Yet spending time with Kate in the kitchen had been her salvation during many a lonely afternoon when Maggie had gone with Grandmother to Worth Lumber and Jake was actually devoting himself to his studies.

Kate cocked her head to one side and rested her hands on her hips, a familiar gesture that showed she was tempted. "Are ye sure ye want to help? Our last time ended in disaster."

"Of course I'm sure." Lenore stood up. Why not? Papa was nowhere nearby and would be none the wiser. "Some of my happiest memories include helping you and listening to the stories and songs your mother taught you from the old country."

"Very well," Kate beamed. "But first, ye must put on an apron. And ye might turn back those grand cuffs on yer sleeves as well."

Kate reached into a drawer and pulled out a bibbed muslin apron. "I'll not have that Jenna Watson taking me to task for a little flour or salt on yer fine dress."

An hour or more had passed and Lenore was elbow deep in a bowl punching down dough for rolls to go with the night's dinner and humming the same tune Kate had hummed earlier, when a familiar voice boomed from the doorway.

"Well, now what is this, have you finally admitted you're getting on in years and taken on an assistant, Kate Butler?"

The deep timbre and baiting tone sliced through

Lenore with a completely unexpected and unsettling effect as it slammed straight through her stomach.

Jake.

Jake Warren. The memories that had revived this afternoon on the porch had not prepared her for the effect of actually hearing his voice again.

Lenore turned with a start and sent the bowl of dough spinning off the table's edge in her haste. As she lunged to catch it she caught a fleeting glimpse of him, framed in the doorway, his face dark in by the sunlight behind him.

Despite the changes the years had wrought in him, she would have known him anywhere.

Staggering, she caught the bowl. Jake's fingers touched hers on the rim. A bolt of heat streaked through her. How had he moved so quickly? She pulled the bowl toward her and his other hand slipped around her back to prevent her from falling against the table.

Pulled close in his embrace, she looked up, past his broad shoulders and the jut of his chin, beyond the curve of his lips and the tip of his nose and straight into the green-flecked depths of his eyes. The scent of sage, citrus, and Jake himself filled the air.

Her breath locked in her chest.

Caught by the fire in his gaze, circled by the strength of his arms, realization dawned. Long before she'd arrived, before she'd taken a pledge to change her life or thought of Maine as her haven, of all the things she'd missed the most from her summers in Maine——Grandmother, the rockers, Belle Cove, Kate, and even her own sister——it was Jake Warren she'd been longing the most to see.

"Hello, Nora," he said with a soft smile. "Welcome home." He bent his head and brushed his warm lips across hers.

She should never have come here.

Two

He was ten times a fool.

Every nerve in his body confirmed the certainty.
His thoughts whirled like dust kicked up beside the
roadway while he clung to Nora Brownley and tried
to reconcile memory with reality.

Nora, the little girl with golden braids and a curious mind, who disappeared one summer, never to
return. Maggie's quiet little sister, matured into a sophisticated and very appealing woman, from her
sleek chignon to the tips of her soft leather traveling
boots.

He looked deep into the smoked amber depths of
her eyes and inhaled a whiff that reminded him of
sun-warmed honeysuckle, and felt both lost and
found at one and the same time.

"Hello, Nora. Welcome home."

The hot shower of sparks that streaked through
him when his lips touched hers warmed his heart.
Her lips were so close, so soft. He could just kiss her
again, kiss her more deeply, and ascertain for himself that he had not dreamed his reaction.

A fool, indeed.

He fought the urge, certain he should have kept
his mouth firmly shut and far enough away from
hers to hide his idiocy for a few moments longer.

With his arms encircling her slender softness and

his fingers tangled with hers on the rim of the bowl she'd rescued, it was difficult to grasp any rational thought, let alone act on it. The warm glow in her gaze burned through him still, scorching away all sensibility. Even the swipe of flour near her jaw-line enhanced her appeal.

Myriad emotions flew through her eyes, but her features remained frozen as if she did not quite know how to react to his embrace. Did she even remember him?

What had made him imagine that baiting the child he'd once teased with impunity would be an apt greeting after all these years? And what had made him think kissing the woman she'd become was even more appropriate?

You weren't thinking at all.

The stern voice in his head closely resembled Sylvia Worth's, who most certainly would not appreciate his offending her granddaughter when she had only just arrived.

Hell, she was practically family.

He forced himself to loosen his hold and fought to get a grip on a more conventional greeting.

"It's been a long time, Nora. How have you been?"

As she pulled herself out of his embrace, the hint of honeysuckle coming from her twined enticingly with the kitchen smells of herbs in the rafters and roast fowl in the oven.

"No one calls me Nora anymore." Vinegar dripped from her retort, belying the honeyed sweetness of her scent. She turned her head slightly, meeting his gaze with a flash of irritation and a disdainful frown as if the contact that had just rocked him to his heels had been no more than an annoyance to her. "Look what you almost made me do, sneaking up like that."

She pulled the bowl from his grasp and moved it to the center of the worktable then flapped a linen square in the air and allowed it to settle over the bowl before she met his gaze again.

"You certainly haven't changed much, Jake Warren, that's for certain."

"Well, well." He fought the urge to laugh at her discomfort. "You've changed in more than appearance, *Lenore*. Grown a backbone somewhere beneath your city finery. The Nora Brownley I remember was a shy girl. Teasing would make you blush rather than provoke a rebuke."

Instead of abating, the odd sensations coursing through him intensified, despite the fact that he no longer touched her.

"Indeed? Is that why you took such liberties in your greeting? To make me blush?"

Her brows arched disapproval and her dagger-sharp tone would have carved apologies from a pirate, but the appealing spark of fury flaring in the smoked amber depths of her eyes kept Jake unable to even speak, let alone concoct anything resembling sincere regret for a greeting he felt all too ready to repeat.

"Well, I've finally got the larder set to rights, thanks to ye, lass." Kate bustled into the room from the back pantry before he could answer. Kate pinned him with a threatening glare and waved an admonishing finger. "Don't ye be harassing the first decent bit of help I've had in this kitchen in almost six years, Jake Warren. I'll have ye banned from my kitchen."

He counted himself grateful for Kate's intrusion and that her timing had kept her in the pantry during his manhandling of her charge. With his attention centered on the appealing softness of Lenore Brownley's small pout, his thoughts had veered along a decidedly improper vein.

"I believe Doctor Warren was attempting an apology." Nora's eyebrow arched a little higher as the anger over the scare he'd given her changed into an amused twinkle.

"Doctor or no, I'll pepper his tongue if he causes ye any trouble at all with his shenanigans." The diminutive Irish woman stopped on the other side of the table and glared at Jake with a look guaranteed to send most men to their knees begging for mercy.

The only time he'd ever seen Kate Butler truly riled was when her employer had been ill with pneumonia last year. It was the housekeeper who had insisted both Sylvia Worth and her physician write to her estranged daughter and son-in-law, requesting they send her some help to run her business concerns while she recovered. That request brought Maggie and Devin Reilly to Maine to stay.

Kate was a force to be reckoned with and he didn't intend to do full battle with her again. He cleared his throat for the apology they both awaited, much easier to formulate now that he had turned his attention to the woman across the table rather than the one standing beside him.

He took a step back and sketched a deep bow. "I humbly beg forgiveness from you both for any offence my intrusion caused."

Straightening, he added, "Particularly if it means I may escape a fate that will prevent me from sampling some of the enticing—" His gaze slid to Nora . . . Lenore. He still couldn't quite believe little Nora had grown into such an incredibly beautiful woman.

"—and delicious smells currently filling your kingdom, my ladies."

"Go on with ye. Don't try yer blarney on me, lad. Dinner will be at seven-thirty sharp, as usual." Kate's tone softened just a bit. "I'll not wait it for ye. But if ye've a call and do not make it home I'll leave a plate warming on the stove as usual."

"Home?"

Surprise sharpened Nora's one-word question. Or was it disapproval?

Her entire body stilled and her features froze into a polite mask. Despite the silly apron and the dusting of flour on her cheek, she looked every inch like the remote china-doll society misses he'd observed while studying in Boston.

Remote and definitely displeased.

"Doctor Warren's quite the hero. Carried his father out of a raging inferno, he did, when their house caught fire just after Miss Maggie and her husband set sail. Mrs. Worth invited Dr. and Mr. Warren to stay here as her guests," Kate supplied.

"I'm glad you and Mr. Warren are all right, Doctor Warren." He could not help but notice her use of his title again instead of his first name anymore than he could ignore the fact that Nora looked anything but pleased. Those lips he'd found so distracting a moment before were set in a firmly disapproving line all too reminiscent of the look her father wore whenever he'd ventured here from Boston.

Jake bristled. William Brownley, Sr. always looked as if he'd eaten something that did not quite agree with him. Whenever he'd opened his mouth it had been to vent some complaint or reproach.

At the moment all signs of the girl from his youth

had fled, replaced by a marbled miss molded in her father's image. Why should Nora care that his father and he were staying here? Pa was usually up at the mill with Sylvia and he himself was rarely here save to sleep or sit down for the occasional dinner.

"Is there something wrong?" The question came out with a harder edge than he expected. But her haughty manner bit him to the quick.

A hint of color rose to her soft cheeks.

"I am just surprised that Grandmother Worth failed to mention the incident in her letter to Mama last week. I had expected Grandmother would be lonely with Maggie and Devin away."

Somehow the answer stung. She had indeed expected to have her grandmother all to herself. Jake's ire rose another notch. *Lenore* Brownley could take her haughty manner right back to the city if she thought to further any familial claims on the grandmother she'd ignored for so long. Save for Maggie, Sylvia deserved far better from her family than she had ever gotten.

"After so many years, what prompts you to believe your grandmother would need to clear her guest list with you or your mama, Miss Brownley? If you've a complaint about the company you are forced to keep while here, you should address your concerns directly to her."

The red stain on Lenore Brownley's high cheekbones deepened. She squared her shoulders and faced him full on. It wasn't fire crackling in the smoky depths of her gaze, but ice. He could see her holding her tongue to keep herself from exploding. Under other circumstances he might have admired the effect.

"I was not complaining. Just surprised." She

enunciated each word carefully as if she addressed someone with hearing difficulties. "This is Grandmother's house, she is certainly free to have whomever she chooses living here with her. For as long as she chooses. I know how highly she values your father's friendship."

The frost edging her tone after his greeting was nothing compared to the chill now. Her gaze held his for a second more and then she looked away.

"If you will excuse me," her voice softened as she turned to Kate. "I believe I will go and check on Jenna's progress with my unpacking."

"Of course, dear." Kate beamed, not the least perturbed by the tension rippling in the air. "Ye've helped me get things well enough in hand for tonight. I've yet to miss serving dinner at the time yer grandmother prefers."

Nora nodded and turned on her heel without so much as a glance. Her leather boots whispered over the bricks as she glided toward the door, every inch the upright, proper Boston miss. How could he have imagined the sparks of desire that seemed to flow from her when he'd held her only minutes before?

"I'll see you at dinner, Dr. Warren." Stiff and polite, her farewell shot back to him as she left the room.

"Poor lamb." Kate sighed.

Jake frowned. "Beg pardon?"

There had been nothing poor or lamb-like in the woman who had just stunned him and left him with so many unsettling questions and unresolved turmoil.

"She's carrying herself so bravely. But I could tell from the way she mentioned her fellow, she's nursing a broken heart." Kate bustled over to the stove and raised the lid of a steaming pot.

"Broken heart?"

Kate added a pinch of salt to the brew and nodded. "It's no wonder she wanted to come here. Her maid Jenna allowed as how she's been sent here to escape some kind of scandal. A broken engagement. Mrs. Worth will know what to do to help her set herself to rights."

A scandal? Jake usually thought of himself as an astute observer of people. His questions about his fitness for solo medical practice aside, he'd always prided himself on his ability to understand his patients needs beyond the obvious. Lenore Brownley hardly seemed the sort to be embroiled in a scandal and if she were suffering from a broken heart it was surely not from being jilted but because it had shattered from the coldness of her soul.

What sort of scandal could cause a miss with all the manners and trappings of Boston's elite to flee to the wilds of Maine?

A clatter in the distant interior of the house stopped any further ruminations on his part or revelations from Kate. They both headed to the doorway Nora had just used. Jake strode through the butler's pantry and into the dining room with Kate on his heels, just in time to hear a panicked scream followed by his name.

"Jake! Jake, come quickly!"

Nora's shout added fire to his steps. Sylvia would never forgive him. Hell, he'd never forgive himself if his taunting had upset her enough to cause an injury.

He skirted the massive dining table and flung open the pocket doors to the foyer. Nora was seated on the bottom step of Sylvia's grand staircase cradling a slight, gray-haired woman.

"There's no need in making such a fuss over a little tumble, Miss." The woman gamely tried to untangle herself from Nora's embrace.

"Don't get up, Jenna." A decidedly white-faced Nora said to the woman. "The doctor is right here. You shouldn't move until he pronounces you fit."

She looked up at him with an appeal for confirmation shining in the depths of her gaze. "Jenna lost her footing on the stairs. It sounded as if she fell the whole way."

"What happened?" Jake crouched beside the pair and carefully began his examination in search of bumps or breaks.

"I only missed the last step or two." The woman was pale and a small band of perspiration rode her upper lip. Her eyes were wide with alarm. Her hands trembled as Jake skimmed his own over her arms and then tested her grip.

"I just got a little light-headed is all," she said in a thin voice as she pressed her lips together in a worried line.

"I knew you should have eaten as soon as we arrived, Jenna. You hardly touched your food at luncheon," Nora fussed. "And Marcus worried over that splash of tea you called breakfast before we set off from the inn this morning."

Jenna's eyes widened further as she looked at Jake. "I don't do well with coaches. I'm better off traveling with an empty stomach."

"Well, Mama will be most vexed if I were to send you home injured—"

"That's enough, Miss Brownley." Jake intervened as Jenna's fingers began to tremble more violently.

He shot Nora a stern look as he skimmed his hands over the maid's ribs and down her legs. "I insist you cease haranguing my patient."

"I . . . I never . . . ," Nora closed her lips to hold back whatever volley she'd been about to unleash as Jenna emitted a sharp moan when Jake moved her ankle.

Nora slipped her hand into Jenna's. "Try to hold still," she said in a gentle voice that belied the fire in her eyes.

"I'm going to have to unlace your boot and have a better look," Jake told her. "Hold tight to Miss Brownley's hand and don't be afraid to squeeze if things get too uncomfortable."

"Is there anything I can do?" Kate asked from the doorway.

"Fetch her husband." Jake worked on the side lacings. "We should move her to some place more comfortable as soon as I'm through. And we'll need some cloths to bind this and keep the swelling down if it is broken."

"Aye," Kate's answer must have been flung over her shoulder as she moved off. "And I'll freshen the tea and warm some broth once I've found him."

Several sharp intakes of breath later and Jake met the maid's frightened stare. "I don't think anything is broken. I think you've just sprained your ankle. A few days rest and you should be good as new."

Instead of showing relief, Jenna's horrified gaze flew to Nora and then down to his hand holding her foot. "But we're to start back to Boston tomorrow. Mr. Brownley was most explicit."

"Don't fret over Mama and Papa." Nora smoothed a wisp of hair off Jenna's cheek then fished in her pocket for a handkerchief and gently blotted her maid's forehead. "I'm sure that if Grandmother writes a letter explaining that I had need of you for a few days here, they will accept it. They are most anxious not to ruffle Grandmother's feathers at the moment, you know."

Jake sat back on his heels and watched as the warm balm of Nora's tone eased the older woman's fears and some of the tension dropped from her shoulders. Nora Brownley had been an arresting sight when he'd first seen her from the kitchen doorway. She'd sparkled with definite allure when he'd held her in his arms. He'd even found her icy reactions and hasty withdrawal from the kitchen strangely intriguing. But the compassion she displayed now carried incomparable appeal.

Incomparable and disconcerting. *She's nursing a broken heart,* Kate had said. . . . *sent here to escape a scandal.* There was certainly more to Lenore Brownley than an attractive façade and a haughty manner.

"Besides," Nora gave Jenna a wide grin. "The last time they threatened to fire an injured servant led to a disaster they will not want to repeat."

That last cryptic comment won a watery smile from the maid. "Aye. Although Miss Maggie seemed happy enough with the outcome."

Ahh, they must be referring to the strange circumstances that surrounded Maggie and Devin's introduction. A tale of high romance and adventure if ever he'd heard one, and he'd heard the newlywed Reillys chuckle about finding hidden blessings and unexpected gold often enough in the past year to make him more than a little curious to hear about the events from an outsider's perspective.

The clatter of heavy footsteps from the kitchen

signaled the arrival of Jenna's husband and cut off any further conversation.

The rapid pounding of her heart grew louder as Jake bent his head toward her.

He was going to kiss her.

Again.

This was everything Lenore had ever imagined in her childish fantasies and yet so much more.

Excitement shot down her spine as she arched up to meet his lips. Her hands rested on the cool hardness of his chest. She wanted to stay in his arms forever—to live in this moment of expectation for eternity.

"Nora. Nora."

Instead of his breath whispering over her cheeks, his voice sounded oddly muffled and far away. And the pounding persisted. Not her heartbeat. Not his. An annoyance that pulled her from the magic of their reunion.

"You have to hurry. It's nearly time for dinner."

Hurry? Dinner?

Lenore sat up with a start. Jake's arms no longer held her. His lips no longer beckoned.

She blinked hard at the gathering gloom of her bedroom at Grandmother's house—familiar and yet still distant. She'd fallen asleep at the small writing desk by the window. How long had she slept? The sky was a deep lavender signaling the last of sunset. Was Grandmother home? Had she missed dinner?

"Nora?" Louder this time, with an edge of concern.

She blinked again. Jake was indeed calling her, but he was only calling her to supper, not to some outrageously inappropriate behavior. She struggled to suppress the edge of regret accompanying that realization.

"If you don't answer me, I'm coming in."

Oh, no. He couldn't come in here. She pushed unkempt strands of hair back from her cheeks. She must look a mess. She was still in her travel clothes. Her cheeks were most likely flushed and creased from laying her head on the desk. No proper young lady would allow anyone to see her in such a state. Mama would be horrified.

She caught herself and nearly laughed aloud. What was she thinking about? A proper young lady could not entertain a gentleman in her bedchamber, disheveled and travel stained or not. At least with the way she looked she wouldn't have to worry that Jake might be tempted to kiss her again.

"I . . . I'm coming."

She stood up from the desk, hating the quaver of disappointment threading her answer. Why should she be the least bit interested in Jake Warren's kiss? Let alone dreaming of a repetition? Especially after the way he'd treated her.

She'd tried to help get Jenna settled into the cozy quarters set up beside Grandmother's stable, but with Jake, Kate, and Marcus fussing she had only been in the way. Jake had finally sent her back to the house with a curt dismissal when all she'd tried to do was plump the pillow for Jenna as he wrapped her ankle.

She'd managed a sedate and dignified exit and then stamped across the yard intending to pour out her aggravation and indignation to Tori in a letter. But the tears she couldn't prevent stopped her from writing more than a short paragraph describing her arrival. She'd only rested her head on her arms for a moment to compose herself. Now she was about to be late for dinner—a cardinal sin at Grandmother's. And she had a decided crick in her neck.

She laid all the blame for her present discomfort squarely at Jake Warren's feet. To her horror, the doorknob started to turn and the door cracked open.

"Nora?" He called softly as if she could still be sleeping after all the ruckus he'd been making.

She crossed to the door and wrenched it from his grasp. "I told you. No one calls me that anymore."

At the sharpness of her retort, he raised one eyebrow and tilted the corner of his mouth.

"So you did."

She thought of his remark in the kitchen as she struggled to compose herself after he'd kissed her. He could think again if he thought to make her blush.

As if rising to the challenge, he held her gaze for a moment then dropped his own to slowly peruse her from head to toe.

She fought to ignore the tell-tale heat creeping up her neck at his scrutiny and tried to think of anything other than her reaction to her former idol. The unique blend of sage and citrus scents that clung to him interfered with her concentration.

He leaned against the doorframe and met her gaze again, smiling. "Sylvia sent me to see if you were exhausted from your travels and required a tray in your room. If you intend to come down to dinner you had better hurry. I believe she is rather anxious to see you."

"Of course I'm coming down. I'm anxious to see Grandmother myself." She turned her gaze to the brown and gold plaid taffeta dinner dress Jenna has laid out on the bed before her accident. It looked so nice on her too, setting off both her hair and the her eyes. "I just need to freshen up, change my dress, and fix my hair."

"There's no time for all that. It's well after seven. The clock will ping the half hour any moment and Kate will be setting dinner on the table." Jake said. "You look fine, anyway." He added as an obvious afterthought although he didn't sound one bit convincing.

"I doubt that." She touched her fingers to the tangles on side of her head and fought not to look at the dress on the bed with longing. She wouldn't be able to struggle into the taffeta on her own, in any case.

What would a man as handsome as Jake know about the work it took to put in a good appearance? Even lounging in a doorway he looked more than acceptable. The broadness of his shoulders stretched his brown wool jacket taut. The simplicity of a darker brown waistcoat that hugged his chest and tapered to his narrow waist contrasted with his white shirt and the tie knotted under a pristine starched collar brushed by the hair at the nape of his neck.

He was every bit a gentleman and he wore his good looks with a casual ease no woman could achieve even with hours to spend and an army of servants. Lenore could have stared at him throughout those hours, but she pulled her drifting thoughts back. She was furious with him after all. Indignant that he'd greeted her with shocking familiarity in the kitchen earlier, irritated that he'd been so unaffected as to be able to make light of the shattering salute with a mocking apology, and angry that he had spoken so sharply to her when she had been trying to help poor Jenna.

How was she going to survive this visit if he was actually living here, underfoot all the time? Her ridiculous reaction to his greeting in the kitchen served as fair warning of disaster looming. Jake Warren was a distraction she could little afford if she were going to find a new path for herself. She'd twisted herself up over this very notion as she tried to write to Tori. She did not have time to examine it further at the moment.

She put her hand on his chest and pushed. "You'll have to give me a minute at least to wash up."

"Wait." Jake's hand closed over her fingers sending a shower of sparks coursing through her before she'd even had time to register that this was just what she'd been both dreading and hoping would happen when she reached out. His palm was warm against the back of her hand. Her pulse quickened. She should have pulled away.

"I wanted you to know that I did not mean to offend you when I asked you to leave while I tended your maid." If he wanted her to follow what he was saying he really ought to release her.

"The room could only accommodate so many people at one time," he continued, seemingly unaware of the effect he was having on her. "Kate knows where things I might need are, and I could hardly send Jenna's husband away."

The ring of sincerity in his voice touched Lenore despite the distraction of his touch. She looked up into his hazel eyes and would have forgiven him anything at the moment. She had forgotten how swiftly the color of his eyes could change depending on his mood. Even in the dim light of fading day and lamps in the hall their appeal reached into her soul.

"That's not much in the way of an apology," she

managed to say as she pulled herself loose from his grip. But she smiled to soften her chiding. If he could make an effort so could she. "All I really care about is that Jenna is comfortable and taken care of. She is, isn't she?"

Jake nodded. "She's fine. I left her with her foot propped up on a pillow and her husband feeding her a plate of Kate's chicken and potatoes. He'll give her some laudanum to help her sleep tonight."

"Thank you—"

The ping of Grandmother Worth's parlor clock cut off their conversation.

"Do what you have to, but hurry," Jake said as he reached beside her and pulled the door shut. "I'll delay Sylvia."

It was only after the door clicked shut that his use of her grandmother's given name registered. If Grandmother caught him speaking so informally of her, she'd pin his ears back but good.

And Lenore decided she wouldn't mind witnessing that at all.

Three

"I am sorry to be late, Grandmother."

Lenore slowed her steps, only too conscious that a full ten minutes had passed since the clock ceased striking the dinner hour. It was amazing how long a quick splash of water on her face and tucking stray locks of her hair on her own had taken. She struggled to emulate the cool assurance her friend Amelia Lawrence always exuded, regardless of the circumstances, and prayed she achieved a modicum of success as she entered the dining room.

Even more amazing was finding Grandmother and her guests still on their feet and not seated as they normally would have been. In all her girlhood she never remembered a meal at Grandmother Worth's beginning at any other time than the appointed hour.

She had apparently underestimated Jake's powers of persuasion.

Or had she?

The sensations provoked by the fleeting touch of his lips on hers had rekindled far-flung expectations and dreams Jake Warren once dominated. Childish dreams. She was seeking new directions, not a juvenile fantasy. She avoided Jake's gaze, unwilling to betray the direction of her thoughts, and focused on the real reason she had come to Maine.

"No apology is necessary, my dear. Welcome

home." Grandmother Worth stood at the head of the table.

Her greeting accompanied a warm smile, unleashing a sharp pang of longing in Lenore. Being here, seeing Grandmother at last, she had the distinct feeling she had somehow found her way home, indeed. How odd.

Her bearing as regal as ever, Grandmother's silver hair glinted in the light from the wall sconces as she turned her cheek to receive Lenore's salute. "As you can see we are just sitting down. I'm afraid all the excitement of your maid's injury delayed Kate."

Lenore smoothed the day-old travel creases in her skirt and prayed Grandmother would not look too closely at her drooping sleeves in the lamplight. Mama would be horrified at her hoydenish appearance and Papa would most likely banish her from the table if she appeared in such a state at home.

Sending a silent prayer heavenward that she might continue to escape Sylvia Worth's censure, Lenore brushed her lips against Grandmother's weathered skin and inhaled a bracing breath of warm oak and violets that had never failed to fill her with a sense of reassurance even when Grandmother had been ringing a peal over her or Maggie's latest escapade.

"Please sit here beside me, Lenore." Grandmother, resplendent in a deep purple velvet dress Mama would have envied, indicated the seat to her immediate right as Kate bustled in from the kitchen carrying a platter of carved chicken.

"Don't blame me if this is a bit cold." The housekeeper looked over the already laden table for a spot to place her main course. "I had everything ready these past few minutes, can't for the life of me remember ye ever ringing the bell so late, Mrs. Worth, if ye don't mind me saying so."

"It smells delicious. I'm afraid the delay is my fault entirely." Jake interposed neatly, taking the platter from her before Kate could get wound up into a full rant.

The housekeeper clamped her lips tight, but raised a skeptical brow.

She proceeded to take the lids off several steaming bowls while Jake continued. "I was so caught up in perusing one of my journals I begged Sylvia to indulge me by letting me finish the article."

After a year away from her older sister, Lenore was unused to having anyone deflect attention away from her actions. She made a mental note to thank Jake later for shouldering the blame for her even as his reference to Grandmother fully registered. She smothered a gasp. Not many dared call Sylvia Worth by her given name to her face and got away with it.

"Oh, go on with ye." Kate laughed. "As if I believe that chip from the blarney stone. It'll take someone a mite more important than the likes of ye to make herself deviate from her routine." But Kate's expression lightened as she moved the gravy boat from the sideboard then turned to exit with a wink for Lenore.

Mr. Warren neatly pushed Lenore's chair in for her and then assisted Grandmother.

"Persistence in calling me by my Christian name, young man, will see you accompanying Kate from this room to eat your supper in the kitchen." Grandmother delivered the stern reprimand with her usual aplomb, but the twinkle in her eyes disarmed the threat. "I would not want my granddaughter to think we have lost all touch with polite society here in the wilds."

"I beg your pardon, Mrs. Worth." Jake ducked his head, the curve of his lips assuring her he wasn't the least bit chastened. "And yours as well, Miss Brownley, if I have offended you with my lack of proper address."

"You do of course remember Mr. Warren, don't you, Lenore?" Grandmother smiled warmly toward her other guest as he took the seat opposite Lenore. Jake sat beside his father. "Young Jake here tells me you renewed your acquaintance with him earlier in the day."

If by acquaintance he meant the pressure of his fingers scorching her back and the heady scents of citrus and sage filling her senses as she stood in his arms, she supposed he was correct.

Jake cleared his throat softly, drawing her attention as he occupied himself with unfolding his napkin. Lenore looked away with an effort though she couldn't stop her jaw from tightening. Surely, he would know she had no intention of relaying the manner of their encounter in the kitchen to Grandmother. Admitting such impropriety to Grandmother would surely send her straight back to her parents.

And that was the last thing she wanted.

She concentrated on Jake's father instead as she placed her own napkin on her lap. "I'm very happy to see you again, Mr. Warren. And so sorry to hear of your recent misfortune."

"Thank you. It is indeed a pleasure to see you again. You have become quite an elegant young woman, Nora, just as I always thought you would."

The sincerity behind his compliment threatened to set Lenore's cheeks aglow. For once she didn't even mind the use of her old nickname. Looking across the table at the older man she realized just how much his son resembled him. Aside from the difference in the color of their eyes, the Warrens possessed the same jutting chin, same noble features, and a genuine honesty that radiated as a refreshing alternative to the artifice evidenced at most supper parties she'd attended back home.

"Jake told me you both have taken up temporary residence here. Have you begun to rebuild your home?" she asked.

"Not yet." Mr. Warren and Grandmother exchanged a curious glance that ended in a shared smile. "But, as it stands your grandmother's generosity will at least allow us to fully enjoy your own visit."

"Jake," Grandmother interposed. "A blessing if you please?"

Jake bowed his head and said a hasty thanksgiving. The light from the sconces on the wall and the candles on the table added a glow to room as his rich baritone rumbled through Lenore. The next few minutes were filled with the passing of dishes and filling of plates. Lenore's stomach growled in an unseemly manner as she helped herself to chicken, stewed apples, squash, and the rolls she'd started for Kate earlier.

"I'm so glad you could join us at table tonight, Lenore," Grandmother beamed after sampling her dinner. "Kate told me how you pitched right in to help this afternoon. After the journey from Boston and the excitement over your maid's injury, I hope you did not overdo."

Lenore's gaze slid up to meet Jake's for the briefest moment before she smiled at her grandmother. "I was not much help with Jenna, I'm afraid. And I feel quite refreshed after my impromptu nap."

"Good." Grandmother smiled again. "We have much to discuss and I would not want you to begin your visit here under the weather. Or feeling rushed. . . ."

Grandmother reached out and rested her hand on Mr. Warren's. A gesture of familiarity rare from her and one which normally might have caused Lenore to wonder at its implications, but her thoughts raced toward where this conversation might be leading.

". . . but there are several matters which need to be brought up before we progress much further." Determination glinted in Grandmother's eyes.

She was using her no-nonsense tone. The one reserved for the most serious of infractions. Lenore's heart plummeted and her own gaze dropped to her plate as her appetite vanished and a lump swelled in her throat. Would she be taken to task for her neglect over the past years? Or was she going to be questioned about her role in the recent Boston scandals tainting the family? Right here? In front of Mr. Warren and Jake?

"What is it, Grandmother?" Her mouth was suddenly quite parched. At least she managed to keep her voice from cracking.

Lenore took a sip from the wine glass by her plate. Her hand barely trembled. *We shall seize our destinies in our own hands.* She'd spoken the vow and taken the first step coming here, surely she'd survive a few sharp questions from her grandmother.

"Now, Sylvia," Mr. Warren squeezed Grandmother's fingers. "Are you sure you want to bring this up tonight? The child has only just arrived."

"Lenore is hardly a child. I was married with Alberta on the way when I was her age, Jacob." Grandmother cast Lenore a glance edged with disquieting tension. In all her life, Lenore had never seen her grandmother nervous.

Grandmother hesitated another moment, then shifted her gaze completely from Jacob Warren to meet Lenore's. "I believe we should start this visit with complete honesty."

Lenore swallowed as the turmoil in her grandmother heightened her own. A part of her was amazed at the intimacy of the conversation between the two older people. The other part felt confused and distressed. What could be on Grandmother's mind? What needed to be in the open?

"Of course, Grandmother. I'll try to answer you as best I can."

"Answer me? About what?" Grandmother sounded genuinely puzzled. "Aside from the length of time it took you to come to your senses and make your escape from your parents' household, I have no quibbles with you, my dear."

Grandmother drew herself up a little straighter in her chair, squaring her shoulders and setting the lamplight shimmering across the pearls at her neck. "I want to discuss a matter of utmost importance with you. A family matter."

She shot a quick look at Mr. Warren and from the corner of her eye Lenore saw him nod once.

"After Margaret and her husband return next month," Grandmother continued after drawing a deep breath. "Jacob—Mr. Warren—and I intend to post our banns at Trinity in Somerset and be wed the second weekend in September. We hope you will wish us well."

Lenore's first thought was profound relief—this conversation was not about her at all. Relief was swiftly replaced by dismay.

"Whatever will Papa and Mama say?" Her first thought popped out before she could stop it.

"I hope they will wish us well, too, Lenore." Grandmother's tone grew distinctly cooler and her expression appeared to have frozen along the sterner lines Lenore had been expecting all along. "At least in time."

Not in this century. Lenore managed to keep that thought locked behind her teeth. As soon as Mama and Papa learned of this wrinkle in their plans to recoup their social standing with the aid of Worth Lumber holdings she would be yanked home as unceremoniously as they had tried to do with Maggie just last year. Only Lenore had no dashing Irishman to swoop in and rescue her.

"I cannot stop you from sharing my intentions with your parents, but it is my hope you will allow me to broach the subject with them in my own time."

Grandmother's comment caused Lenore to look up from the gravy congealing on her plate. Three pairs of eyes were fixed on her.

"I beg your pardon. I was so . . . so—"

"Aghast?" Jake supplied, his gaze filled with disapproval. "Dismayed?"

"Overwhelmed." Lenore shot him back a look she hoped would quell further prompting. The last thing she needed to fill the awkward silence reigning in the dining room right now was sarcasm. "You have my congratulations, Mr. Warren."

The sympathy in Jacob Warren's blue eyes bolstered her as she turned back to his intended bride. "And my best wishes of course, Grandmother."

"Thank you, my dear." Grandmother's rigid features relaxed a trifle and she returned the smile Lenore was giving her with a small upturn of her own lips. "I truly hope you mean the sentiments you have just expressed."

"Indeed." Jake folded his arms across his chest, looking decidedly out of sorts as his gaze bore into Lenore.

"That's enough goading, Jake," his father warned.

Grandmother released Mr. Warren's hand at last and picked up her knife and fork. "Perhaps Jacob is right and I should have waited until later to disclose our news. Let us finish our meal and continue this discussion elsewhere."

"Begging yer pardon, Mrs. Worth." Kate burst into the room just as Jake opened his mouth to reply. "Young Daniel's here to fetch Dr. Warren. Seems Job Pruitt's in a poor way and Martha was hoping he could come over tonight instead of tomorrow on his way home from Somerset."

Jake was out of his seat before she finished speaking.

"I'll get my bag," he shot over his shoulder as he headed for the hall.

"I've a mind to ride along with ye," Kate called after him then looked at her employer. "If ye don't mind helping yerselves to the tarts in the kitchen. I'll see how Martha is faring and clear up here when I get back."

"Of course." Grandmother nodded her assent, as she stood and moved over to Mr. Warren with a new line of worry creasing her brow. Jacob stood and reached out to her.

"I'll go, too." The words shot out of Lenore's mouth before she could call them back. The last thing she wanted was a carriage ride to the other side of the cove with Jake Warren, especially when he'd been glowering at her so across the dinner table.

Looking at her Grandmother and Mr. Warren standing so close together, almost in an embrace, made her bite back any rescinding of her offer. Maybe going somewhere with Jake was the *second* to the last thing she wanted. She also was not ready to spend an evening with her grandmother and her soon-to-be grandfather. At least, not until she'd had some time to get used to the notion. What could possibly possess two people at their stage of life to want to marry? Surely the age of romance was long past for both of them.

"Are you certain you are not too tired from your journey?" Grandmother looked dubious.

"She's young. It's a beautiful night." Mr. Warren slipped his arm around Grandmother's shoulder. "And it will give the two youngsters a chance to visit."

The feel of Jake's hands on her back, the strength of his arms around her, and the touch of his lips on hers in the kitchen sprang all to quickly to Lenore's thoughts—they had already visited far more than necessary. While she had no interest in any further conversation with Jake—at least for this day—a ride in the night air, especially a silent one, might just help her order her thoughts and focus on the reason she had come here and how she could keep this latest news from forcing her to return to Boston before she could make other plans.

"Martha always was partial to Lenore. Even the time she trampled her prize rose bush." Kate offered.

"Jake was chasing me with a live lobster!" Lenore protested. "Mrs. Pruitt was most kind as she tended my scratches and pinned his ears back for scaring me so. I was seven and he made me ruin my dress."

"See?" Mr. Warren gave Grandmother's shoulder a squeeze. "That's the liveliest we've seen her all evening."

"Young Daniel went to harness the horse to the trap. He should be bringing it round to the kitchen door any minute." Kate said. "Ye'll have to hurry."

Grandmother looked up at her beau and over to Kate before she finally gave her assent. "If you're sure . . . ?"

What was it Tori said once—*better the devil you know than one you didn't?*

Lenore nodded. "I'll just fetch my hat and gloves."

"What's that?" The devil himself stood in the doorway, dressed in a bowler and carrying a black valise.

"Thank your grandmother and Kate for the tarts, Nora. Job's always been partial to Kate's sweets." The gray-haired, gaunt woman stood in the doorway haloed by the lamplight in her kitchen as Jake handed Lenore into the small cart they'd ridden over in an hour before.

"I will, Mrs. Pruitt. Goodnight." Lenore looked up at the sky and marveled at the number and brightness of the stars in the black velvet canopy. She'd forgotten how bright the night sky was here compared to Boston.

"And don't be a stranger while you're down here. It's hard to believe our little Nora has grown into such a beauty." Mrs. Pruitt clutched her shawl around her shoulders as the wind sharpened a bit. "Perhaps Job will be feeling up to company next time you come. He always brightens when your dear sister comes to call."

"Tell him I'm counting on a chess game," Lenore answered. It was Job Pruitt who'd taken time out from his dairy farm to sit on his porch every so often and teach chess to a shy ten year old.

"Get some rest while you can, Martha," Jake swung up beside Lenore, cutting the exchange off. His thigh rested against hers on the narrow seat, and she could not put even an inch between them. The scents of sage and citrus which clung to him blotted out the tang of salt in the breeze for a moment.

"I increased the dosage of Job's drops, you should both sleep easier tonight. And I'll call tomorrow as usual." Jake clucked to the horse and they set off, out of the splash of light from the farmhouse and into the night.

They rode down the lane, past the Pruitt's barn and pastures, in silence. Or in what passed for silence as far as Lenore was concerned. Despite the jingle of the harness and the jolting of the trap's wood and iron wheels on the rutted road, a soft quiet surrounded them as the lane merged with the trees and darkness enveloped them.

The man beside her could be carved in stone he was so still and tense—lost in his own thoughts no doubt. Just as well, she'd wanted the ride to be one she could use to arrange her thoughts, plan some way of showing Grandmother she was happy for her and Jacob Warren. Even if she was not sure that was exactly how she felt.

We shall no longer bow to the dictates of others.

Grandmother was the living embodiment of the pledge Lenore had taken. Perhaps that is why coming to Maine had seemed her own best first step.

Grandmother Worth already walked along the path Lenore was attempting to find. It would be odd to think of her as Grandmother Warren.

"Thank you."

Lenore jumped as Jake spoke directly to her for the first time since dinner. "I beg your pardon?"

"I said, 'thank you.'" He shifted his position so that he was looking directly at her.

At least she thought he was looking at her. The pine trees pressing the sides of the narrow road seemed to soak up the meager light from the ribbon of stars overhead. She shivered. "Whatever are you thanking me for?"

"That was the second time this night you did not bristle when someone called you by your old name." His voice, so close and intimate in the darkness, blew warm against her cheek. He spoke softly, without the edge of anger he'd shown over her reaction to the nuptial news. His tone rushed through her leaving a wash of wonder in its wake just like it had when she had indeed been *little Nora*. She shivered a second time, but this time it was not from the cold sting in the air.

Jake pulled the horse to a stop and leaned away from her for a moment. "The first time was when my father slipped, despite my warning. Then back there, with Martha. She's . . . she has a lot to bear right now. It's nice for her to revisit happier times unhampered by rebukes."

His scented heat enveloped Lenore as he draped his coat over her shoulders. The wool was warm from his body, but she felt warmed more by his praise. Even if it were only for *not* snapping someone's head off the way she had done to him over the same trifle.

"One of the few of Grandmother's traits my mother actively cultivates is addressing people by their full given name. Now that I am grown I suppose I just expected everyone to recognize that fact and address me accordingly." Lord, that sounded exactly like the haughty miss she was trying to escape.

Jake clucked to the horse without further comment and they started off again. The white of his shirt sleeves almost shone in the night. She clutched his coat tighter about her.

"I'm sorry if I reacted too harshly earlier," she said over the suddenly loud noises of horse and harness. "I have a few things to resolve while I'm up here. To think over. I suppose being prickly over a name is not all that important in the scheme of things. Especially to someone like you."

"Exactly what does that mean? 'Someone like me'?" The hardness in Jake's voice arrested her.

"You're a doctor. You know what you want from life. Other people respect you for what you can do. Your future is assured."

So unlike a socialite on the run from the only future she'd prepared for herself. A socialite with no idea what an alternative for such a life could possibly be. Little Nora Brownley with no prospects except a loveless marriage to the highest bidder. Sentenced to an empty life of luxury with a stranger. She was whining about a future most women would envy. Why had she thought coming to Maine would change that? Would change her?

"So you think I know what I am doing." Jake finally replied into the night. "That my future is assured. Everyone else seems to think so, too. They act as if I have done something that changed the situation in their illness or recovery. As if I have any control. I am not some sort of miracle worker. I'm a sham."

Deep bitterness etched his words and fairly scorched Lenore with the burn of his self-contempt. She didn't know how to answer him or even if she should.

He let out an exasperated breath as Grandmother's cottage came into view. "The only thing I know is how little I know. How little control I actually have over who lives or dies. How hollow I am compared to everyone's opinion. No one understands."

That's just how I feel. Lenore hesitated. How could she tell Jake she understood what he was feeling when their worlds—their problems—were so different. She might not understand exactly a doctor's experiences, but she did understand feeling hollow, feeling as if you could not measure up to everyone's expectations. She understood the loneliness in his voice.

Just before they pulled into the spill of light from Grandmother's windows she leaned up and brushed her lips against his cheek in a gesture of comfort, of wordless sympathy.

"Evening, Miss. Dr. Warren." A shadow detached itself from the side of the porch before Jake could react to her impulse.

Jake tugged the reins and they halted by the steps. He didn't look at her. What must he be thinking? Was he as shocked by her action as she? And what about the man who had just observed them?

The shadow proved to be Marcus, puffing on his pipe. She recognized the vanilla scent of his tobacco in the air. Marcus would never betray what he had just seen. At least she was safe there.

"I'll take care of your rig for you if you like, Dr. Warren," he offered.

"Is Jenna all right? Does she need Jake?" she blurted out before Jake could answer the coachman.

"She's sleeping as sweet as a babe." Marcus reached up to help her down from the seat while Jake climbed off the other side. "I dozed off in the chair for a bit and just came out for a stretch when I heard you coming back."

"Enjoying the quiet?" Jake asked.

"Actually, it's too quiet here for a city lad like me. Each time I come up here I seem to forget how unnerving the nights are." Marcus grabbed the mare's harness as Jake rounded the cart. "There's no sound from a hundred vehicles bearing their loads over Boston's cobbles."

"No dogs howling in a distant alley. Or lonely cats seeking a mate for the night." Jake answered with a twist of humor.

"No buildings close together, teeming with the sounds of business and family life." Marcus chuckled and tapped his pipe against the ground before stamping on the small hill of embers. "I heard your cart from far away. Over the peepers in the woods and the waves crashing in the cove. And I was grateful."

"Here I was just thinking that as loud as the peepers seemed tonight, I'd be lucky to get any sleep at all."

Both men laughed.

Lenore looked at Jake joking so easily with Marcus. It was obvious that her companionship, any solace she might have to offer, was not necessary. She had thought she'd detected a crack in him that matched her own, a dissatisfaction with the masks society forced on them. She must have been wrong.

"I'll say good night now, Jake." She hit just the right note of quiet cheerfulness. "Please tell Jenna I will come to see her in the morning, Marcus."

"Good night, Miss."

"Good night . . . Nora."

The nickname followed after her in the dark, but she'd already turned and started up the steps. She wasn't about to rise to the bait. She entered the silent house and picked up the note on the hall table.

I'll see you in the morning, Lenore.

Fondly,
Grandmother

Well, that was some progress. She hurried to go up the stairs herself to avoid any further awkwardness with Jake. He could turn out the lamps. She made her way to her room and was grateful to see a lamp lit and waiting for her on the nightstand.

The pages of her letter to Tori lay scattered on the desk. Her brown taffeta dress was still spread on her coverlet. She'd have to hang it in the wardrobe before she could sleep. She'd never thought about all the small things Jenna did for her until she looked around at this disarray. She was the one to do the cleaning up tonight.

"Best get to it." She spoke to herself.

As she pulled off her gloves and untied her bonnet, Jake's coat slipped from her shoulders. Something else to put away. She nearly groaned, all the exhaustion from the day's exertions and the emotional tumbles descending on her. She had no idea what time Dr. Warren left in the mornings, but he'd need his jacket and there was no guaranteeing how long it would take her to dress herself and do her hair without Jenna's help.

She draped the coat over her arm and opened her door. She was certain she'd heard the tread of Jake's boots on the steps coming upstairs just after her. She did not want to seek him out again tonight, even if she could figure out which was his room.

Never before had she kissed a man of her own volition. She had kissed Jake Warren twice today. The first time had taken her by surprise, but she had certainly enjoyed it. She needed to keep a comfortable distance from Jake if she was going to keep her thoughts clear. Surely, if she put the garment on the peg in the hall below, he'd find it.

A bar of light fell across the darkened hallway from under Grandmother's door. Perhaps she should look in and tell her goodnight and try to wish her well again with her plans to marry Mr. Warren.

Her hand closed on the cool glass knob and she turned it before she could lose her nerve. The sight greeting her shocked her to her core. Grandmother, dressed in a blue silk nightdress, was seated at her dressing table with her long silver hair cascading down her back. Sitting on her massive four poster bed in his nightrobe was Jacob Warren. They were deep in conversation.

"Don't fret over the chit anymore tonight, Sylvia," he was saying. "You'll find out what is troubling her in the morning. Come to bed."

Lenore was speechless. They both were turned enough in their seats to have not yet noticed her presence.

"I suppose a night's rest will do us both good."
Grandmother answered in a soft voice Lenore barely
recognized.

"Rest is not exactly what I had in mind," Jacob
chuckled. "At least, not just yet."

That was too much. Lenore could not bear to
hear another word. She opened her mouth to let
them know she was standing just outside the threshold when a hand clamped firmly across her mouth
and she was yanked backwards into the darkness.

Four

Jake kept his hand firmly over Nora's mouth as he half-dragged, half-carried her down the hall, then down the stairs toward the front door.

He was quite certain she aimed one or two very unladylike kicks at his shins as he hustled her away and he was equally sure the words being spat against his palm were nowhere near fit for a drawing room tea.

"If you raise your voice I'll haul you right out to the woods and leave you there," he warned when he finally got her, squirming and writhing, out onto the relative safety of the porch.

Out here, with distance between them and Sylvia Worth's bedroom, Lenore was much less likely to disturb anyone if she decided to vent whatever she might be thinking about the interchange she witnessed upstairs. And if she chose to berate him for his hasty handling of the situation, she could do that as well, provided she didn't get loud enough to draw the attention of the two people she'd been unreservedly spying upon just a few moments before.

She struggled against him as he debated whether to release her fully or just allow her the use of her mouth. Enticingly round parts of her decidedly female anatomy moved against him in a manner he was quite certain she would not have continued had she any awareness of the seductive havoc she was wreaking on his body and his patience.

He gritted his teeth and smothered a groan. The faint scent of honeysuckle swam in the night air. It was definitely time to either let go of her or suggest they follow the example of their elders and find a more secluded spot. Before his inclinations got the better of him, he released her.

"I hate you, Jake Warren," she said with all her pent up fury.

"What did you think you were doing back there?" he demanded, steadying her arm a moment longer to help her keep her balance and prevent her from striking him with her full force as she seemed all too ready to do.

She pulled free and backed up against the porch rail. Her pale hair was a wild tangle spilling over her shoulders and her breasts heaved in a distracting manner as she fought to gain control of herself. Even in the scant illumination the night and the shadows from the porch roof afforded he knew she was glaring at him with all her might.

"I was going to wish my grandmother good night." She almost choked on the last words. "What is it you think *you* are doing?"

"Stopping you from ruining what has been a very sweet awakening for two people who deserve a chance at happiness."

"Is *that* what your father was doing in my grandmother's bedroom—in his nightshirt? Because it certainly looked far more like he was trying to entice Grandmother *into* bed than awakening her from it."

She was shaking, whether more from her anger or the chill in the air he could not tell. A dark mass lay in a heap on the floor between them. He bent to retrieve it and recognized the coat he had draped over her on their ride home.

"And what if he was?" He straightened and held the garment out to her.

"She's my *grandmother!*" Outrage underscored the last word. She snatched the coat from him and flung it over her shoulders, then spun away to look across the darkened ground toward the rocks and the cove.

"My grandmother." This second reference was spoken so quietly he had to strain to hear her. She hugged herself and rubbed her arms under his coat as another wave of shivers wracked her.

He supposed a girl Nora's age might well be shocked by what she almost interrupted. It wasn't every day a young lady walked into her grandmother's boudoir and found her entertaining a lover. His lips twisted at the thought.

But Sylvia Worth had spoken of a broken engagement and hinted at a scandal when she'd informed her household of her granddaughter's impending arrival. How she knew, what she knew was anyone's guess, but she hadn't built and run Worth Lumber all these years without having her way of keeping track of what was important to her. Sylvia might not have shared the untoward details, but Little Nora was not quite so innocent as she appeared, of that he was certain.

Whether or not she was tainted, Miss Lenore Brownley had spent the last few years preparing herself for a life built on lies and evasions. A life populated by men who kept mistresses *and* wives, and wives who, having done their duty, took lovers. A life where scandal was merely a word for those who did not follow the unspoken rules of the game and got caught.

He'd seen it all during his years attending lectures at Harvard Medical. He would not allow the brittle façade of society to ruin the joy of the two people upstairs, discovering each other and their future. He would not allow her to shame his father and her grandmother with an artificial standard that satisfied her understanding of right and wrong.

They had wasted enough time already.

"And he is my father." He moved to stand beside her. He gripped the rail in an effort to keep his hands from snatching her up and shaking her. "But that doesn't mean they owe either one of us a scrap of explanation for the way they conduct their lives. Don't you think they deserve some happiness, especially after all this time?"

"They have been practically inseparable for years." Her cheeks glistened wet as she pressed her fingers over her mouth. She was crying, though from shock or anger was hard to tell. "Have they been carrying on like this all that time?"

"Would it really matter if they have? The one thing I have learned from medical practice is, that life is precious." He shifted his stance and put his hands on her shoulders so he could see her face more fully. "At best, happiness is fleeting. Look at Job and Martha, after almost fifty years together, they are being torn apart. I'd wager they would give anything to have a few more nights to share together without the shadow of illness."

Nora did not pull away as he had half expected. She tilted her head to look up at him for several heartbeats. The soft scent of honeysuckle filled the air. Everything inside him tightened in response. He wished he could see the deep amber glow of her eyes, try to gauge what was going on behind them, what she was really thinking, really feeling. She turned her head back toward the cove.

"If two people finally find their way to one another as your grandmother and my father have, they should not waste the opportunity." He offered her the reality he saw in his own adjustment to the relationship that had blossomed between these two old friends. Two people he both respected and admired.

"But . . . but . . ." said Lenore, "they already share a deep mutual . . . regard, surely they should be past . . . past the need for . . . that kind of . . . intimacy. For there to be any . . . *pleasure* in the exchange." She blew out a shuddering breath after stumbling through what seemed more thoughts spoken aloud than any true observation.

He took her chin in his hand. Her skin was cool satin beneath his touch. This was not the little girl who'd tagged along behind him on summer expeditions. She was an all too stirring woman with quite obvious wants and needs, whether she was willing to recognize them in others or not.

He pulled her closer. "Perhaps pleasure is a thing best measured on a more intimate level."

The silk cloud of her hair spilled over his fingers as he held her shoulder fast. Her honeysuckle fragrance filled him and he bent his head—knowing he should not, yet convinced he could do nothing else.

The instant his lips touched hers he was lost: Lost to his point in the argument, lost to his purpose for bringing her outside. Lost to everything sane and sensible in the world. He could do naught but savor the wonder filling him and the madness pounding through his veins here on the darkened porch, holding Nora Brownley close in his arms.

He moved in to taste the sweet fullness of her lips. She held back, but did not pull away. Reluctant innocence or shocked outrage? It did not matter. He could not stop now.

He gently took first her upper, then her lower lip into his mouth and moved his fingertips along her jawline to thread through her hair. She tasted sweeter than nectar, felt more right in his arms than he would have imagined possible, even a moment before.

The heat of her breath, coming in little gasps as he touched and released her lips with his mouth, warmed his skin. His hand slid from her shoulder to her back as he pulled her closer, kissed her closer. His coat fell from her shoulders and bunched over his arm while at last her hands crept up the front of his vest to rest at the base of his throat. Even through the starched linen of his shirt, the cool softness of her palms set fire to his suddenly scorched skin.

With a sigh she leaned in closer still and moved her lips against his, returning his attentions full measure. Pure male satisfaction poured through him at her response even as his mind noted her reaction was definitely not that of an innocent.

Poor lamb, she's nursing a broken heart, Kate had made a point of telling him earlier. Warning him, or warning him away? Doubtless, he must listen. Had Nora's betrothed played her false, or had she been the one to use sensual wiles to hide empty promises?

He pulled back, raw and bereft.

She nearly fell. Only his arm around her and her hands clutching his shirt saved her. He pushed the coat back up to her shoulders and let go as he stepped back. It took a moment for him to find his voice, and even then, the husky sound was almost unrecognizable as his own.

"If two strangers can find enjoyment in as simple an exchange as a kiss, would you deny two people in love such moments of enjoyment merely because of their age?"

He knew she had witnessed his father and her grandmother in a far more compromising circumstance than the kiss he had just pressed on her, but he wanted her to think about her response. Both Sylvia and his father were so overjoyed with their late-blooming romance he'd hate it to be spoiled in any way by Nora's disapproval.

Her chin lifted and she met his gaze with haughty assurance. "What makes you think I enjoyed your kiss?"

That question was the last one he'd expected. He snorted. "Either you are far more practiced in the arts of deception than I imagined, or you are more innocent than I've noticed."

He reached out and brushed a few stray strands of pale blonde hair from her cheek. "You do not kiss like an innocent, Nora."

She stiffened beneath his fingers, withdrawing just enough to break the contact as the last barb hit home. For several minutes the only sound on the porch was their breathing and a few soft woodland peepers in the distance.

"They are not even married yet." Nora chose to ignore his accusation as she used a tone which held every ounce of the same imperious quality of Sylvia Worth at her finest.

"Can you not see past the hurdles of convention and just accept that their happiness is something best left to them and how they chose to pursue it?"

"What will people think once the banns are posted?" she demanded. "Especially with you both living here?"

"Those who truly love them will be happy for the two of them. The rest will think what they like. The only important opinions to your grandmother, besides yours, are Maggie's and Devin's—who both applauded the match before they left for Ireland, by the way."

"Your father didn't live here then. Your house burned down after Maggie left—" She stopped herself in midsentence with a gasp. "Unless they *have* been . . . visiting . . . like this before."

"As I said earlier, that would be none of my business." He took a step toward her. "Or yours."

If her eyes had become daggers he could not have felt the thrust of her glare more keenly.

"So your father is upstairs enjoying my grandmother's *hospitality.*" She twisted the last word to make it sound as dirty as all the other pictures that must be flying through her head. "And you decided to drag me down here and kiss me until I agreed to ignore what is happening beneath my grandmother's roof?"

"Did it work?"

He longed to grab her again and this time give her the shaking she seemed to need. His father was shaky enough about people speculating that he was marrying Sylvia only for her wealth or that indeed he was finally making an honest woman of his longtime mistress. If Miss Lenore Brownley of Boston tried hard enough, could she push a wedge between her grandmother and his father?

"If I say it has," she said, "will you let me go back upstairs? Will I be allowed to seek my bed, or do you think to hold me hostage out here all night and give them the time they need?"

She moved as if to step around him, but his hand on her arm stopped her.

Silence reigned again between them as she turned her head to stare at his fingers against the black of his coat. Myriad possibilities cascaded through him as she stood close enough so that her breath fanned the back of his hand as it clutched the brushed wool. Whatever she said next, would he believe her? Could he believe her?

She tipped her face up to him at last. "You say you have learned that life is precious and happiness fleeting. You use that to excuse otherwise scandalous behavior because it involves someone you love."

She retreated a step and pulled free of his coat, leaving him holding an empty garment. "Yet only a few minutes ago you accused me of being fast when you said I did not kiss like an innocent. Is there not a double standard in your beliefs? Or were you thinking that wantonness ran through my family line?"

She stepped forward, brushing the coat he still held aside, and put both her hands on his cheeks. "If I kiss you again, will you believe me if I tell you I will not trespass in my grandmother's bedchamber again this night. Will you let me go?"

Before he could protest, she tugged him down to meet her lips even as she pushed against him and stretched up. His hands closed around her to keep them both from tumbling over as well as to keep her away.

Her lips touched his, repeating his earlier pattern. First, she suckled his lower lip, then she released it to gather in his upper. His response was instantaneous and ferocious. He could no more force himself to pull away than he could stop his heart from beating.

Instead of pushing her away as the sane corner of his mind insisted he should, he pulled her closer. She was soft in his arms, but demanding against his mouth until he kissed her back, measure for measure.

Her fingers clung to his cheeks and jaw sending a cascade of color whirling through him as she stroked his skin with the tiniest of movements. His very core opened in response to this woman he barely recognized as the girl he once knew. It did not matter. He burned to know her now in a way he'd never thought possible before.

He pressed her tight along the length of him. Her breasts pushed against his chest and his manhood swelled against her softness. His tongue lightly stroked the outer rim of her mouth. She tasted as sweet as her honeysuckle scent promised. He would have plunged deep inside her mouth to taste her more, but as abruptly as she had begun the kiss she wrenched herself away and released him.

He stood there stunned and lost, his chest heaving and his rigid flesh protesting, with her still close in his embrace.

"Have I convinced you?" She spoke in a deadly cold tone that showed how outraged she was. "Will you let me go?"

He was still speechless, both from what had passed between them and by how abruptly, how completely she had changed direction. As if the heat of the kiss had been nothing to her at all.

She traced her finger along his jaw. "Tell me was I an apt pupil! Or was I the tutor?"

"Go to bed, Nora."

His voice was harsh with denied longing and self-loathing as he released her and turned to clutch the porch rail. What had gotten into her? What had gotten into him? Who indeed was the tutor and who the student?

He drew a deep breath of the bracing night air. Whatever had just passed between them, neither of them could afford to let it happen again. "Anything you have to say to your grandmother can surely wait until morning, Lenore."

The slap of the screen door as she left him was her only answer.

He wished she'd never come to Maine.

"That's it, Miss. You've almost got it."

The hair cascaded down her shoulders, pins showering to the floor.

Lenore sighed. "It's hopeless, Jenna. I'm all thumbs. I am doomed the whole visit to go around with my hair in plaits as I did when I was a girl. And Maggie will not even be here to help me keep them straight."

"Why don't you come here and let me have a go?" said Jenna.

Lenore turned to look at her maid sitting atop the coverlet, fully dressed, with her foot wrapped and propped on a pillow. Tempting as the offer might be, she had to learn to do for herself. How could she even think to change her whole life if she couldn't master her hair or change her own skirt and petticoats?

"Nonsense." She shook her head and bent to pick up the wayward hairpins. At least two appeared to have escaped by sliding beneath the bureau. "If all the other women in this little corner of the world can get along without someone else to help them dress or fix their hair, surely I will be able to manage. Eventually."

She straightened and gave a dubious look at her image in the small mirror atop the dresser in Jenna's cozy room, and tried again to gather and twist her hair, holding it with one hand and pinning it with the other.

Haunted by what she imagined transpiring in her grandmother's bedroom and tormented even more by her own scandalous behavior with Jake, she'd tossed and turned most of the night. What must he think of her? Why did it matter? What was she to do? She'd come to Maine to seek a change in her life—but certainly not a change like that.

The worst of what had kept her wakeful and restive had been how much she had enjoyed those kisses shared in the dark of night. Only once had she been kissed by a man before yesterday. The sweaty, ham-fisted embrace her nearly-betrothed, Jonathan Adams Lawrence, III, had pressed on her after producing a tattered sprig of mistletoe last Christmas was revolting.

Horrified as she was by her grandmother's behavior and righteously angry with Jake for his high-handed treatment in dragging her away from the scene she had nearly interrupted—she still found no escape through the long night as her lips continued to tingle from Jake Warren's kisses.

The sensation of his mouth over hers, the beckoning smell of him on her cheeks and the scorching pressure of his fingers on her shoulders and back as he held her in his embrace tantalized her even in her dreams. She had been grateful when Kate woke her with a small pot of chocolate an hour ago.

Perhaps wantonness really did run in her family.

"There you are, Miss Lenore. You really do have it this time." Jenna's exclamation brought her back to their present surroundings.

She looked at herself from side to side. There indeed was her usual sleek chignon, or close enough to pass for it. "I do, don't I?"

She was inordinately pleased despite the fact that it had taken her a good half hour to master what most women must be able to do daily in no time. "Not that I won't miss your touch when you return to Boston, Jenna. Especially should there be an occasion that calls for something more elaborate. But that's hardly likely here in the wilds."

The daily possibilities of running into Dr. Jake Warren were nowhere near an occasion of note, no matter how her pulse might quicken at the thought. She planned to avoid Jake as much as she could.

"Well, now. Miss Maggie surely managed all right here and Mrs. Butler allowed as how her nephew's wife would be able to lend you a hand from time to time." Jenna patted the small pile of clothing on the bed beside her. "Once I've made a few alterations to these, you should be able to dress yourself in most of the clothes you brought along."

"My, I shall feel quite accomplished by the end of this visit. Able to dress myself and do my hair. Who ever would have thought?" Although she laughed, Lenore was only half-teasing.

"Certainly not that stiff-necked Amelia Lawrence."

Jenna's observation very nearly mirrored Lenore's own line of thinking. She shook her head. "I can't imagine Amelia having to rough it on her own no matter where she ends up going. Tori Carrington, however, manages quite well all the time."

Surely both her friends were faring better in their quests to seek new direction in their lives. Amelia always knew unequivocally what she did or did not want and Tori always behaved in a dignified manner. Neither of them would be capable of participating in, let alone enjoying, such a scandalous evening as she had last night.

Footsteps outside the door halted further suppositions. Could it be Jake come to check on his patient? Jenna had assured her he had already popped his head in early in the morning. Suppose he had come back? Was her heart pounding in anticipation or dread? Her mouth went dry as the doorlatch pushed up.

"Hello, my love. How are you faring?" Marcus's greeting entered the room just before he did.

Not Jake. Lenore breathed a sigh of relief, as the coachman stopped in the doorway and ducked his head in Lenore's direction. "Morning, Miss Lenore. Mrs. Butler asked me to tell you that your Grandmother was waiting for you in her study."

Lenore's relief turned to a cold lump of dread that froze in her throat. How would she face her Grandmother, knowing what she knew? How could she reveal her shock over the situation she'd witnessed without causing a rift between her grandmother and herself?

Don't you think they deserve some happiness? Jake's questioned haunted her. *Especially after all this time?* Maybe they did. And who was she to judge anyway? She swallowed hard.

"Thank you for delivering the message, Marcus." She gathered up the extra pins and her hairbrush. "And thank you for your expert tutelage, Jenna."

Just as Tori had said at the outset, she would begin

her interview with Grandmother one step at a time. "Good morning" ought to be a good start, she'd gauge what to say next by Grandmother's words. She left the cozy room attached to the stables and crossed to the cottage.

Five

"Please sit down, Lenore." Grandmother glanced up from her correspondence after Lenore greeted her. She pointed to the chair on the opposite side of the polished cherry library table, which served as her desk. "I am nearly finished with these."

Lenore crossed the expanse of floor covered by a large floral Persian carpet, with muted tones of green, brown, and soft blue edged in cream. She looked around, as much to reacquaint herself with another of her favorite parts of her grandmother's cottage, as to distract herself from her nerves while she waited.

Now that she was here, the thought of actually confronting her grandmother about what she had inadvertently seen last night made her quake. Why had Grandmother summoned her? Was it to continue their conversation from dinner last night or was it about events from later in the evening?

She took a deep breath, reveling in the smell of ages-old paper rising from the leather-bound volumes on shelves in floor-to-ceiling cases in the back half of the room. A massive granite fireplace stood opposite the door with a cushioned settee and several wingback chairs clustered before it, along with two tables, one bearing a tall lamp, the other a carved marble chess set—the perfect spot for whiling away a rainy summer evening.

She couldn't count the number of contented hours she'd spent sprawled by the fire with Maggie and Jake, helping him study or challenging him to chess just to watch his eyes light up each time she came close to defeating him. How young and foolish she must have seemed to him then, and she surely had sunk even lower in his estimation after her goading display last night just before she fled the porch.

The pressure of his hands on her arms, the breath-stealing kisses they'd traded with such ire harrowed her anew. Especially because there had been more than anger swirling between them—longing, unfulfilled hunger, and an unsettling desire for something more still lingered from the encounter.

She turned from the scenes revolving in her mind and sank onto the edge of the chair to await her grandmother's attention. She had come here to change the direction of her life and discovered that her grandmother was in the process of doing exactly what she herself had hoped to accomplish. Well, not exactly—she had not come here seeking a lover, let alone a husband.

Looking at her grandmother who was dressed in a dove gray worsted day dress, with her silver hair neatly rolled and pinned at her nape and her glasses perched on the end of her nose and absorbed in what she was reading, Lenore saw her in a new light—not just as the matriarch of the family and as a formidable force in business and the community, but as a woman who was seizing an opportunity. Her grandmother was getting married after nearly forty years of being a widow. What had made such a change appealing at this stage of her life? Why now? Why never before?

Perhaps that is what she should be asking her grandmother, not contemplating taking her to task for entertaining her betrothed in her bedchamber. Lenore suppressed a sigh and the pictures those thoughts elicited. The bank of mullioned windows behind Grandmother looked out toward the cove. The screech of a gull diving from heights outside echoed in from the side panels, which were cracked open to let in the morning breeze. She laced her fingers to help fight her nerves and the urge she had to bolt from the room and scramble over the rocks to see the creature emerge from the waves with its prize.

Grandmother closed the journal in front of her with a bang that immediately brought Lenore's thoughts back to her current surroundings. She took off her glasses and placed them on the desk.

"The rest of this can wait until I return from the office." Grandmother smiled ruefully as she looked over several stacks of papers on the table. "For the first time in years I find it is easier for me to deal with certain things at home. The office at Worth Lumber does not feel as safe."

"Why is that, Grandmother?" Lenore's ears perked up. Her grandmother had always seemed impervious to trivial things such as nerves.

"Mischief. Most likely boyish curiosity." Grandmother wrinkled her nose. "Someone entered the offices at Worth Lumber a few weeks ago and left the window open overnight. There was some wind damage and rain. Papers in Devin and Margaret's office were strewn everywhere. I felt somehow violated. As if someone were spying on me."

Just as she herself had when she opened her grandmother's bedroom door last night. She nodded, guilt overtaking any lingering outrage.

"But I did not ask you here to listen to an old woman's prattle. I trust you had an enjoyable ride with Jake last evening. How did you find the Pruitts?"

Her grandmother was also seldom one to indulge in idle chatter. She generally got right to the point in her conversations. Lenore wondered at the change as she answered. "Mrs. Pruitt seemed very tired and sad, although she tried not to show it to me while Jake was in with Mr. Pruitt. Neither of them said much, but I assume he is very ill?"

Grandmother nodded. "Cancer. Job is just wasting away and Jake cannot seem to stop the progress no matter how he tries. Job and Martha are devoted to one another. I honestly do not know how she will go on without him. Nothing in life is certain beyond today."

A kernel of insight dropped into Lenore's lap. Perhaps that was the key to her grandmother and Mr. Warren's plans. To their actions. Could seeing old friends losing something so precious made them look at themselves?

Grandmother was quiet a few moments longer, lost in her own thoughts. Then she looked at a pile of envelopes on her desk and selected one. "This came for you my dear. I had no idea you and Miss Carrington were friends. I know Margaret speaks quite highly of her, and they correspond."

"Tori and I belong to the same charitable organization."

"Ah, yes." Grandmother nodded. "The Brookline Daughters of Grace, for young women of good character. I believe your mother informed me when it was established. The sweet cream of society extending themselves for the benefit of those less fortunate."

"Yes, Grandmother." The way she said that last part almost made Lenore wince. She'd never paid much attention to the actual efforts of the Daughters of Grace. She'd always enjoyed their gatherings more for the tea and gossip than any other reason. Tori and Maggie had been the ones blathering about helping others.

"Are you aware that you girls help support several projects right in this area?"

When Lenore shook her head, Grandmother smiled ruefully. "I thought not. You not only sponsor Jake's clinic in Somerset, providing medical help for those who cannot pay, but also a small workhouse associated with the cloth mill which trains girls not as fortunate as you so that they might better themselves."

Better themselves working in a mill? Lenore could not fathom such a prospect.

"I see," she answered tentatively. Why did her grandmother persist in speaking of these beneficiaries of the Daughters of Grace as if she herself were personally responsible for the efforts?

"The mill teaches the girls a good work ethic, the rewards of being on time and doing assigned tasks. At the home you provide, they receive regular religious instruction and are taught household tasks, along with how to make a good appearance and proper modes of address. In time, employment is found for the girls and they move on so that new girls can avail themselves of this."

"It sounds like a very worthwhile endeavor. I'm sure Tori will be quite pleased to know how they are progressing. I'll be sure to tell her when I answer her letter." Perhaps that would satisfy whatever point her grandmother was trying to make.

"Margaret has a great deal of correspondence regarding the work house. I was hoping you would be so kind as to organize the correspondence again, as it was among the papers scattered about at Worth Lumber." Grandmother leaned forward in her chair.

"Devin, Jake, and she were looking into some important matters earlier this spring," she continued. "I know Jake is eager to locate some key information. I had everything crated up and sent here. It is in the corner over there."

Grandmother waved her hand at the far side of the room near the bookcases. Lenore turned. Sure enough, beside a smaller cherry table was a good-sized traveling trunk. It could not possibly be full of correspondence for a workhouse, could it? A sinking certainty bloomed in her stomach. While she hadn't exactly planned to come up here to actually accomplish anything, and she hadn't a clue how Maggie would want things organized, how could she refuse? Besides, a project initiated by her grandmother would give her a legitimate excuse to avoid Jake for a few hours at least.

"If that is what you would like me to do I'd be happy to help." She hoped she sounded sincere at least.

Grandmother nodded. "Good. I was certain you would be willing to pitch in. I find I have grown quite dependent on your sister's support and I would be pleased if I could say the same about you."

Grandmother took a deep breath and put her palms flat on the polished wood before her. "But that is not the purpose either of us is here to address at the moment, is it?"

Here it comes. The sinking feeling in Lenore's stomach turned into a cavern. Her grandmother's face had settled into her serious look, the one where it seemed as if she could see into your very mind and know all your thoughts before you'd even formed them.

"I know you are disturbed by my prospective marriage to Mr. Warren, my dear. And possibly by the fact that he is already in residence." Grandmother pressed her lips together for a moment before standing up and continuing. "While you are still young enough to be shocked by details, I respect you enough to be forthright."

She leaned forward, keeping her gaze fixed keenly on Lenore's. "Mr. Warren and I are willing to obey the proprieties and wait to say our actual vows, but we are not willing to waste any further time in expressing our affections for one another to our fullest. Do you understand the meaning behind what I have just told you?"

Lenore nodded her head, praying there was no stain of color tracing embarrassment across her cheeks. She had no clue what she was supposed to say to such a declaration. To her great relief, her grandmother did not look as if she truly expected a response at this juncture.

"If your sensibilities are too outraged to accept our current arrangements, I will regretfully wish you well on your journey home to your parents and rely on your discretion in allowing me to relay any information I deem necessary on this matter to my daughter and her husband, in my own good time."

With that Grandmother clamped down her lips and raised one eyebrow. Apparently now was the appropriate time for Lenore's response. If only she could find the right thing to say. Was there a right thing to say when one's grandmother revealed she had taken a lover? And that you could either accept this or leave?

The silence ticked by on the mantel clock. Outside, the gull screeched anew. Lenore chose her words carefully. "I'd very much like to stay, Grandmother, if that is still all right with you."

"Of course you may stay. For as long as you like." Tension she hadn't realized Grandmother must be feeling eased from the older woman's shoulders as she smiled broadly. "I knew there was still more to you than party dresses and the latest style to wear one's hair."

Grandmother rounded the desk and took Lenore by the arm. "Come and sit with me, my dear. There is more I have to say. More I have to ask you now that we have settled the most urgent matter. I want us to be candid with one another. To develop a new trust."

Warmth spread through Lenore, a warmth she hadn't realized how deeply she missed until this moment. Grandmother chose one of the buff padded-leather chairs in front of the fireplace and Lenore took a seat on the royal blue velvet settee.

"In her letter, your mother implied you needed to take a breather from your social calendar. She went so far as to hint at some sort of scandal involving Jonathan Lawrence necessitating such a break." She reached over and patted Lenore's hand as the shock of what her mother intimated must have registered on her face.

"I don't know anything about your suitor, but I do know you. And that neither Margaret nor Devin had much good to say about him." Grandmother paused and laced her fingers together in front of her as she rested her elbows on the arms of the chair and gave Lenore time to digest what she had just said.

The heat of humiliation stung Lenore's cheeks. Trust Alberta Brownley to twist events to her advantage. No wonder Jake felt so free to make advances toward her. Her mother had practically painted a scarlet *A* on her forehead.

"I need to ask you if your lack of dismay over my change in my life is because you yourself have become more experienced in the ways between men and women? Is there anything I can do to help you? Are you escaping an indiscretion of your own?"

Indiscretion? The exchange of searing kisses on a dark porch rose to mind. She shook her head, but she couldn't quite meet her grandmother's eyes. "Jonathan's disgrace was not of that nature."

She took a deep breath and met her grandmother's appraising gaze with the truth. "After Maggie married Devin, Jonathan did turn his attentions to me. I was flattered at first, but found I could not return his regard."

Remembering the horrible sense of betrayal she'd felt about what had almost been forced on her, she drew a shuddering breath, before continuing. "He and Father were in negotiations for a possible marriage despite my opposition. When his financial dealings with several shady characters from the docks came to light, he disappeared to Europe with what was left of the family fortunes. He left his property mortgaged to the hilt and his mother and sister bankrupt."

Compassion shone in the depths of Grandmother's hazel eyes. If she reached out again Lenore was quite certain she would burst into tears.

"I imagine William had some involvement with these ventures?" Grandmother summed up the crux of the matter.

Lenore nodded. "I realized I was lucky this time, but that I might not by the next time someone offered for me, especially with father's shortfalls looming."

"So you escaped using the opportunity to ingratiate yourself in Margaret's absence as your excuse. Very good. It is as I had hoped." Grandmother smiled and rose from her chair. "I believe I shall send William a nice fat bank draft as evidence of how well you are doing."

Grandmother moved back behind her desk and pulled a large black ledger out from the shelf. She dipped a pen in the inkwell and started scribbling as she talked. "Do you think this week is too soon for you to have wound me round your finger? I will be traveling next week and this may get delayed in transition otherwise."

Lenore's mind whirled. Grandmother knew Lenore was using her visit as an excuse to escape? She was willing to bribe her father so she could stay here? Grandmother was going on a trip? Everything was confused.

"I think I shall make it clear that your father can expect more of the same as long as he does not feel the necessity to visit himself. I saw more than enough of my son-in-law and his wife last summer." Grandmother looked up and fixed her with a stare. "Don't just sit there gap-mouthed, Lenore. You can hardly set yourself on a new path in life if you remain mired in the past."

"Where are you going?" Lenore's last coherent thought was the first thing out of her mouth. She pushed up from the settee and crossed to the desk.

"Jacob and I are touring an investment in Portland I've had my eye on. Then I have some shopping to do for my trousseau." Grandmother tore the page from the ledger and left it on the desk to dry. She looked her granddaughter up and down with a decided twinkle in her gaze. "I had thought to bring you with us if you were in need of emotional support, but since you do not appear to be either despoiled or devastated by a soured romance, I hope you won't mind if I leave you with one or two projects sadly neglected in Margaret's absence and enjoy the journey with my future husband, alone."

"Oh." Whatever would people think? *Those who truly love them will be happy for the two of them. The rest will think what they like,* Jake's words from last night echoed back to her.

"Yes." Grandmother was using her determined voice. "We will of course be very discreet. I do have your reputation to consider now, too. You could still accompany us, I suppose, but I think Kate and Jake will be able to look after you adequately while we are gone for a few days."

"Certainly, Grandmother." Lenore nodded, her thoughts flying back to the sweet heat of Jake's kisses and the spirals of pleasure his fingers on her shoulders caused even when she'd been her most outraged. "I'm sure we'll be able to get along quite well."

Provided she stayed as far away from Jake Warren as possible.

"Oh," she said, her jaw nearly dropping a second time when she saw the size of the draft Grandmother had made out to her son-in-law along with one of equal proportion to Mama.

"I'll write my letter informing your parents that the Watsons will be delayed by a few days and send the packet out after lunch. I'm sure these drafts will ease any dismay they may feel. You might want to include messages of your own at the same time. I'm quite sure your parents will be anxious to know how you are getting along."

"I'll go up and write a note at once, Grandmother." While she hadn't the faintest idea what she'd say, she knew it would not be anywhere near the truth, beyond that she'd arrived safely and in good health.

"Well, don't forget your own letter." Grandmother nodded toward the cream vellum envelope from Tori, clearly ready for this interview to be over. "I think I have given you enough to contemplate for the moment. Will there be anything else?"

Lenore lingered. This new feeling of rapport was too fascinating to abandon. And she needed to voice her question before she lost her nerve. "May I ask you something personal, Grandmother?"

Instantly, the tension from earlier was back in the line of Grandmother's shoulders. A wary spark widened her eyes. Sylvia Worth was not someone who delved lightly into personal matters. "Go ahead, my dear."

"How did you know that now was the right time to make such a change in your life? How do you know you are making the right choice? That this is what you should do?"

Grandmother was quiet for a few moments as she looked at Lenore. A smile curved the edges of her lips and a soft gleam replaced the wariness in her hazel eyes. She seemed much younger and softer than the no-nonsense business woman she normally appeared.

"Sometimes you do not recognize you are on the right path until you have trod it for awhile," she said at last. "Sometimes a blessing missed turns out to be a curse."

Lenore knew her face must be reflecting her confusion as Grandmother tried to explain. "Something Margaret said when she first arrived with Devin last summer made me open my eyes."

"Maggie?" Something Maggie had said set their grandmother on the path to matrimony?

Grandmother nodded. "Even someone as old as the hills can still learn if they are willing to listen, really listen. Especially to their own heart."

Grandmother sat down and gestured for Lenore to follow suit. She leaned back in her chair and raised her chin. "Albert Worth was a man too much like your father. Even worse, in that he was a gambler."

She paused and pressed her lips together as if to keep herself from saying more. "The best thing he did for me and our child was die shortly after winning the lumber mill in a poker game. As I struggled to make Worth Lumber grow, I vowed I'd never depend on a man again. For anything. Especially not for fulfillment. Love was a sign of weakness. That philosophy kept me at a distance from my only daughter. By the time I realized that fact, it was too late. I vowed that would not happen with Alberta's children."

It was true. Grandmother had never made any pretense, despite her busy schedule, that she was anything but devoted to Maggie and to Lenore when they had come to visit. She was eager to hear about their days and devised new treats and entertainments to keep them amused while she was busy. And she had written to them both every week throughout the rest of the year. At least, until the argument with Lenore's father.

"But what changed your mind about Mr. Warren?"

"Jacob Warren was devoted to me almost since your grandfather died. He would have done anything for me. In fact he did, even finding another woman to love when I told him to. He was my best friend, my confidant, and my stalwart support through all the years, but there was so much more we could have shared if I had not been so blind.

Grandmother shifted her gaze to the portrait over the mantel. Herself in younger days looking very serious, even grim. "When Devin brought Margaret to me he planned to continue on to California. She was willing to pay a terrible price, to sacrifice her heart in order to have what little bit of time he had to give her. To share one moment of happiness even if that was all they'd ever have."

Lenore nodded. "Papa was so angry when he figured out where she had gone and who had accompanied her. He swore to clap them both in irons. I don't know how you managed to change his mind, but I have even heard him go so far as to boast about the shipping magnate his daughter married."

"Their love gave them the strength to win the day." Grandmother shook her head, refuting any credit for herself in maneuvering events so that Maggie and Devin were wed literally under her parents' noses.

"When I saw all she was willing to risk—all she was willing to surrender and still not consider it a loss— I knew I had lived most of my life as a coward. I hid my feelings for Jacob in order to protect myself and cost us both countless moments of happiness in the process. Faced with Margaret's example, how could I do less?"

Now, Grandmother smiled broadly. "Jacob just took a little longer to convince."

Lenore had enough to contemplate without trying to picture how Grandmother had convinced Jacob Warren she was ready to love him after all the years they had worked together. She clutched her letter from Tori tightly in her hand and rose from her chair.

"Thank you, Grandmother. For telling me, for trusting me." She felt oddly humbled by the confidences her normally reticient grandmother had shared with her this morning. She had much to digest. So many changes to consider. "I'll go attend to my correspondence now."

"Very good, my dear." Grandmother rose from her chair as well.

"After luncheon I usually take a short rest. Doctor's orders since my bout with pneumonia last year." She wrinkled her nose and made a face that nearly set Lenore to giggles.

"Before I leave for the Worth Lumber offices I'll show you what I'd like you to do for the next few days. Unless you have suddenly developed an interest in sawmills and would like to accompany me?" A speculative gleam accompanied the raising of one of Grandmother's eyebrows.

"No, thank you, Grandmother." Something about the sound of the massive blades moving through the timbers at her Grandmother's mill had always sent a chill right down her spine. "I'll be happy to assist you in any way you would like, but Worth Lumber has always been Maggie's interest, not mine."

"Very well." The mantel clock began to chime the eleventh hour. "I will see you at luncheon. I trust you remember Kate serves that meal at noon. Any later and she gets quite testy."

"I remember." Lenore smiled. "I'll see you then."

She reached the door as the eleventh chime died away and turned to look back. Grandmother was already seated with one of her books opened, studying the contents—absorbed by the task in front of her. Not everything about Grandmother Worth had changed it would seem, only Lenore's perceptions of her.

Six

There was no need to elude Jake after all. He hardly came home long enough to even notice Lenore's determined and pointed avoidance of him.

She stretched her arms up over her head and arched against the ladder-backed chair she'd been using in Grandmother's study—wishing she could straighten her knotted emotions as easily as she straightened her spine.

If only she could discern whether she was more grateful for his absence, or irritated by it, she might make headway toward achieving some understanding. As it was, the debate raging inside her grew more maddening with every meal he missed and each time she heard the early morning tread of his boots on the staircase as he left the house, or his quiet return long after the household had retired.

Too often these past days had found her staring at the piles of Maggie's papers while her mind flew far from the tasks at hand. Focused on a pair of enticing hazel eyes alight with enough laughter to warm any heart or burning with such cold anger they could slice clean through any girl unwary enough to stand in his path.

She kept back a sigh, disgusted with her thoughts and more than frustrated at her inability to concentrate on the task at hand.

After the way he had treated her, why did she even care?

She supposed she would find a new path for herself, and not relive their brief indiscretion as though it was the pinnacle starting point in her new life. Seeing Jake again, showing him how little importance he held in her plans, would surely put an end to the echoes of desire and excitement he'd awakened in her. Then she might be able to accomplish any number of tasks without being teased by imaginary whiffs of his scent around every corner. And remembering the pressure of his firm lips against her own.

"But of course I need to be in the same room with him in order to show him how little he means to me." Her frustration echoed across the empty study. He'd been hiding himself in his clinic work for days.

She looked over the piles of papers again. Perhaps the hours he kept had nothing to do with her. He was a doctor after all, finishing his time with Dr. Michaels and working in Somerset to boot. The files piled before her showed that part of his efforts, as did the bills for clinic supplies. She had never guessed the cost involved in dispensing what she estimated as a few bandages and dosing syrup for a few coughs. No wonder Tori and Maggie had been so diligent in their efforts to keep the rest of the Daughters of Grace working on their fund-raising efforts. Shame touched Lenore again that she'd been so out of touch with the group's real focus. Her life in Boston had truly been a shallow and vacuous existence.

And it had taken her along time to notice.

What did that say about her?

She gave herself a shake and bent to remove the last of the papers from the box beside her makeshift desk. With Grandmother preparing to depart for

Portland with Mr. Warren this morning, she needed to finish sorting and get her grandmother's advice on what to do next. She smiled, pleased at least with this unexpected bonus. Her task had helped her forge a new rapport with her grandmother. And that turned out to be far more important to her than she had ever expected.

In that respect, she was more than relieved by Jake's absence. By avoiding her, he had also escaped revealing her shocking behavior on her first night in Maine. Grandmother's peace of mind would have been all but destroyed if she thought something untoward might occur in her absence. The relationship Grandmother shared with Mr. Warren notwithstanding, Lenore could easily imagine the disapproval that would shower her way if even a hint of her behavior with Jake came to her grandmother's attention. She needed to ignore what had happened in favor of peaceful coexistence.

Even she couldn't decide whether to kiss him again or do him injury.

Another sigh rolled through the study. Would Jake come home to bid his father farewell as Kate had mentioned earlier?

"Not that I want to spend any more time with Jake Warren than politeness dictates, mind," she warned herself.

The heavy tread of male footsteps tromped across the foyer, heading toward the study. A quick dash of fear streaked through her. For a moment she was certain she had conjured his presence merely by thinking of him.

She tensed as the door cracked open.

"Miss Lenore?" Marcus Watson called from the hallway. "I'm sorry to disturb you. May I come in?"

"Certainly." She pushed back the chair and stood to greet her father's coachman as he entered, relieved and disappointed at the same time that he wasn't Jake. "I suppose you've come to tell me you are ready to go?"

"Aye." Marcus nodded, clutching his cap in hand, his gaze anxiously checking for any sign of dirt tracked in from the yard. Lenore nibbled her lip and held her peace, wondering if Marcus heard the same lecture in his mind as she did in hers. Even here her mother's supervision could still be felt.

"Seeing as how Dr. Warren declared my Jenna sound as a cobblestone once more and ready to travel, she sent me to thank you for all your kindness to her while she's been indisposed."

"Yes, of course." Lenore waved away his gratitude as an unexpected wash of homesickness swept through her. "You just make sure you take your time heading back to Boston and give her that much extra time to rest and heal."

"Yes, Miss." Marcus nodded again. "You have a nice visit and when you're ready to come home, send word and I'll be right along to fetch you."

Marcus took a step toward the door, clearly anxious to be on his way. She remembered what he said about missing the city the other night and she understood.

"Wait." She halted him at the door. "I'd like to see Jenna, to wish her a good journey, if you can spare the time."

"She'd like that." Marcus smiled. He stood aside to let her pass. "I'll slip out to the kitchen and see if Mrs. Butler's ready with the lunch she promised to do up for us."

Lenore crossed the foyer, moving past her grand-mother's trunk toward the back porch and her parents' waiting travel coach. She stopped in the doorway a moment to blink at the sun's brightness. She had definitely been spending too much time indoors. The fresh breeze, salt air mixed with the scent of pine, filled her lungs and reminded her of some of the good things found outside the city. Marcus was too late fetching his lunch, Kate was already standing by the carriage handing Jenna a jar wrapped in a red-checked napkin.

"Here ye go," she said. "Miss Lenore said ye suffered from travel sickness. Just sip this ginger tea as ye go and ye should be right as rain. It's a recipe from Mr. Reilly's family. His granny's own, guaranteed to stop the queasies."

"Thank you, Mrs. Butler." Jenna took the gift and set it on the seat between herself and a large picnic hamper. "When you see her, please tell Miss Margaret we all miss her terribly at home. We wish her and Devin the best, but all the joy and laughter seemed to go out the door behind her when she left us."

A painful knot formed in Lenore's throat. She'd always known Maggie was the favorite daughter with the Brownley household—save for Mama and Papa. It had never bothered her before. Still it was quite unsettling to actually hear the sentiment expressed so freely by the people who were her last link with home. Should she protest what she knew to be true, or retreat back into the foyer and pretend she was just coming out?

"No good comes from eavesdropping, Lenore." Grandmother Worth's voice behind her made Lenore jump. "If you do not intend to go out, kindly cease dawdling in the doorway and allow me to pass."

Lenore stepped hastily onto the porch just as Marcus rounded the corner from the kitchen. "All set then, Mrs. Watson?" he called to his wife. "Said your goodbyes and got yourself settled in, I hope?"

"If I might have a word with you, Mr. Watson. I believe my granddaughter has yet to bid your wife farewell."

Grandmother emerged from the cottage resplendent in a gray watered-taffeta pointed basque traveling dress trimmed with silver buttons and forest green velvet ribbons. A small green velvet hat with net trim nestled in her upswept hair. She crossed behind Lenore to meet Marcus half way, but the small pat she gave Lenore's arm as she passed told Lenore she had been excused for her momentary lapse in good manners just now.

Lenore realized both Kate and Jenna were looking at her expectantly, no doubt wondering how much she had heard. She swallowed the lump still clogging her throat.

"Take care of yourself, Jenna." She offered, praying she'd managed just the right note of cheer in her greeting to past muster. "I'll miss you."

"And you, too, Miss Lenore." Jenna's features relaxed ever-so slightly as the sharp words she'd obviously been expecting didn't pass Lenore's lips. "Just look at you—Mrs. Butler here tells me you've been up since early in the morning and you still look just as fresh as can be. Country living and simple dressing becomes you."

"That is mostly from necessity at this point," Lenore admitted and smoothed her hands over the silk poplin of her simple russet skirt. With only one flounce and three rows of gold braid at the hem to match the cuffs of her plain white silk blouse, she felt very plainly dressed. "Even with your alterations,

I believe Grandmother's sense of style and abilities far outshine whatever I can manage on my own. I don't know how she does it."

"Necessity, my dear. Sheer necessity." Grandmother pressed a small purse into Marcus's reluctant hand before she turned and glided over to join the other women. "The days when I looked as radiant as my granddaughter in a simple white blouse and skirt are long past. Wouldn't you agree, Jacob?"

"I've never noticed any dimming of your countenance, Sylvia." Mr. Warren chuckled as he joined them on the porch, his gaze warm on her grandmother. "Although now that you mention it, Lenore does looked quite lovely today. Your hair is especially becoming, my dear."

Lenore felt her cheeks warm with the praise. It had taken her far too many attempts to achieve the simple braided chignon, but she thought she finally had perfected this style at least. She smiled her thanks to her grandmother's beau.

Jacob Warren winked and turned to shake Marcus's hand. "Have a safe journey. There's a hint of rain in the air. We'll be setting off ourselves as soon as possible. Do you think Dan needs any help with Mrs. Worth's own carriage?"

"No, sir. Soon as my Jenna and me get on the road, he should be ready to bring the landaulet around for you. Unless you'd like me to help him load your baggage before we go?" Marcus turned a wary eye toward the cloudless sky.

"That won't be necessary." Grandmother answered. "Thank you for the offer. Jake promised he would be home before our departure. I'm sure we'll manage."

"Very good then. We'll be off." Marcus jammed

his cap on his head and then tugged on the brim. "Good journey to you both, Mrs. Worth. Mr. Warren. Take care, Miss Lenore."

With that he shut the door to the coach and scrambled up to the seat. Kate stepped back.

"Give my regards to Mama," Lenore called as they pulled away. Jenna yelled something she could not hear and waved from the window.

"And now it is our turn to be on our way." Grandmother slipped her arm through Mr. Warren's and looked up at him with a smile that sparkled with warmth and affection. She looked at Lenore, "Are you sure you do not wish to accompany us after all, Granddaughter?"

As if the conversation she'd overheard between Kate and Jenna hadn't been awkward enough. True to her word, her grandmother had been discretion itself regarding Mr. Warren since their interview in the study, at least as far as Lenore could tell. Still, she barely suppressed a shudder at the thought of traveling with the two elderly lovers. Watching them squeeze each other's hands or exchange surreptitious glances as they'd feigned decorum for her sake, was even less appealing than staying behind with Kate and a man who was little better than a ghost.

"No, thank you, Grandmother. I am looking forward to some quiet time for . . . re-reading some of Mr. Shakespeare's plays." Lenore prayed that didn't sound as forced to her grandmother as it did to her own ears. Grandmother Worth had always been an advocate of her granddaughters' education, particularly the classics, and especially because she knew her son-in-law did not approve. At least, Papa had not risked offending his wife's mother over something he considered a waste of time when she footed the bill for the their tutors. "Before you go, would you like to hear about the papers I have organized? Or at least tell me what you would like me to do with them?"

"Jake was interested in the matter. He and Devin were working to help Margaret. I believe you should tell him what you have discovered and he will know what to do."

"Here comes Dr. Warren now," Kate pointed to the far side of the clearing. "I wonder what's become of his cart?"

Lenore craned her neck. Sure enough there was Jake trotting out of the trees on the gray mare that normally pulled his cart. Just from his rigid seat on the horse's bare back she could tell he did not seem to be in a mood to hear about the correspondence she had reorganized for her sister. She fought the urge to flee the porch and avoid facing him altogether. That would never do with grandmother's departure imminent.

"I told him the front wheel on that cart did not sound quite right to me just the other day," Mr. Warren commented with a shake of his head. "He never listens."

"Now, Jacob. We must allow the children to learn from their mistakes. Experience can be very educational." Grandmother patted his arm, watching Jake wince as he dismounted after dropping the satchel he'd been clutching in front of him. He did not yet acknowledge the party near the steps as he tethered the gray mare to the hitching post in the yard.

"Experience must be an especially fine teacher when it's yer own rump that's receiving the lesson," Kate observed in a dry tone.

Grandmother Worth's lips twitched with humor and her eyes twinkled, but she managed to suppress a smile at her housekeeper's remark.

"Kate, would you please inquire as to what is keeping your nephew?"

Kate nodded and hustled away.

"Speaking of experiences, Lenore." Grandmother Worth turned her full attention toward Lenore with a thoughtful frown. "I believe I neglected to mention the arrangements I made for you this week."

"Arrangements?" A tingle of danger raced through Lenore. "Something beyond sorting through Maggie's work for the Daughters of Grace?"

"Something I believe will put your nimble mind and organizational skills to good use." Grandmother's tone was light but her face held the look of a woman who would not be gainsaid. "If you are looking for a new direction in your life, you cannot stay cooped up in the study day and night, no matter how important those papers are to Margaret. Jake has been so very busy of late: I'm sure he'll welcome your assistance."

"What's that?" The felt bowler jammed on his head hid Jake's face in shadow as he climbed the steps, but there was no mistaking the cold displeasure in his tone.

The warning vibrating along Lenore's spine intensified despite the rebellious flutter in her heart as his voice rumbled through her. Her palms grew damp and she clenched her fists, fighting to retain her composure as she faced Jake with all the dread and anticipation that had built since the slap of the door separated them following their kisses on this very porch.

"If you are concerned about keeping your grand-child busy, Sylvia, I suggest you take her with you. I have better things to do than play nursemaid."

Jake struggled to keep a grip on his reaction to Nora Brownley now that they were finally meeting again in the light of day. His comment had obviously found its mark as her chin lifted and her spine drew up to an ultra correct straightness. He had both dreaded and anticipated this anger since she left him alone not far from this very spot her first night here. His father and Sylvia acting as two keen-eyed witnesses had played no part in his imaginings which ranged from shaking some sense into Nora or kissing her senseless.

"Do not take your ill-temper out on the girl, Jake. . . ."

His father's advice bit through the unwelcome rush of reluctant desire coursing through Jake. He drank in the cool perfection of Nora's features like a man parched, even as he cursed himself for a fool.

". . . I told you about that wheel—"

"Jacob." Sylvia's hand tightened on his father's sleeve and halted any further discourse as his father subsided for the moment. From the way his lips pressed together, it was clear to Jake he'd hear more on the subject later.

He should have listened the other day when his father first mentioned the wheel, if only he hadn't been so preoccupied. He knew Father and Sylvia might be disappointed if he'd missed their departure, but so far they had adjusted to the demands of his profession and would have chalked it up to a lengthy call—surely not the book by Hawthorne he'd been occupying himself with after he quit the cottage each morning.

The bolt breaking on his axle had almost been a relief, granting him a solid reason to miss facing the fact that he would be alone in the cottage with this maddening temptress for the better part of a week.

"If you had not rushed off after the church service yesterday, young man, you would have heard the whole story and you would not need to interrupt." Sylvia fixed him with a stern look. "Just as you clearly paid no attention to the rector's homily on the importance of paying due respect to one's elders."

Sylvia's frown did not bode well. Usually she enjoyed his irreverent use of her first name, notwithstanding her outward reaction and the proper reproof to which she usually treated him. He hadn't meant it to slip out just now however, and certainly not in the tone he had used. Yet another thoughtless folly to lay at Nora Brownley's dainty, distracting and proper feet.

"I beg your pardon for any offense I gave." He tried to appease Sylvia, wondering if propriety would allow his apology to stretch enough to cover the advances he'd pressed on her granddaughter and the penchant to press her further that swirled even now in his thoughts.

"I've no stomach for insincerity, as you well know." Sylvia's features still relaxed a shade. "I'm placing Lenore's welfare in your hands. You might at least behave as if you understood the trust I am putting in your promise to look after her. You do remember your promise the day her letter arrived, do you not?"

"Of course I remember." When he'd promised Sylvia he'd keep an eye on Nora, he'd assumed he'd be making sure the child he still pictured in his mind was safe each night and occupied during the day. He could think of several occupations for the tempting minx who had pressed her winsome charms on him the other night, but he was quite certain neither Sylvia nor his own father would approve.

Hell, *he* didn't approve.

And if it wouldn't put them all in a very awkward situation and shame Lenore into the bargain he would tell the tale of it right now and scare the two of them into taking her with them or providing some other chaperone for her.

He'd been dreading this group farewell ever since Nora had made such a fool of him on the porch. Seeing her now, looking so deceptively innocent in her pristine white blouse and simple skirt, brought an unwelcome rush of desire sweeping through him. Her parting taunt from their last encounter—*Was I an apt pupil, or was I the tutor?*—echoed through him still. And so did the even more galling urge to drag Nora back into his arms teach her a lesson she'd not soon forget.

He'd made sure to keep his distance since then.

"Elmira Gallagher's second youngest daughter has just had her first child. . . ."

Sylvia's reasonable tone only thinly hid the iron will behind her explanation. Whatever she had in mind to keep Lenore amused for the duration of her trip, Jake knew they would both be scurrying to do her bidding as soon as she was done.

"A boy. Your father and I are taking Elmira to Westbrook to visit them and Lenore has graciously agreed to act in her stead at the clinic."

Lenore looked as stunned by this announcement as he felt. What possible interest could she have in his clinic?

"Elmira's mind was set quite at ease by the offer, so she will enjoy her visit." Sylvia continued without appearing to take notice of her granddaughter's dismay. Or of the open displeasure he was quite certain registered on his own face. "You know how faithful she has been to the clinic after her oldest son came so close to dying from fever last summer."

Jake held his peace for the space of several heartbeats as he sought the right way to squash this plan. The thought of Nora working in his clinic was almost too absurd. Still, no one refused Sylvia Worth lightly.

"I thought Elmira had arranged for Sarah Moore to help at the clinic when her daughter's confinement began?" There, that didn't sound half as terse as he felt.

Sylvia shook her head. "Sarah is still away in Portsmouth for her brother-in-law's funeral and helping her sister with the business. They don't expect her back for at least another two weeks."

"Grandmother, if Jake would prefer I not accompany him to the clinic, I'll understand. I truly don't know what I can do to assist him anyway." Nora looked perplexed. The pallor of her complexion since her grandmother's announcement added a luminescent contrast to the stormy amber gaze she had fixed on Sylvia. His groin tightened in response and he pulled his gaze away.

His immediate and visceral reactions to her were becoming more and more disturbing each time he was near her. Spending more time in her presence was definitely the wrong direction to travel. Nora Brownley in his clinic—anywhere in his vicinity— would be more a distraction than a help. Enough was enough. Better to end this before it progressed any further.

"You will not assist me at all—"

"At least not with the actual examinations, my

dear." Sylvia edited his response, preventing him from endorsing Nora's offer to bow out. "Elmira merely keeps the waiting area in order and makes notes on the various patients and their complaints so that everyone can get through the afternoon and evening as smoothly as possible."

During his time at Harvard Medical he'd observed that people of the Brownley's social circle barely acknowledged the existence of factory workers or their children, let alone spent any time or effort assisting them. Even if he could endure the rides to and from the town with Nora, her elevated presence in his clinic would surely prove unsettling for his patients.

He had to quash this scheme. He drew in a breath and struggled to attain his best doctorly tone.

"I cannot imagine what interest a woman—a girl—of Nor . . . Lenore's class will have in sorting the ills of my patients or what possible use she will be to them—"

"Then you lack imagination." Nora's dry observation cut through his bluster as effectively as anything her grandmother might have tried. The brows she raised and the gaze she cast his way echoed the effect.

"If nothing else," she continued with a lift of her chin, "the young women of my acquaintance have been taught to be gracious to guests and see that they are comfortable. I believe I will be able to deal kindly with a few sick people, especially if it will set Mrs. Gallagher's mind at ease so she can enjoy her visit."

She turned a dazzling smile on her grandmother.

Her swift change from reluctance to defiant acceptance was stunning. Jake felt quite certain she'd twisted the end of her declaration to drive home the

contrast to her own visit. His mind was made up.
Once they were alone he was going to shake her
quite thoroughly.

Sylvia beamed approval. "I knew I could count on
you, my dear."

Dan Butler and the Worth traveling carriage,
complete with his aunt Kate, rattled around the side
of the house at that moment. He pulled Sylvia's new
pair of bays up to the porch with a flourish.

"I'm glad that's settled then," Sylvia said as Dan
handed Kate out of the landaulet. She looked quite
pleased with herself. "No need to thank me for my
foresight in arranging assistance, Jake. You have
been working entirely too hard of late as your frequent absences attest. Now please help your father
bring my trunk and his valise out for Dan to load so
we may be on our way."

"Come along, son." His father was already heading toward the door as Sylvia walked down the steps
with Nora in her wake.

As soon as they were safely over the threshold,
Jake let some of his frustration out by tossing his hat
unceremoniously across the foyer to land just short
of the table. He blew out an exasperated breath and
raked his hands through his hair.

"What am I to do with a spoiled Boston socialite
in my clinic? Even if she deigns to lower herself to as-
sociate with my ordinary patients she is not going to
know the first thing about what to do."

"I think Nora might surprise you, Jake."

Nora had been nothing but surprises since she
arrived, that's what he dreaded: Teasing kisses and
tempting curves pressed against him in the dark.
The smell of honeysuckle lingering on his jacket:
A week of nights alone with her in the house, Kate's

presence notwithstanding, without even the safe harbor of his work, his clinic, to deter his wayward thoughts.

His father put the valise and small strongbox on top of the trunk. "She has proved very dedicated to the correspondence and filing Sylvia set out for her, accomplishing it in nearly a third of the time we anticipated."

Jake picked up one end of the trunk. "Dealing with some paperwork for Worth Lumber is hardly the same as working with people who are ill or injured."

"She seems to have come here looking for a new beginning. Surely helping others can only help her in her quest."

A new beginning—added to expertise she'd displayed the other night, the certainty that the innocence Nora Brownley bathed herself in was a sham hit Jake like a punch right in his gut. His father picked up the other end of the trunk and they moved back toward the porch. The weight of the luggage precluded any further discussion.

By the time they had everything loaded onto rear of the landaulet they were both perspiring profusely. The women had moved aside a few paces while Kate received the last of her instructions and then returned to the house. Even at this distance, Jake caught a teasing whiff of Nora's familiar honeysuckle fragrance and nearly groaned as an involuntary rush of yearning coursed through him. His father pulled a handkerchief out of his breast pocket and mopped his face.

"Just how many rocks did you pack to take with us, Sylvia?"

"It is not loading the trunk into the carriage here

that should worry you, Jacob. It is unloading it when we return. I have a great deal of shopping to accomplish." Sylvia arched her brow as Dan helped her into the carriage.

"About your cart—" His father began as he stuffed his handkerchief back into his pocket and fixed Jake with his no-nonsense look.

"You were right about the bolt," Jake attempted to divert the lecture sure to follow the reintroduction of this subject. "It snapped clean off about a mile from here. Luckily there does not seem to be any damage to the axle."

"You cannot always count on such luck. You have got to maintain your equipment. Your patients depend on you to arrive when they need you."

"Dan says young Daniel should have a few hours this afternoon to assist Jake with repairs." Sylvia leaned over the edge of the carriage.

"Aye," Dan nodded. "He's got the Pruitt's herd to tend to, but you could perhaps give him a lift once you're done."

The sunlight glistening on Nora's spun-gold hair as she said her farewells to her grandmother distracted him from answering immediately. With a start he realized some sort of reply was expected.

"Thank you. I'll gather some tools and seek him out once you are on your way," he managed with effort. If he could not collect his thoughts—his reactions to Nora—here, how was he going to survive the week, let alone tomorrow afternoon in the clinic?

Why couldn't she have gone with his father and her grandmother?

"Jacob, will you stop ringing a peal over the boy so we can be off. I am quite certain he will manage to

repair the wagon and have better care in the future."
Sylvia frowned again.

Pa nodded to his betrothed with a bemused look
on his face and then shook Jake's hand. "Never
argue with a woman who is ready to go. Take care of
yourself son. And look out for Nora."

Had he meant the last as a warning to take care of
Nora or beware of her, Jake couldn't help wondering as Nora moved within a tantalizing arm's-length
while Dan and his father climbed into their respec-
tive seats.

Sylvia leaned over as Dan gathered the reins and
chucked to the horses.

"Since you will be busy with your repairs for the
rest of the day most likely, Jake, the ride to and
from Somerset tomorrow will give Lenore plenty
of time to tell you all she's discovered about the
matter of the workhouse girls. Don't give Kate too
hard a time, children," she cautioned as they began
to move.

"The workhouse girls?" He turned to Nora. What
on earth would she know about the situation of the
workhouse girls in Somerset? "I cannot believe you
have any interest in the plight of orphans from
Boston's poorest neighborhoods, or your sister's efforts to rescue them."

*Let alone what was happening to these girls once they
left Somerset.* The question they had been asking for
several months now. He now found himself in
agreement with Devin on one point of the investigation in particular. The less the Brownley sisters
knew of the matter the better he'd like the situation. There was no need to expose either of them
to the full ugliness of life. He refused to examine
his sudden need to protect Nora just as Maggie's

husband wanted to shield his wife even over her vigorous objections.

"Believe whatever you like." Nora stood her ground.

The storm brewing in her amber gaze was disconcertingly like her sister's. The thought helped him hold his untoward reactions to Nora at bay. Maggie was his friend and there was nothing more between them. There never had been. Perhaps if he could bring himself to look at Nora in that light they could muddle through this week.

"Grandmother said the matter was of particular interest to you just before Maggie and Devin departed for Ireland," she continued. "You can listen to what I have to say or not, as you please."

He ignored her tart tone as he considered the matter. The inquiries Devin had sent out at the last should have come back to him, not gotten mixed up in Maggie's papers. Whatever Nora had pieced together could not possibly have any value beyond the little they already knew about the girls who had disappeared after leaving the workhouse.

He was really struggling to think of Nora as a friend, not a tempting annoyance. Struggling and losing. The fire in her eyes, the stubborn lift of her chin and set of her shoulders as she faced him begged for a far different reaction. He had to get away from her and practice his new approach for a bit.

"Your grandmother was right, this will have to wait until tomorrow. I have to see to the cart if I'm to get you to Somerset and back tomorrow." He left her standing with Kate and went to retrieve his satchel.

"Be ready to go tomorrow, right after luncheon," he tossed over his shoulder. "Bring an apron. And

be sure to wear something simple. You'll make the
Somerset women uncomfortable dressed in such a
frippery fashion."

He made his escape without once looking back at
her, certain he could feel her agitated amber gaze
boring into his back.

Seven

I believe I will be able to deal kindly with a few sick people, especially if it will set Mrs. Gallagher's mind at ease so she can enjoy her visit.

The breeze from Belle Cove blew the prior day's declaration right back in Lenore's face as she clung to the words in the vain hope of strengthening her composure to face whatever lay ahead.

She'd spent the better part of the morning in the kitchen with Kate removing all hints of decoration from her plainest gray skirt, even going so far as to remove the lace collar from her simple linen blouse. She put her apron, straw bonnet, and ordinary green wool shawl on one of the rockers behind her, and she'd been cooling her heels out here for over an hour. She'd even left her hair down, plaited into one braid that swung across her back each time she paced down the length of the porch and back.

Still no sign of Jake.

Surely he had not decided to go directly from Kittery to Somerset and fail to stop for her in defiance of her grandmother's dictates. Not that she would know what his plans for the day were, as usual he was ignoring her. He'd arrived home late and left before dawn. Even the small pile of papers he'd requested she leave for him in the study appeared to be undisturbed.

As irritated as he had seemed, she could not bring

herself to believe he would purposefully have lied to Grandmother. She couldn't think of anyone foolish enough to do that. The echoing tap of her demi-boots against the porch boards did little to release her own growing ire as she returned to her post at the porch railing.

But she couldn't lay all of her turmoil at Jake's feet. Neither his defense of their elders' scandalous behavior, nor his high-handed treatment of her could be blamed for the wasteland looming in her own future. Though she'd been in Maine for an entire week she had yet to feel as though she had begun anything more than a social visit. Nothing was going as she had hoped. But then the entire problem with her hasty escape from Boston was that she had no plan. No direction. And wasn't likely to have one in the near future.

In a few weeks she would have to admit that she had no prospects beyond the one Papa was no doubt setting up for her right now.

The thought chilled her clear through.

She bit her lip and completed yet another circuit of the porch, heels clicking just the tiniest bit faster than before against the oaken boards. If only Jake would come to fetch her. At the very least going to Somerset would prove a distraction from the dark clouds gathering on her personal horizon.

"If he has made me go through all this preparation only to forget me, I'll . . . I'll. . . ."

Just what did a well-bred young woman do when a so-called gentleman stood her up? Especially one she was supposed to be doing a favor for? She leaned out over the porch railing, ignoring the protests in her mind, and tried to gain a view of the road to see if he was coming.

"It's not as if I really want to spend all afternoon with someone as arrogant as Jake Warren doing Lord-knows-what with whoever shows up at the door."

"Have I come at a bad time?"

The unfamiliar voice jolted through her and she straightened abruptly, nearly stepping back onto the rocker that held her shawl. Heat spread over her cheeks to have been caught talking to herself in broad daylight by anyone, let alone the very proper looking gentleman who made his way onto her grandmother's porch dressed in an impeccably tailored riding habit.

"I—I beg your pardon, sir." Years by her mother's side in stiff-necked Boston society came to her rescue as she composed herself.

"No, no, I assure you it is I who beg your pardon for startling you. That was most inappropriate of me." He doffed his fine bowler, revealing shiny dark hair, and bowed to her with a flourish. "Richard Moore at your service. I hope my sister and I have not chosen an inopportune time to pay a call?"

"Your sister?" Lenore knew she sounded stupid, but the intense scrutiny of the man's dark gaze and the utter surprise of his approach still had her heart racing. He was one of the most handsome men she had ever met, but he was also most definitely alone.

He laughed, the deep bass sound filling the porch as he stepped closer. The sheer masculine perfection of his features was almost overpowering. She fought the urge to step back a pace.

"I don't mean to shock you," he said dropping his voice to a conspiratorial tone, "but I'm afraid Deirdre regrets the second dish of tea she had a luncheon before we undertook the ride over from

Somerset. She dashed to the necessary as soon as she dismounted."

"I see." Lenore nodded, more than a little taken aback by his frankness. "Was my grandmother expecting you?"

She fervently hoped he did not know Grandmother was away for the coming week and that Jake would come home at last, impending clinic visit or not. Being alone with this stranger made her uneasy, though she supposed it was only her own inner turmoil that made it so. He appeared younger than she first thought, especially when he smiled. Not quite as tall or broad-shouldered as Jake, the aquiline line of Richard Moore's nose, his jutting chin, the twinkle in his eye, and the neatly-trimmed mustache over what appeared to be a perfect bow-shaped mouth was the markings of a young gentleman who would have set most of the members of the Daughters of Grace a-twitter. Even Amelia Lawrence would have been hard-pressed to find something to pick at in his appearance and manners.

He pulled off his dark kid riding gloves, folded them with a single flip of his wrist and tucked them into his pocket. "We came over expressly to make your acquaintance, Miss Brownley. Kate told me I would find you out here when I stopped by the kitchen for a glass of water. You are Nora Brownley, are you not?"

The knowledge that Kate had sent him in search of her, that someone in Grandmother's household at least knew this charming stranger, alleviated part of Lenore's anxiety. "Yes, I am. But I prefer to be called by my full name, Lenore."

"Something we have in common." He laughed again and leaned against one of the rail posts. This time the sound curled in the air more invitingly, enticing her to join in even as she refrained. "I too suffer from my childhood name. No matter how many times I've told my sister I prefer Richard, she persists in calling me *Dick.*" He pursed his lips in a moue of distaste that dissolved into another of those charming smiles. "Or worse, *Dickie.*"

He gave a shudder.

"How is it you and your sister made the decision to ride all this way just to meet me, Mr. Moore?"

"My mother and your grandmother were once great friends—" he began when the door behind him swung open.

Jake emerged onto the porch with the most dazzling woman Lenore had ever seen at his elbow. Dressed in a rich burgundy velvet riding habit trimmed with black satin braid, the woman was unmistakably Richard Moore's sister with her cascade of black curls spilling over her shoulders and her flawless milk and cream complexion. The small matching bowler nestled atop her head was cocked at a jaunty and very carefully artless angle.

"Why, you were so right, Doctor Warren." The woman practically purred as she took his arm and glided across the porch. "Here they are. Already becoming fast friends, if I know Dickie."

Jake's gaze could have cut glass he was raking Lenore and Richard so intently with it. The grim set of his features softened when he glanced down at the diminutive woman who clung to his arm very familiarly. Too familiarly. The sight made Lenore's stomach churn.

"Dearest Dick." The woman gave Lenore a thorough once over with her wide dark gaze as they reached the railing. "I do hope you have been behaving yourself out here with Nora, unchaperoned as you are. Aunt Sylvia would never forgive you if you corrupted such unspoiled innocence."

"Aunt Sylvia?" The question popped out of Lenore's mouth before she could stop it.

"Perhaps I under-represented our families connections just now. Your grandmother is my sister's godmama."

Richard had the grace to look uncomfortable. "Let me introduce you."

He straightened up and squared his shoulders. "Miss Brownley, may I present my sister, Mrs. Deirdre Moore Johnson. Deirdre, Miss Lenore Brownley."

There was only one word to describe Deirdre Moore Johnson and that word was ripe. From her lustrous black curls, ample curves, lush red lips and floral perfume to the way she still clung to Jake's arm. She was a very sophisticated and appealing package. She was older than her brother, but that only added to her appeal.

Lenore had seen women like her before, women who walked into a room and captured every man's attention. They were so vividly alive they made all other women fade into the wallpaper. She felt very gauche and plain at the moment, overly large, and utterly without any grace. Her mother had always sniffed and made sure they avoided the women whom she dismissed as *obvious.*

"How do you do, Mrs. Johnson?" Lenore managed to maintain her civility even as she wished she could just flee this whole encounter. If only the woman would let go of Jake.

"And how timely of you to arrive at this point, Doctor Warren," she added, meeting his piercing gaze with her own.

"Pray do not call me Mrs. Johnson, dear child."

The trill of Deirdre Johnson's laughter grated on Lenore's frayed nerves. "My husband has been gone these four years or more. You simply must call me Deirdre and I shall call you Nora. We will be bosom companions in no time at all."

Lenore sincerely doubted that. Something about this woman made her uneasy.

"She prefers Lenore." Jake spoke for the first time.

Deirdre finally untwined her arm from his.

"Why of course she does," she smiled prettily up at him, pouting her lips just a little before turning her gaze back to Lenore.

"It sounds ever-so-much more grown up. I am so glad Dick is the one who found you first, though," she added as she smiled again at Lenore. "When Aunt Sylvia asked us to drop by and see how you were making out, I was expecting someone far younger. In fact, from your attire, I probably would have mistaken you for the child's nursery maid."

"Deirdre!" Dick protested.

His sister blinked her eyes innocently for a moment. "Not that such simplicity of dress is not utterly charming in one so young. Nor . . . Lenore." Deirdre made a show of stopping and correctly herself that included the faintest of blushes.

She was good, Lenore had to admit that even Amelia on a tear could not have been so charming and still worked the conversation so that no matter how you looked at it Lenore was both too young and too old, and utterly lacking in sophistication. Old family friend indeed.

What was her real reason for making this call?

"Lenore is coming to assist me in the clinic today as Mrs. Gallagher is out of town. I asked her to come prepared to work." Jake explained before Lenore had a chance to speak.

"Now, I would have gladly offered to assist you. . . ." Deirdre pouted up at him again and Lenore suspected that this visit had been meant to assess the threat Sylvia Worth's visiting granddaughter might pose to the obvious interest the Widow Johnson had in the town's handsome doctor. "But I am quite certain Colette would not have been able to conjure such a serviceable ensemble from my wardrobe."

Having dished out more than her share of thinly-disguised hostility in the company of Amelia Lawrence, Lenore knew full well what this woman was up to. The urge to stamp her foot in frustration and scratch the smile from the woman's flawless face swept through her in full force. It had been quite some time since such a childish urge had held full sway in her thoughts. She forced her hands to remain by her side and held onto her composure with an effort. Not only did Deirdre have glossy black curls that even Maggie would envy, an outfit sewn in the latest and most flattering style, but she had a French maid as well. And there was Jake just drinking it all in as if every word were dipped in gold.

Which shouldn't bother her anywhere near as much as it did.

"I think you are to be commended for your generosity in offering to assist those less fortunate who must avail themselves of Doctor Warren's services, Lenore." Richard rose to her defense. "I only wish my sister could find such a satisfying use for her time. Especially one so beneficial to others."

"Thank you, Richard." Lenore managed a genuine smile. It wasn't often she had been commended for her part in any sort of charity work. The fact that this day had been Grandmother's idea seemed immaterial at the moment.

"I am very mindful of the plight of those less fortunate as you well know, Dick Moore. You just stop your shameless flirting this instant." Deirdre protested sharply. "Why, just last week Colette took some of my cast-offs up to the orphans you employ at the mill so they might see how a true lady dresses."

"Deirdre," her brother cautioned.

"You own the cotton mill?" That portion of the widow's declaration sparked Lenore's interest.

"Why, yes," Richard answered. "Are you familiar with the business? Its quite fascinating. I could give you a tour one day if you'd like."

"Actually, it's the orphans that caught my attention. I've been doing some reading about your employees in my sister's papers lately."

"Nora." Jake was issuing the caution this time.

"If you have read through the papers I left on Grandmother's desk for you, you'd know that there are some questions that Mr. Moore might be able to answer," she shot back at him.

"This is not the time," Jake answered sharply.

"Exactly," Deirdre Johnson chimed in as she turned an appealing gaze up at Jake. "We were discussing charitable works, not stuffy business. I think Dick was being terribly unfair. Don't you? After all, I have been picking up your mail at the general store to save you the trip when you are so busy at the clinic."

Jake's eyebrows shot up at that news, as though he'd had no idea the widow had been performing this service for his benefit. That tidbit of insight provided Lenore with entirely too much satisfaction.

"Both Mrs. Gallagher and I appreciate your efforts," he answered gamely. "And speaking of the clinic, we are regrettably late in leaving for Somerset. If you will excuse us?"

"But we have had almost no time to visit with Lenore." Deirdre looked more than a little put out. "And I am quite parched from the ride over."

"I'm sure Kate can provide you with some refreshment before you set out for Somerset," Lenore offered, grateful she would not have to stay and play hostess.

"I think we can manage until—" Dick answered.

"That would be lovely," Deirdre interposed. "Would it be all right if we partook inside? The sea breeze is quite harsh on my complexion. If you come to call on me, Nora, I will ask Colette to give you the recipe for the treatment she uses to keep my skin soft and fresh. I'm very delicate as the doctor here knows."

"Have your headaches returned?" Jake asked, a slight frown wrinkling his brow.

Deirdre sighed prettily. "Not as severely as before I sought your advice, but they have never truly gone. You are so kind to worry over me when my own brother can think only to chide me for all I cannot do."

Lenore seethed anew as the widow recaptured Jake's full attention. She thought she saw Richard rolling his eyes. She had no intention of calling on the widow Johnson and endure more of her less-than-subtle digs.

"Perhaps we should try a different course of treatment. I will consult with Doctor Michaels and then discuss the possibilities with you."

"Whatever you think is best," Deirdre purred and put her small gloved hand on Jake's upper arm. "I always enjoy your visits."

Jake covered her hand with his. "I'll see what I can come up with within the week."

"I'll look forward to that day," the widow purred. "I hope to see you again," to Nora.

Not if I can help it, Lenore thought as the other woman's intense gaze filled her with unease.

Turning to Richard, Jake held out his hand. "Good to see you, Dick. Will you let Kate know about your sister's refreshments or shall we, on our way out?"

Richard shook Jake's hand with a somber, almost grim air. "Thank you. I'll take care of my sister's needs. As always."

He took Lenore's hand in his, a smile lighting his dark gaze once more. "It was a pleasure meeting you at last, Miss Brownley. You are every bit as charming and delightful as I expected from one of Sylvia Worth's granddaughters. I hope to see you again soon."

"I'd like that, too," she answered sincerely, smiling. Her earlier qualms about the man had been allayed by his support in the face of his sister's veiled antagonism.

"Gather your things, Nora," Jake ordered. "We're late enough without you lingering."

Lenore Brownley in his clinic was even more a disaster than Jake had imagined. The faint scent of honeysuckle teased him each time a patient opened the door that separated his examination room from the one where of his clients sat and waited their turns.

Swathing her in an apron did little to disguise her charms. The pert bow at the back only seemed to accentuate her narrow waist. All male eyes and most of the women seemed to follow every graceful twitch of hers as she calmly asked their names and complaints then ushered them in one by one to see him.

Expecting her to be overwhelmed, or at the very least flustered, by the volume and variety of his patients, she'd surprised him by smiling sweetly at one and all and not even wrinkling her nose at some of the more noisome of the patients who tromped past her on their way in to tell Jake their symptoms.

The ride to Somerset had been a very quiet one indeed. After the eyeful he'd gotten of her flirting shamelessly with Richard Moore, he hadn't quite trusted himself to speak civilly. She'd even had the nerve to act as if he'd done something to offend her. Keeping her head turned to the side with her gaze averted through most of the journey, she'd pretended to be absorbed in the passing scenery. If only the long golden braid hanging down her back had not swayed so bewitchingly, he might have enjoyed the peace and quiet.

Now, it was anything but quiet in his clinic. Several families had been waiting outside the door when they'd pulled up. Several more had arrived after seeing his cart roll through town. So far he'd treated three sore throats, a badly sprained ankle, sewn up a gash one of the lobster men had acquired from his haul, and checked a dog bite from last week.

"Keep changing the bandages, Mrs. Phillips," he advised the mother of the dog bite victim, eight-year-old Jimmy. "Clean ones every day, but I think you can dispense with the comfrey compresses. There's no sign of infection. If area around the wound feels hot or turns dark red, send for me right away. Otherwise bring him back next week."

"Tell the doctor thank you, Jimmy." Geneva Phillips beamed at her son whose carrot-colored hair matched the shade her own had been at his age.

"Thanks." Jimmy hopped down from the stool. "Can I have my peppermint stick now?"

"Of course. You know where Mrs. Gallagher keeps the jar," Jake ruffled the lad's hair. "And stay away from the Aldrich's berry patch, at least until the one leg is healed. Then you can give that mutt of theirs a shot at your other one."

Jimmy hid his red-stained fingers behind his back, but grinned as his mother shooed him out the door into the largest room of the small structure.

The wails of a baby filled the clinic so Jake peeked out at the number of figures waiting on the benches that lined the room, ready to signal to Lenore that it was for the next patient. There was no sign of her at the small table Elmira Gallagher used as a desk. Jimmy's mother snatched his fingers back as he dove into the large glass jar perched on the corner and tried to snag another treat to match the one hanging out of his mouth. Geneva took her protesting son by the shoulder and dragged him to the door with a rueful shake of her head.

"Who's next?" he called, since Lenore was nowhere to be found. Despite his misgivings about her abilities to deal with the chaos of clinic days, he'd never expected her to just up and leave without so much as a word.

"I am," Lydia Jenks, the mother of the baby stood up and jiggled him to quiet him. The eight-month-old babe settled against her shoulder sucking two fingers and looked very unhappy. Her other two children clung to her skirts. "But you might want to take a look at Mrs. Aldrich first. She was not quite herself after walking here, so Miss Brownley went to fetch her a drink."

She pointed to the white-haired woman sitting in the corner near her. It was Constance Aldrich, once famous throughout the county for her strawberry jam. Her eyes were fixed straight ahead as if she were looking at something well off in the distance. He crossed the room and crouched in front of his elderly patient to take her cold fingers in his. "Mrs. Aldrich does your daughter-in-law know you are here?"

"Dorothy?" The woman looked at him in confusion for a long moment before her gaze began to clear. "You're Jacob Warren's boy aren't you?"

"Yes ma'm," he answered. "Can you squeeze my fingers?"

To his relief, her hand clamped on his with an iron grip.

"Why aren't you down in Boston?" Her voice grew stronger as she came back more to herself. "Thought you wanted to be a doctor or something?"

"He's been a doctor for close to two years now, Mother Aldrich." A stern-faced woman bustled through the side door followed by Lenore holding a pitcher that sloshed water on the floor as she walked over to set it on the table.

"It took me a bit to get the hang of the pump and then it wouldn't stop." Lenore's face was flushed either from embarrassment or exertion as she explained herself to no one in particular. She garnered several sympathetic looks from the waiting area's occupants with her admission. It had never occurred to Jake, when he'd explained that part of her duty was to keep the pitcher full, that a girl used to being waited on by servants might not know how to work a simple pump.

"You had me quite overset, Mother Aldrich." Her daughter-in-law exclaimed as she eased herself down onto the bench and fanned her flushed cheeks with her hand. "I've been looking for you this past half hour or more. I even left the jam you were helping me put up simmering on the stove."

"She was standing outside looking a trifle lost so I invited her to come in out of the sun." Nora poured some water into two glasses and proffered them to the first and second Mrs. Aldrich. "I am sorry for the delay."

"That's quite all right, my dear. Thank you." The elder Mrs. Aldrich fixed Lenore with a gaze grown suddenly quite keen and clear. "You have the look of your mother, but you possess a far sweeter temperament than Alberta Worth could ever claim."

Jake noticed more than a few heads nodding in agreement to that sentiment. He might have agreed also, but he was concentrating on the transformation in Mrs. Aldrich. She appeared to have recovered herself. He would have to commend Lenore for seeing her and thinking to bring her inside for a rest.

After taking a sip, the elderly woman handed her glass to Jake. "It was lovely to see you, Doctor Warren. But I must be going. There is jam simmering on the stove that requires my attention."

Using Jake's shoulder for support, she propelled herself to her feet and set out for the door. "Come along, Dorothy, you may help me seal the jars. Please stop by on your way home, Doctor Warren, and take a jar or two for your kindness," she called over her shoulder.

"I am sorry if she was a bother." Dorothy Aldrich rose from her seat. "Her memory slips away much more easily these days."

"She was no bother," Lenore reassured.

"I was reading in one of my journals that a tea of ginseng root may help to stimulate mental vigor. It also works to build appetite. I'll see if I can locate some if you like."

"Thank you, Doctor Warren. She keeps me on my toes, that's for sure. Good thing my youngsters are all school age or better." Dorothy smiled sympathetically at Lydia Jenks who had been standing with her children all this time, then hastened after her mother-in-law who had disappeared down the path.

"This way, please," Jake indicated the door to his examination room still holding Mrs. Aldrich's glass which he promptly returned to Elmira's desk.

"Can the twins stay here with you?" Lydia looked hopefully at Lenore as she detached first one's hand then the other's from the death grip they had on her skirt. "Mrs. Gallagher did the last time and it was so much easier to deal with Doctor Warren alone."

"Of course," Lenore answered although Jake thought he glimpsed a flare of panic in her eyes. The children were far more openly wary as their mother gushed her thanks and hastened away. Jake followed, certain the two four-year-olds would protest being abandoned at any second.

"Perhaps you can show me your dolly." Lenore had crouched in front of the children. As he closed the door behind him he could just see the little girl holding out what looked to be little more than a very grubby rag with strategic knots.

Peace still reigned fifteen minutes later when he ushered Lydia Jenks back into the waiting area. "Doctor Michaels's wife swears by comfrey lotion after a bit of fresh air each day. Says it got her through five children and a dozen grandchildren so far."

Lydia looked skeptical but accepted the bottle he held out to her as he opened the door.

"A young gentleman never pushes his sister. Even when she has provoked him by lobbing her doll at his head." Lenore explained as she cuddled Lydia's daughter Rachel against one of her shoulders while seated on a bench by the windows. The other occupants of the room were all staring in rapt attention at the trio.

Lenore's other shoulder was occupied by the lad who nodded his tear-streaked face as they all huddled together on the far bench. Lenore looked up and met Jake's gaze with her own melting amber one. She looked strained as she continued speaking in a gentle tone to the twins. "And young ladies do not strike at a gentleman, even their brother, no matter how vexing he may seem. So I think you should both apologize to one another, then go greet your mother."

"Aye, Miss." Kyle Jenks scrambled down, casting a guilty glance at his mama. "I'm sorry I said Isabelle was just a rag, Rachel. And that I pushed you."

"And I'm sorry I hit you, Kyle." Rachel too pushed herself off Lenore's lap and raced over to their mother. "Mama, mama. Miss Brownley is ever so nice! She told us all about the city and gave us each a peppermint stick and made Kyle say he was sorry he was mean to Isabelle."

"They have so many horses in Boston, no one can count them. Can we come back tomorrow?" Kyle asked as he joined his family. "Next time, Miss Brownley says she'll tell me all about the big boats that dock there. I bet she knows almost as much about ships as Devin."

Given that Devin Reilly had been born and bred

a ship builder, the last statement raised Jake's eyebrows.

"I'm sure we'll see Miss Brownley again soon, Kyle. Both of you tell her thank you for keeping you entertained." Lydia smiled her own thanks as she shooed her children outdoors.

Lenore barely glanced at Jake as she brushed by him to go gently shake the older gentleman in the corner. "Mr. Connor. It's your turn to see the doctor," she said.

The grizzled farmer blinked his bleary eyes. "A man could get used to waking up to a face like yours real easy," he said as he shuffled to his feet and ambled to the door. "Real easy."

Still mesmerized by the gentle sway of Lenore's skirts and long braid as she glided across the room and tantalized by her warm honeysuckle scent when she passed, Jake was unable to suppress memories of holding her, kissing her. He barely stopped himself from nodding his head in agreement. This side of Lenore was a complete surprise. She was indeed behaving as a gracious hostess, able to enchant each of her guests into thinking they alone were special to her. Too bad it was a sham. Bitter reality played havoc with the warmer memories enticing him. He followed Hank Connor out of the waiting area.

The afternoon stretched into evening. Lenore was graciousness personified addressing his patients, and even displayed due deference to him in front of them, but she almost never met his gaze or addressed him directly if she could avoid it.

The last of his patients, one of Johnson's millwrights, left through the back since his house lay right behind the clinic. The overly long consultation had included a recitation of every ache and pain in the man's joints as he bent to tend the cotton mill's various machines.

Jake walked into the waiting area to find Lenore, haloed by lamplight, attempting to dust one of the shelves while a carrot-haired adolescent entered the side door with a small bucket of glassware. Neither of them seemed to notice Jake's presence.

"There you are, Miss Brownley. All clean." Gerald Phillips offered her the bucket as if he were offering her the sweetest bouquet.

She rewarded Gerry with a dazzling smile that erased the tired circles under her eyes as she accepted the bucket. "Thank you. It was very kind of you to offer to help me clean up. I don't know how I would have managed without you."

Was there no man safe from her flirting? Enough of his male patients had offered compliments on his change in staff today to set his teeth permanently on edge.

The gangly lad flushed bright red from his neck up to his ears. "I told you that pump is a bit cranky. Mrs. Gallagher complains about it all the time, but Doc Warren don't seem to pay her no mind."

"I'm not surprised, Gerald." Lenore glanced up and saw Jake standing there at that moment. Whatever else she might have added was lost.

"Gerry, is there something I can help you with tonight?" Jake asked the young mill apprentice who had turned an even darker shade of red. "Did your mother send you back about your brother's injury?"

"No, sir," he answered. "Jimmy just told me that you had an angel working for you today so I came to see for myself while Ma finished with supper."

"Well, I'm sure she is ready for you now." Jake's patience was ready to snap. "If you'll excuse us, I have to stop at the Pruitts before I get Miss Brownley home to her own supper. Get your hat, Nora, and blow out the lamps while I go fetch the cart."

"Good night, Gerald. Doctor Warren has had a week of very long days and is quite out of sorts. I'm sure he appreciates your help as much as I do." Lenore cast Jake a sharp look before he grabbed his bowler from the peg by the side door and went to retrieve his rig.

He was not looking forward to the ride home to Sylvia Worth's cottage. Not one bit. He'd intended to bring up the investigation into the girls who had left the workhouse and seemingly disappeared. He'd intended to diffuse Lenore's questions and allay any lingering concerns to keep her well away from Richard Moore and his suspicions. He'd intended to thank her for her help in the matter, and for her work today. But all he could think about where Lenore Brownley was concerned at the moment was how much he'd enjoy putting space between the two of them.

Or worse, kissing her to soften her sharp tongue.

Eight

"What have you done?"

Jake's voice behind her made Lenore jump. He did not sound the least bit pleased about the transformation of his waiting room, but then she hadn't ridden into town early this morning with young Dan Butler with pleasing Doctor Jake Warren foremost in her thoughts.

"And who told you could do this?" Accusation added bite to Jake's reaction to the alterations she had worked so hard on all morning.

Still gripping the broom in her hand she turned to face the man she had not seen in almost two days, not since she'd fallen asleep against his shoulder almost before they left Somerset following her first afternoon working in his clinic. The brief stop he'd made at the Pruitts's farmhouse that night, and even his carrying her into Grandmother's cottage were all a blur until Kate was tucking her into bed with a glass of milk and a warm bowl of soup. The part of her that wanted to thank him for his kindness that night stopped the exasperated part of her, who wanted nothing better than to take the broom to him now, from acting.

A lady does not strike a gentleman . . . no matter how vexing his behavior. Was that not the advice she had been handing out so freely just the other day?

"I'm waiting for an explanation, Lenore." He took his hat off and strode further into the room. A frown furrowed his lips and his brow.

"The mark of a good hostess is making certain her guests are comfortable," she proclaimed, raising her chin a notch and meeting his intense gaze with her own.

He looked around, drinking in her day's work and shook his head. Why on earth would he object to her improvements to his facilities. It was not as if she'd gilded the furnishings—all she'd done was add a few simple amenities.

"Those benches were not made for the long waits," said Lenore. "Too many of your patients are stiff and sore already, coming here shouldn't add to their ills. I rooted around Grandmother's attic and found some cushions for them. I'm sure she won't mind."

And too bad if she did.

A newly discovered well of rebellion swelled from deep inside Lenore. It had been Grandmother's idea to send her to help here. If Lenore chose to help in the only way she knew, so be it. She intended to make the best of things, to do her best under trying circumstances, just as Tori said Amelia was doing in the Berkshires according to the letter she received just yesterday.

"What about those? Sylvia might well object to you taking something directly from her porch." With his hat in one hand and his satchel clutched in the other, Jake used his own chin to indicate a point just over her shoulder.

"The rocker will help mothers with young babes soothe them and make the wait better for all. The rug will give children a little older a softer area to crawl around."

"And the sketches?" He swept the hand that still clutched his hat at the row of neatly framed drawings she'd hung on the wall. "What useful function will they supply for your patients, *Doctor Brownley?*

"Perhaps they will help divert people from their troubles. Give them something else to think about."

She gripped the handle of the broom tighter. While she'd hoped for his approval, she'd sworn a hundred times yesterday she would not allow Jake's opinion to sway her from this effort to make the clinic a comfortable haven. He might be the doctor, but it was her friends and her grandmother and sister who were supporting this place. She should have the right to make some improvements free of his censure.

The sketches had been Kate's contribution when she'd outlined her plans. The housekeeper produced quite a pile of Devin's artistry. While Lenore had especially liked some of the ones he'd done of Maggie—her sister looked so happy—she'd chosen scenes depicting Somerset's wharfs and cottages, a group of millwrights gathered at the gate early in the day, two fishermen cleaning the day's catch, two boys playing hoops, and a group of housewives emerging from the church—everyday images from the lives of the clinic's patients and neighbors.

"My brother-in-law has a talent for capturing not only the surface, but what lies beneath. They can come down when he returns, if he prefers that. I think your patients will find them interesting and distracting."

She bit her lip as Jake continued to look around the room with a frown. She was not going to mention Kate's assurance Devin would be delighted. Jake needed to take her seriously on her own. He'd picked

up the papers she'd left him regarding the workhouse
girls, but had yet to seek her out to discuss the matter.
She'd checked Grandmother's desk just yesterday
morning. There were definitely further inquiries to be
made, but if she could not gain his respect in regard
to a few cushions she held little hope for a reasonable
discussion on weightier matters.

"Are ya open for business, Doc?"

She looked past Jake to the open door and recognized one of the retired fishermen from the other
day. "Come in Mr. Connor. Doctor Warren was just
admiring the new cushions."

"Cushions?" The man's wizened face lit up.
"Them benches gets a sight hard on my hips. That's
why I come as soon as I saw the Doc's cart rolling
past. Wanted to beat the crowd."

"Will ya look at this," the man blinked after wrapping his fingers around the doorframe and hauling
himself up the small step into the clinic. "Wait 'til
Elmira gets a gander at this. She'll be tickled pink ya
finally listened to her and spruced the place up a bit,
Doc."

The fisherman gave the room a thorough once
over as he ambled stiff-legged over to the nearest
bench.

"I—" Jake started.

"If you think this room has changed, wait until
you see the examination room," Lenore interposed.

With a soft curse, Jake spun on his heel and
headed toward his inner sanctum. She almost
laughed out loud.

The afternoon sun took bold advantage of each
infinitesimal dappled opportunity afforded by the

pattern of the parlor's lace curtains to assault the polished walnut table and glare against Richard Moore's well-trimmed nails. He trimmed his nails daily—the hallmark of a man of means, a man who had nothing better to do with his hands than to keep them clean and neat.

Who would have thought he'd ever find such a life so terribly confining?

He frowned, pondering the significance of getting everything one had once wished for—or very nearly everything. The rapid tattoo of dainty heels on polished marble did not bode well for the immediate future.

"I do so hate the sunlight, Dick. It is not at all good for my complexion." Deirdre exclaimed as she joined him in their luxuriously appointed front parlor.

"I'll see what I can do to hasten the setting of the sun for you, dearest," he answered in as neutral a tone as he could manage.

Although she'd once possessed quite a keen sense of humor, able to laugh at her own foibles and find humor in the worst of their circumstances, she'd changed—hardened—some time ago. Now, nearly any chance remark, teasing or otherwise, could set Deirdre into one of her spells.

"Don't be a goose," she snapped, true to her waspish nature, he noted with a inner wince. "Today is clinic day and I must deliver the mail I have collected from the store for the good doctor."

Alarm bells rang for Richard whenever Jake Warren's name arose, as it had so often of late. *Widow* or not, his sister could not afford the scandal of an affair in such a small community as Somerset, let alone the strain such an attachment would cause for a woman as delicate as Deirdre.

He sighed, there was no use in reasoning with her on that front this afternoon from the look of her. He stretched his legs out in front of him, crossing them at the ankle and offered a discerning glance to the shine on his boots before transferring his gaze up to meet Deirdre's as she paced past him and the windows.

"Ohhhhh." She practically shook with anger. What had set her off on such a tear? "How can you sit there so placidly? Have you no feeling at all for me?"

"Deirdre—"

"Don't 'Deirdre' me. Everything was working out so well since our return to Somerset. We have the life we always dreamed about. The life Mama should have had. There is too much at stake for us. Too much, Dick!"

Her voice rose nearly an octave as her pacing picked up speed. Each swish of her shapely hips whipped her skirts from side to side, hissing against the plush parlor carpet. If he didn't divert her soon she would work herself into another fit. What was really behind Deirdre's hysteria? All this could not possibly be over an afternoon of glorious sunshine. No matter, he needed to distract or divert her.

"You could always send the mail by way of Colette."

This suggestion was met by frosty silence.

"Or I could go," he said.

The chance to chat with Lenore Brownley if she happened to be assisting at the clinic seemed an appealing diversion. She had proved an intriguing mix of city sophisticate and refreshing innocent the other day. The sparkle of intelligence in her amber eyes and her willowy form enhanced her appeal.

He would not mind running this particular errand at all, especially if Deirdre was soon to be prostrate with one of her headaches or increasingly frequent attacks of nerves. Perhaps he could even use the errand as a means to discuss his sister's case with the doctor or garner some suggestions for specialists he could take her to visit. He'd travel the world to see Deirdre made well again, he owed her that much and so much more.

"Hoping to catch a glimpse of that simpering little socialite?" Deirdre flicked imaginary lint from her dark blue gown, the one chosen to highlight the glossy black in her hair and the pale perfection of her features as she finally paused in front of the carved mantel. "Now that she is underfoot I can just imagine how close I am going to get."

Perhaps the irritating grain rubbing his sister was jealousy. Had his sister's flirtation with the doctor progressed further than he'd thought? Although he'd never seen her react to another woman with jealousy before, Lenore Brownley's pale beauty held a definite appeal at odds with Deirdre's lush attributes. "You accomplish nothing by torturing yourself over a mere visitor."

Her brows raised and he could almost see the delicate hairs along the back of her neck rising like hackles. Her dark eyes burned cold flame at him, almost as keenly as when he had questioned her about the packet she had removed from Sylvia Worth's desk the other day. It had taken Colette nearly three hours to calm her mistress and he never had gotten a straight answer to his question. Nor seen the contents of the packet. Perhaps this time it would be better to let her exhaust herself with words.

"Visitor?" She huffed her discontent with such a mild label for the girl she had shredded at every opportunity since their meeting.

"Yes, visitor. That's all Lenore Brownley is. She will be gone in a month's time and allow you to resume your pursuit of the doctor, if that is your aim."

"As if such a piece of fluff as that one could deter me." Poison dripped from Deirdre's full red lips. "Although you have failed to take into account the fact that her sainted sister arrived for a *visit* just last year."

He never failed to marvel that such stark venom could issue from such ethereal features. But then, Deirdre only used her beauty when it suited her. What was she up to with the doctor if it was not a discreet dalliance? Would she confide her motive to her brother? There were many things he knew her capable of, many things they'd been capable of together. He liked to think their struggles had left them closer than an ordinary brother and sister. Much closer. But still there were facets of her he did not know, dark corners she would not let him see into.

"I doubt fetching his own mail is one of the more onerous details of Doctor Warren's medical practice." He couched his question casually as if it did not matter to him whether she answered him or not. "If not to guarantee regular contact with the doctor himself, why this dubious interest in local charity work, dearest? You clearly find it taxing."

She gave him an all too familiar wouldn't-you-like-to-know look, but no answer to his barb was forthcoming. If it was not the doctor's person that attracted her interest in the clinic, what then? He smoothed his mustache and tried to consider the possibilities calmly and rationally.

"Don't you have some pressing matters to attend at the mill, Dick? Surely your profits could use some of this attention you are lavishing on how I choose to spend my days or the company I keep." Trying to shift the conversation was one of Deirdre's favorite ploys when she was indeed up to something.

"The mill practically runs itself as you well know."

For a man used to surviving by cunning and a good portion of luck, the security of a well-run business seemed much more appealing as a goal than when it actually came to fruition. The mill might provide the means and veneer of respectability to protect his sister from the dark life they had once led, but it was dreadfully dull looking at contracts and account columns all day long, day after day.

"Well, why should you care if I am attracted to Jake Warren? The more distraction I provide him, the easier your pursuit of Sylvia Worth's insipid granddaughter." Deirdre batted her lashes at him in mock innocence.

"Lenore is of no more interest to me than the girls at that workhouse down the road." He examined his nails in the dappled sunlight rather than meet her gaze and have her read anything there she would not like to recognize. Lenore Brownley *was* a visitor after all, a subject for a mild flirtation and nothing more, no matter what her appeal.

"Since when do you have a interest in the orphans you employ? What do you know of them?"

The sharpness of her tone surprised him. He looked up to see her rubbing her temple, another sign that one of her headaches threatened.

"Little more than my foreman tells me. They arrive on time, change the bobbins through the day, and return to the Hawkins household on the other side of the hill each night. We employ girls of that age because their hands are small and nimble enough to slip inside the machinery quickly." He threw the last information out hoping to divert Deirdre's thoughts from whatever spirals they were attempting.

Deirdre's eyes were closed and she was rubbing her temple in earnest now, rocking ever so slightly back and forth on her heels, not the least impressed with his small display of knowledge. "Of that age. *Of that age.* I did not have such options. I did what was necessary to protect you. To protect us. I had no choice. Look how well it turned out."

She was speaking in a low monotone, more to herself than to him at this point. Her face was pinched, her skin washed out and gray. The transformation was alarming. He rushed to her side.

Deirdre opened her eyes and fixed him with a dark gaze rife with anger and roiling with haunted sorrow. Everything she had been through, all she had suffered for his sake, lurked in the depths of her eyes. His heart twisted with memories best left forgotten.

"The least you could do, the very least, is take care of our investment here. Our life here," she said.

"Of course, dearest," he soothed. "I'll go to my office at the mill directly."

He reached out and pulled her into his embrace. She did not resist, a good sign that she could still be calmed. He stroked his hands down her slender back, tracing along her spine to the curve of her waist and back again. She sighed and nestled against his shoulder. He smiled against her hair.

Deirdre had always enjoyed being touched. It was one of the things that had made her part in their past endurable for her. And for him. Knowing she garnered some small pleasure from the things she had been forced to do made the past easier. But his guilt was never completely alleviated. He had to protect her now. Even if it meant protecting her from herself. He owed her that, he owed her everything.

"Oh, Dick." She sighed again.

"Yes, love?" He stroked with a bit more pressure, kneading her back, pressing lower down her spine.

She tilted her head back, her dark gaze sparkled into his. She could be a lovely woman.

He smiled. "Feeling better?"

"Tell me things will work out the way I want them to." She wrapped her plea in her huskiest tone. "Tell me again that we will succeed in all the dreams we once had."

His heart tightened in his chest. For too long it had been just the two of them pitted against the rest of the world—a demanding purgatory with no room for softness or compassion except what little they could wring from each other. Everything she had been through, all she had done for him tore his conscience anew. Sometimes the boundaries of familial affection still blurred despite the best intentions. Surely she had suffered enough outside the bounds of society to make the tedium of his life here a small sacrifice in comparison.

"We will." He dipped his head and pressed his lips to her temple, breathing in the magnolia scent of her perfume and trying to absorb her frustration. "We have."

She swayed against him. He could feel the strain begin to uncoil from her limbs. He stroked her back again, releasing more of her stiffness, lessening her tension.

They would continue to succeed at this pretense of respectability because they had to. That's how it had always been for them. He knew this in the tattered depths of his soul and he would do whatever he could to keep that determination alive in Deirdre as well, because she needed his faith even more than he did.

"Everything will continue to work out exactly as we always planned. I promise."

"Thank you." Her whisper fanned the pulse point at the corner of his jaw.

They had pledged to leave behind everything in their past that didn't meet the needs of their current life. All their secrets and desires were best left unspoken. They were straying dangerously close to old patterns. He brushed one finger down her cheek and released her.

The unnatural brightness was gone from her eyes. She smiled up at him as if the storm had not only passed, but had never threatened.

"Why don't you go fetch that bonnet I believe I saw Colette unpacking this morning? You may show me how dazzling you look in it before I head off to my office and you run your errand of mercy in town."

"What a wonderful suggestion." Deirdre's face lit with anticipation. "I not only have Doctor Warren's mail to take to him, I must remind him that the ice-cream social is this Sunday afternoon. And I can use the time to get better acquainted with your little friend, Nora, too."

With that she blew him a kiss and hurried from the room, leaving behind a haunting whiff of her perfume and an increasing sense of alarm.

Deirdre Moore Johnson could not have picked a worse moment to glide through the door of the clinic. Lenore was still dabbing water on her apron where the Jenks's baby had lost a goodly portion of his last meal. Lydia had both twins in to see Jake while Lenore rocked the babe for her. As dusk settled outside the clinic, Lenore, the sleeping child, and Mr. Connor, dozing in the corner, were all that remained in the waiting room. Although she'd had precious little to do with infants before, holding the small bundle and listening to the tiny breaths and noises he made proved surprisingly satisfying.

Mr. Connor looked to be their last patient and he had only returned to ask if he should use the liniment Jake had given him earlier twice a day or every two days, he'd forgotten. She'd just been thanking her lucky stars the afternoon was winding down when the child had fussed a moment, expelled the contents of his stomach, and then settled back down to his nap. Alarmed that she'd done something wrong, she'd nearly bolted to the other room only to find Mr. Connor roused enough to comment that his grandchildren did much the same and then he too closed his eyes again. If someone as old as he saw nothing to worry about she had no desire to betray her own ignorance.

She continued to rock the child nestled on one shoulder and dab at the stain with her free hand as the widow swept into the room. Deirdre Johnson's snide reference to her looking like a nursery maid the other day echoed sharply as Lenore faced her with a child in her arms. The sweet scent of other woman's perfume twined unappealingly with the soured milk soaked into Lenore's apron.

"Good evening, Mrs. Johnson." Lenore clutched the wet rag in her hand and prayed she did not look as unkempt as she felt after a morning of cleaning and her afternoon greeting the clinic's patients.

The trill of the widow's laughter filled the silence.

Lenore fought not to wince at the shrill falsetto and stroked the babe's back lest he rouse. The brilliant blue cashmere gown the other woman wore was the perfect shade to offset her flawless complexion and the glossy black curls that fell below her straw bonnet. The cut of the walking dress' bodice accentuated her figure without appearing in the least bad taste. Lenore felt quite the dowd, indeed.

"Oh, you dear thing." The other woman's lips parted into the broadest, most condescending smile Lenore had ever seen. "I thought we settled this the other day. You do not need to be so formal with me, given our close family ties. Please call me Deirdre."

"Very well, . . . Deirdre." Lenore patted the babe who stirred again ever so slightly against her neck.

"Is Doctor Warren busy at the moment?" Deirdre enquired.

"If you'll have a seat and tell me the nature of your complaint, I will make a note of it as soon as I can. Doctor Warren has only one patient ahead of you." Lenore gestured awkwardly toward one of the benches.

Deirdre looked at the seat and wrinkled her nose. "You must be as tired as you look, poor thing. I am not here to *see* the doctor, just to visit. I thought I'd mentioned my little contribution to the good work being done here. I so enjoy the walk through the village, fetching the doctor's mail has become quite my favorite pastime, practically the highlight of my week."

I'll bet. Lenore struggled not to giggle over the inanity of Deirdre's last remark.

"But since Jake is occupied we can use the time to get better acquainted." Deirdre arched a delicate brow. "Or to make arrangements to meet under more comfortable circumstances. Perhaps tea?"

Nothing had changed in Lenore's reactions to the lush older woman. Something about Deirdre Johnson made her distinctly uncomfortable. "I am very busy helping here. Perhaps once Grandmother returns."

Deirdre pouted. "I get the feeling we got off on the wrong foot. Tell me how I can prove my friendship if you will not give me a chance to get to know you better without Aunt Sylvia to run interference?"

"I appreciate your offer. Really. But so little of my time is my own." Lenore searched for a polite way to continue to decline. Luckily the door to the examination room opened just then forestalling any need for her to answer the widow directly.

"I will fetch the candy sticks from the jar for you, Kyle." Lydia cautioned her son as the family emerged. "You and your sister each need to thank the doctor for bandaging your hands so expertly."

"That's quite all right." Jake followed his young patients into the waiting room as they mumbled their thanks while staring intently at the bandages on their hands. "But next time you wish to present your mama with a fresh-picked bouquet, leave the poison ivy out of the offering."

"Those are the ones with three shiny leaves together, Kyle." Rachel informed her brother.

"He already told us that." Kyle shot his sister a withering look. "So did Mama."

"What adorable children," Deirdre exclaimed. "But how will you manage to enjoy the ice-cream social with your poor little hands wrapped like that?"

Two pairs of panicked eyes turned to their mother. Jake frowned at Deirdre who fluttered her long lashes in innocent confusion at him and then smiled with exaggerated sympathy at the twins. "I'm so sorry I upset the little dears," she exclaimed.

"Doctor Warren said that if you were good and kept the bandages on until Saturday I could unwrap them then, in plenty of time for Sunday's treats." Lydia soothed her two older children with the peppermint sticks Jake fished from the jar for her.

She accepted her sleeping babe from Lenore. "Thank you again, Doctor. Putting a rocking chair out here was truly inspired, I must say. Come along children. The mill is letting the workers out and your father will be coming home looking for his supper."

With that she ushered her children out of the clinic giving Deirdre a wide berth. Lenore rose from the rocker. She glanced over at the gentleman snoozing in the corner oblivious to all. "I believe Mr. Connor is next. He is confused about using the liniment you—"

"If I might have a word with you first, Doctor Warren." Deirdre spoke right over Lenore as she crossed the room to stand practically in Jake's shoes and smile prettily up at him with her wide dark eyes. Jake nodded, obviously dazzled enough by her charms to ignore her rudeness as she continued. "I already explained to Little Nora here that I will only require a minute of your time. I have brought your journals and correspondence from the general store."

Little Nora. Lenore wanted to scream, and held her peace with great effort. Part of her wouldn't give the other woman the satisfaction of knowing her barbs worked so effectively. The other part wondered why Deirdre Johnson worked so hard to make her appear as an awkward child in Jake's eyes. Not that she herself cared what Jake thought of her. But why did it seem to matter so desperately to a beautiful woman like Deirdre?

"Thank you, Deirdre. It is quite thoughtful of you, as always." Jake accepted the small bundle she fished from her reticule. "But you really needn't worry yourself over this. I pass the store on my way out of town and can fetch it from Mrs. Hampton myself."

"I don't believe you appreciate my thoughtfulness at all, Jake Warren. Were you not the one who told me I needed fresh air and an interest to help me with my nerves and my headaches?" Deirdre pouted her full red lips at him. "And here I planned to inquire if you might like to join my brother and me for luncheon following services on Sunday. Then we could attend the ice cream social together afterwards."

She turned to Lenore. "You are of course invited too, Nora dear. My brother was quite taken with you the other day and would like to further our acquaintance. We will make such a charming little party."

New Hampshire sugar maples during a warm spell could not have dripped sweeter than her tone. Lenore's hackles rose, ready to refuse flat out.

"I believe Mrs. Butler has asked both Miss Brownley and me to help in setting up for the social." Jake slapped the mail on the table. The effect of Deirdre's effusive charms had apparently evaporated in the dryness of Jake's refusal. "Perhaps another time."

"Thank you anyway for the gracious invitation." Ordinarily Lenore would have been annoyed at being volunteered for yet more work and for Jake's refusal on her behalf, but she was too grateful at having an excuse.

Deirdre's protest was interrupted by a call from outside.

"Doctor Warren. Doctor Warren!" Gerald Phillips burst through the door, panting. "There's been an accident, Sir. Mr. Moore sent me to fetch you straight-away. I came as fast as I could."

"Dick?" Genuine alarm tore across Deirdre's face as her gloved hand flew to the base of her throat.

"Where?" Jake was already heading to the door.

"At the mill." Gerald managed between gasps.

"Fetch my satchel, Nora," Jake called over his shoulder. "Send it up with Gerry when he's had a moment to catch his breath."

After that, he was out the door with Deirdre Johnson on his heels.

Nine

Lenore had not run as if her life depended on it in years, probably not since that horrible day so long ago when Jake had been hurt in a terrible accident. She shuddered away from the memory of the blood and the terror. Jake was fine, just fine, and he was counting on her to bring the bag with his supplies.

With her chest burning from exertion, she followed Gerald up the path to the stone and mortar base of the factory and stayed right behind him as he pushed through the small crowd of workers gathered at the base of a metal staircase.

Towering well over the crowd, the narrow steps led up to a small landing just outside an upper floor exit. Lenore eyed the length of the rickety stairs. How far could someone fall and still survive?

When they reached the center, a myriad of impressions flew at her at once—Deirdre Johnson sobbing softly against her brother's shoulder; the millwrights with brows furrowed, standing a pace or two away and shaking their heads; a clutch of girls all dressed in gray homespun clinging to one another, fear etched on their faces; but the only one Lenore could focus on, the only one they were all staring at was Jake bent over a tiny figure laying so very still—too still—at the bottom of the stairs. Her face was as white as the caps on the waves in the cove, her eyes closed as if in sleep with a dark swath under each one, and her long, blonde braid curled against the stones like a snake.

After checking her arms and shoulders, Jake ran his hands down the girl's legs. When his hands touched her ankle, the child moaned and she jerked her foot.

"Lizzie's not dead!" One of the girls exclaimed and then burst into tears.

"Course not, you goose. Mr. Carter wouldn't have sent fer the doctor if she weren't breathing." The tallest girl answered her as she dabbed at her own eyes with her apron.

"My bag, Nora."

Lenore started. Jake held out his hand to take the bag she'd grabbed from his examination room. She crouched beside him and put the bag on the gravel. He jerked it open and rummaged in the contents, finally extracting a small vial.

"Ammonia salts," he answered her question before it had fully formed and turned back to his patient as he uncorked the bottle. Taking her head in one hand he waved the bottle under nose.

To Lenore's relief the girl sniffed a few times then gasped, coughed, and her eyes fluttered open. Fear and confusion dulled the startling blue of the child's eyes as she looked around frantically for a moment.

"Callie?" She hiccupped a few short breaths.

"You're all right, Lizzie." The tall girl from her group of friends called. Callie had beautiful chestnut hair pulled into a tight plait and looked to be the eldest and leader of the group by the way they all looked at her. "We're all here with you."

Lizzie's eyes cleared a little as she focused on Jake

bending over her. To Lenore's horror, panic widened the girl's gaze. She stiffened and tried to throw herself out of his grasp.

"Don't worry." Lenore slipped around Jake and knelt so the girl could see her. She touched her shoulder. "You're in good hands. The doctor is going to check you for injuries."

The girl reached over up and grabbed Lenore's hand, and fixed her blue-eyed gaze on her. The grip of her slender, callused fingers was surprisingly strong. "You won't let him bleed me will you, Miss? Aunt Beatrice never recovered."

"Lizzie, that's your name?" The girl nodded and swallowed hard. The fear and appeal etched in the girl's pallid face as she continued to take small gasping breaths touched something deep within Lenore. She squeezed the girls hand. "Doctor Warren will be very gentle. He's not doing anything that is not going to help you. You must let him see if anything is broken. You had a bad fall."

The girl nodded and released Lenore's fingers. "My head." She touched the lump on her temple that was turning a deep lavender and red.

"I see that." Jake nodded. "Try not to move your head too quickly, it will likely make you dizzy. What about when you take a breath, does that hurt?"

"A little." Lizzie tried a deep breath that she cut off with a little hiccup as Jake put his hands on either side of her chest.

"I think you've just bruised your ribs," he said after a few more breaths. He smiled a reassuring smile at Lizzie, who seemed to have relaxed her wariness of him just a bit. "I'm going to take off your one shoe. I think your ankle needs some attention, Otherwise, I'd say you're a very lucky girl."

He looked over his shoulders at her friends who had crowded closer. "She's going to be fine."

"No one's ever said I was lucky before. Mrs. Hawkins says a dark cloud follows me." Lizzie confided to Lenore before she bit her lip and winced as Jake removed her shoe. Her hand reached over to Lenore's again as he pulled a handkerchief from his bag. Lenore thought of how he had bound Jenna's ankle, and held tight to Lizzie's hand.

"Is that the Mrs. Hawkins from the . . . from the place where you live?" Lenore could hardly bring herself to think of this delicate-looking girl in a workhouse—a place she'd always pictured as dark and rough, forbidding even. None of the small cluster of girls looked anything like what she'd expected. Dressed in the right clothes and with their hair fixed, every one of them would look as if they could belong to the Daughters of Grace, not be the objects of their careless benefaction.

"We all live with Mr. and Mrs. Hawkins, Miss. Hawkins Home for Wayward Girls, though Lizzie was never wayward." The girl called Callie spoke up. "She came from Medford way, Medford, Massachusetts. Her aunt took sick and couldn't keep her no more. That's how she came here."

"All done." Jake sat back on his heels.

"That didn't hurt near as bad as I thought," Lizzie said.

Lenore had to bite her own lip to keep from laughing at the surprise in the girl's voice. "Doctor Warren's very good at this you know. A friend of mine hurt her ankle a little while ago and he had her good as new in no time."

"Really?"

"Really."

"Here's the root of problem." Jake held up a canvas boot that was obviously too big for Lizzie's small foot.

"Mrs. Hawkins says I'll grow into them." Lizzie sat up a little and then closed her eyes from the efforts. "She'll be mad if I ruined them. Mrs. Hawkins says I'm the clumsiest girl she ever laid eyes on."

Lenore desperately wanted to give Mrs. Hawkins a piece of her mind. First, the girls who disappeared after leaving Somerset, now, evidence of the shabby treatment they received while here. The workhouse was supposed to be a charitable effort, a full set of good deeds in action. Wait until she wrote Tori about this. A scathing letter of rebuke from the Reverend Anthony Carlton might burn a little charity into the Hawkins.

"Mrs. Hawkins only buys things in two sizes. We have to make things fit or make do." Callie explained as Lenore realized the skirt the girl wore was woefully short for her. "I told Lizzie to put newspaper in the toes."

"Do you need some of the men to make a litter and take the girl home?" Richard Moore disengaged himself from his sister and stepped closer.

Jake shook his head. "I think I can manage carrying her myself. I need to give Mrs. Hawkins some directions for her recuperation. She will not be back to work this week."

Richard nodded.

"All right, fellas. The doc says she's going to be fine, time to get home to your suppers." Mr. Carter, the foreman waved the still-waiting audience of millwrights and apprentices. The men nodded and turned to head down to the village wishing Lizzie a speedy recovery as they moved off.

"We'd best go on ahead and tell Mrs. Hawkins you're coming." Callie gathered Lizzie's boots and shooed the other girls up the path winding behind the mill. "She'll be overset enough that we're late without us bringing some forewarning."

"If you're sure you have no need of my assistance, Warren, I'll take my sister home." Richard put his arm around Deirdre. "She's most distressed by all this. Would you care to join us for some tea, Miss Brownley, while the doctor is occupied?"

Deirdre looked more distressed by this invitation than by the injury to the little girl Jake was scooping into his arms. She clutched her brother's sleeve with one hand and rubbed her temple with the other, but refused to meet Lenore's gaze.

"Thank you, but—"

"But I need Nora to bring my bag and help me get Lizzie settled." Jake interrupted before she could refuse for herself. That was two invitations he'd turned down for her today without so much as a by-your-leave. Still, she was grateful enough not to reprimand him. Instead, she dutifully picked up the satchel she'd carried from the clinic and shrugged as she smiled at Richard.

"Very well." His mustache twitched into a half-smile. He tipped his hat. "I'll have to content myself with seeing you Sunday, Miss Brownley. Perhaps you will share a dish with me at the social. Good evening."

"Good evening. I hope you feel better, Deirdre." She returned Richard's smile and nodded to Deirdre before she turned to see Jake already climbing the path carrying his patient.

"I'll fetch your horse and cart to the Hawkins place for you, Doctor Warren." Gerald Phillips called as he dashed away without waiting for an answer.

"Are you planning to join us, Nora?" Jake paused long enough to turn and glower down at her from the opening in the trees the girls had disappeared into a minute ago. "With your admirers disbursed there is little reason to linger."

Lenore scrambled to catch up to him, determined to not even acknowledge the jibe. How could she have entertained the thought earlier that they'd managed to work a bit more comfortably together today? Of course, that had been before Deirdre Johnson had sashayed into the clinic or her brother had expressed some solicitude for Lenore's own well-being. Jake could learn a lesson or two in treating women with respect and thoughtfulness from Richard Moore. She was fairly certain he would not appreciate her pointing that out, however.

"Is Mr. Moore sweet on you, Miss?" Lizzie peeked up over Jake's shoulder as Lenore caught up to them on the narrow path through the trees.

"Mr. Moore was just being polite—"

Jake snorted.

"—Unlike some gentlemen, he has manners."

Lizzie nodded, then closed her eyes and rested her head back against Jake's shoulder. Nestled in his arms, she looked so very young and pale, especially in the gathering gloom of an overcast evening sky and the shadows from the trees.

Jake's satchel was as heavy as it looked, but Lenore was determined not to complain as she found she needed to use both hands to keep hold of it. Lizzie appeared to be sleeping and Jake stayed grimly silent as they trudged down the dirt path, keeping his eyes fixed on the ground to avoid the roots growing across the way. The chirps of crickets and tree frogs singing into the evening were the only sounds besides the tread of their feet and thumping of Lenore's heart.

"Watch your step, Nora. The meadow grass is slippery sometimes." Jake cautioned as they emerged from the small wooded patch. It was the first time he'd spoken since they'd left the mill behind, but at least he did not sound annoyed any longer. As they began the downward descent through a stone-fenced pasture toward a small farmhouse, Lenore could just make out the group of girls on the back porch.

So this was the Hawkins Home for Wayward Girls. It was smaller than Lenore had pictured, given the number of occupants. Smaller and far humbler than its name implied, that much was certain as they drew closer. The two outbuildings, a shed and a crude stable were tumbledown. The whitewash on the clapboards of the house had faded until the house was nearly as gray as the sky above it. She could have sworn there had been a hefty fee for paint included on one of the invoices she'd sorted last week.

Gerald Phillips rattled Jake's cart around a bend in the road at an alarming rate and startled Lizzie awake. One of the girls on the porch waved and ran out to meet them as the rest disappeared inside the small house.

"I hope he tightened the rigging," Jake muttered. "What is he thinking making a show like that?"

"Gerry is sweet on Callie." The girl picked up the thread of her earlier conversation as if her small nap had not occurred. "But Mrs. Hawkins says nothing will come of it cause Callie's going to be leaving for her new situation soon."

"You shouldn't trouble yourself about that right now, Lizzie." Jake warned her. His voice was gentle enough, but there was something behind the softness that raised the hairs on the back of Lenore's neck in warning. Would Callie disappear like the girls before her?

"You just rest and keep your foot up and do whatever else Doctor Warren instructs." Lenore tried to think of a good incentive. "That way you may be better enough to still come to the ice-cream social Sunday afternoon."

"Oh, none of us Hawkins girls will be there." The genuine sorrow in the child's voice tugged at Lenore. "Sunday's our day to learn how to keep a respectable home. We come straight home from service and Sunday School and spend the rest of the day cleaning the house from top to bottom."

How awful. The girls worked full days at the mill and then had to spend their one day off doing chores? As far as Lenore could remember, she'd never missed a party unless she'd had to choose between invitations. She almost never stopped to think just how pampered and privileged a life she led, even when Maggie or Tori had tried to point out those very facts. Her usual worries were if she had been seen in the same dress too many times or who she would be seated beside at supper.

Well she'd come here to change things, to change herself. Why couldn't she change things for a few other girls while she was at it? Perhaps if she appealed to Mrs. Hawkins, especially as one of the members of the group providing her husband's stipend, they would forego their routine this one time.

Jake started up the steps. "Put my bag on the step and wait at the cart with Gerry and Callie, Nora."

"But I wanted a few words with Mrs. Hawkins."

Those too big boots and the upcoming community treat figured prominently in the words forming in her thoughts.

"Not tonight." Jake stopped and looked straight at her. Even with just the reflected lamplight from the window, she could read the appeal in his eyes. "Lizzie's care comes first."

He was right. Lenore hated to acknowledge it, but he was. Mrs. Hawkins would have her hands full dealing with his instructions. She would most definitely not appreciate any further interference with her routine, at least this evening. She set the satchel on the step. "All right, but ask her if I might call on her tomorrow sometime."

He nodded and proceeded to the door being held open for him by one of Lizzie's friends. Lenore turned to go to the cart to wait. Grateful as she might be to sit down, she realized she was tired of waiting already. She had been waiting all her life it seemed, and although she hadn't known what she would find when she came to Maine seeking a new direction, somehow she felt just a little bit closer tonight.

A low murmur of voices reached Lenore as Jake took his leave of Martha Pruitt. The breeze sharpened and she drew her shawl tighter around her. Which Jake would join her for the rest of the ride to Grandmother's cottage? The cold forbidding one who had been judging her and finding her lacking since her arrival? Or the companion of old—the one she'd caught a flash of as they left Somerset and headed for here?

At least waiting here, even alone, she felt none of the unease she'd felt outside the Hawkins's.

Night had fallen quickly once they'd left the Hawkins's place with Gerald Phillips. Jake assured her Lizzie was resting comfortably as the center of attention from all her friends as they dropped Gerald off at his door. They'd stopped at the clinic long enough to close up and to wake Mr. Connor who had snoozed on in the corner there through all the excitement. They'd even shared a laugh that felt almost natural after the farmer had ambled away. Through the recent strain between them, she'd forgotten how Jake's eyes twinkled when he laughed or how his voice tickled her from the inside out.

As he climbed into the cart next to her now, Lenore could feel the difference in him. The man who took the reins from her was the forbidding Jake, stiff and frozen like a wave of cold air icing the warm contentment that had marked their ride to the Pruitt farm. They hadn't talked much then, but the ride over had at least been companionable in its silence. She hadn't wanted to break the fragile peace even to mention the irregularities with the Hawkins girls. At least his present mood released that impediment.

The gathering clouds obscured the stars and the cold wind signaled an approaching storm, which prompted her offer to stay outside and drive the cart up the lane to keep the horse from getting stiff, while he checked on Job and Martha. He'd even thanked her for the offer, but that was before he'd gone inside. While she'd driven the cart and horse along the lane to the far pasture and back she'd resolved to confront Jake regarding the unknown fates of the former Hawkins girls. She swallowed, now was as good, or as bad a time as any to carry through on that resolve.

"How was Job tonight?" she asked, unable to think of a way to break the now forbidding silence between them.

His attention snapped toward her with an almost audible crack. She fought to keep from squirming as she felt his gaze probing hers through the darkness. Though she couldn't see his features well she could feel the disapproval pouring from him.

"I beg your pardon?"

Tight jawed, that was the mildest way to describe him as he shook the reins and urged the horse forward down the dark lane. She didn't have to be able to see the details of his face to recognize the sound of grinding teeth. He definitely did not appreciate her intrusion. But she couldn't back down now.

"How is Mr. Pruitt this night?" A second try to goad a response.

"Much the same." The edge of his despair, honed by inexplicable anger, cut through the chill in the air.

She caught back a sigh as her heart twisted within her. Jake's frustration was as palpable now as it had been the first night she'd accompanied him. She thought they'd shared some common ground that night, perhaps they would again tonight.

She took a deep breath to steady herself. "I'm sorry to hear that. I know how hard his illness is on you."

"Kindly save your sympathies for those who either need or desire them. I am neither."

He might as well have slapped her and been done with it. The wind scouring the trees and the creaking of the cart on the rutted lane whistled through the void between them for what seemed both an eternity and the time it took her to blink back the unwanted tears that hovered near her lashes. What had she done to deserve his wrath?

And then her own anger rose. Whatever spurred this current distemper, she was not at fault and she had no intention of cowering from Jake's injustice.

She'd come to Maine to change the course of her life, truth be told, to avoid turning into her mother. Mama always mollified Papa and acquiesced to his wishes when he was on one of his rants, no matter how outrageously he behaved or who was at fault. He heaped the blame for all his failures on her mother's shoulders and her mother let him. She herself had shrunk before her father's wrath over the years and transformed herself into a perfect society darling to please him, but she had no need to please or change for Jake Warren.

"That's about enough, Doctor Warren."

"Enough of what, *Lenore?*" The sharp emphasis he put on her entire first name was like a stab next to the soft beguilement contained in the shortened Nora he usually used. She'd noticed he only used her full name when he was most perturbed by her. Good, she was thoroughly perturbed by him as well.

"Enough acting as if you can barely stand my presence in your world. Enough treating me like a child unable to grasp complex situations or the realities of life. Enough avoiding me and the job Grandmother asked me to help you with."

Thunder rumbled off in the distance. Lenore could only hope the storm building about them would hold off long enough for her to get to the bottom of the one she was deliberately brewing with the other occupant of this cart.

"What would a pampered young city chit like you know about life?" He snorted. "I have endured your *help* at the clinic with a great deal of forbearance for Sylvia's sake."

His ire was at least thawing the frost from his voice as it lashed her in the dark. He flicked the reins to encourage the horse to a faster pace. "With any luck, she and Elmira will be back early next week and you need suffer no further imaginary mistreatment at my hands."

"I am not talking about the clinic."

"Since the only time we have spent together has been at the clinic, how have I offended you, Miss Brownley, save for failing to dance attendance on your every whim at other times?"

"What do you think happens to the Hawkins girls when they leave Somerset?"

Again, his attention snapped toward her with an almost audible crack and more disapproval poured, cold and unwelcoming through the darkness.

"I beg your pardon?"

He definitely did not appreciate her question. But she couldn't back down now. Callie was due to leave soon. She was not a name on a list, she was a real girl, only somewhat younger than herself. The thought of her disappearing was too unsettling.

"The summary and correspondence I left for you on Grandmother's desk, surely you've read them by now. What is it you and Devin suspect is happening to the girls who have finished at the workhouse?"

Thunder rumbled again—louder, closer.

"There was no list for me on Sylvia's desk beyond some purchase orders and correspondence at least four years old. You needn't have fabricated a connection to our investigation to try to prove your diligence to Sylvia."

"Fabricated? How dare you!"

The first splat of rain hit at that moment. The flashes of distant lightning gave her a few glimpses of Jake's rigid profile as he concentrated on the dark road ahead and did not react to her outrage.

Anger squeezed the breath from Lenore's chest. "I left you a stack of papers. Lists of the girls and their addresses. Correspondence that ceased abruptly almost two years ago."

The raindrops cut the night and began to pelt them, she pulled her shawl tighter around her shoulders as the wind tugged at the brim of her bonnet. Another flash revealed Jake's gaze boring into her.

"Although I knew Sylvia told you to sort the files, I suspected it would prove too challenging for a flighty socialite to organize those wind-blown papers and actually find anything of value. It's amazing how convincing you can be when you want."

His words lashed her. His gaze glittered in the flash of light that streaked overhead.

"What do you mean by that?" she demanded.

The wind ripped the bowler from his head, it flew away into the night. He never flinched. "I was fool enough to actually look through the stack of papers you left on her desk. I'm sure Sylvia was equally misled into believing you had actually attempted to comply with her wishes."

He was as much as calling her a liar. Fury roiled in her stomach. No one, anywhere, dared to speak to her in such a manner. The mystery was real. Her concern was real. The papers she had organized were just as real. What would Maggie or Tori do? She bit her lip and counted to ten, slowly, then tamped her feelings down. If the girls were disappearing, someone needed to speak for them. Someone needed to look for them. That is what was important here. If she were going to enlist the aid of Tori's father, she would need as much information as she could pry out of Jake.

"The girls are indeed disappearing, are they not?" She finally ground out, surprised at the reasonable tone she managed. Tears hovered at the corners of her eyes and her throat tightened.

"Why you of all people would concern yourself over a handful of society's forgotten is beyond me. Unless it was for the drama of the moment, to add some excitement to the boredom of your visit." Another flash, brighter and followed by loud thunder, showed Jake shaking his head, his lips pressed in a thin line.

He put out a steadying hand as a jolt in the road sent her sprawling against him. She pulled herself back from the solid contact, barely able to stand his scorn much less his assistance. The pace of the rain increased.

"Well, I am concerned. Why is none of your business. Suppose something dreadful is happening to the girls? We sent them from the city to find a better life."

He blew out an exasperated breath. "No word does not necessarily mean that there are nefarious forces at work." His voice in the dark lost none of its edge. "And if there are, they would still be none of *your* concern. Devin and I have the matter in hand."

The wind blew rain into her face. Water dripped down her cheeks, mingling with the stray tears she didn't remember beginning to fall. She swallowed again, trying to clear the lump from her throat.

"How?" Her challenge came more as a croak.

"How what?" His voice rose over the wind as the heavens opened up. "We don't have time to indulge your fancies right now, Miss Brownley. Perhaps back at your grandmother's over a hot cup of tea."

The way he twisted the words the image was anything but appealing. It took all her will to continue probing despite his scorn. She put her hand on his sleeve and tugged. "I am not going to let this go until you tell me what is being done. Even if you don't care, I do."

She wiped at the water streaming down her face. He pulled the reins and the cart slid sideways to a stop. She no longer needed the lightning to know he was glaring at her, most likely ready to throttle her.

"You are no position make such a demands or accusations." His tone lashed at her like the rain. "You cannot tell me you even knew there were such creatures as Hawkins girls before this visit."

The keen knowledge that he was all too right in his assessment stung her to the core. After today however, little Lizzie with her too-big shoes and Callie with a too-short dress were vividly alive for her. She couldn't let her past failings get in the way of their futures. "But I know about them now."

"Fleeing Boston to come here and try to figure out what to do with your own life hardly qualifies you to render assistance to these girls. You don't really care about them and you certainly don't know me any better than you know yourself if you think I am go to let you continue to point an accusing finger at me."

"But I'm not—"

"You're not what?" He turned the full force of his dark humor toward her, she flinched. "You're not asking questions that are none of your business? You're not trying to interfere in a situation you know nothing about? You're not playacting your compassion for the Hawkins girls or at the clinic, with the very work that *is* my life?"

His words were like blows. Who was she to think

she could change her life? That she could make a difference in someone else's? Sheer stubbornness and pride pushed her onward.

"I know you don't think very highly of me, Doctor Warren. My life is very pointless next to yours." She spoke evenly despite the tight knot coiled in her stomach. "But my intentions to help are true. All I am asking is for some enlightenment."

He pushed the water soaked fringe of hair out of his face and blew out a long breath. "Very well. If it will get you to drop the subject and let us continue home before we are both soaked through I will offer you this much. Perhaps the new employment agency Hawkins engaged is not forwarding the girl's letters. Perhaps these particular girls have not thought to write of their new situations, not every one ever has."

Again he used that teeth gritting tone as he all but growled at her. "If I get word from our investigator in Halifax before you leave I will consider sharing the information with you."

It was a grudging concession. Hardly life altering. But after years of observing Mama and Papa she realized it would be better if she did not push him for more right away. With the rain splashing around them and the dark shrouding them, it would be enough for now. When they reached home she would probe for more details about this investigation in Halifax. She nodded.

Jake turned back toward the horse and urged the animal forward. Nothing happened. The mare strained and still nothing.

"Hell and damnation!" He bit the curse out, shoved the reins at her and jumped from the cart. After circling quickly, he came to a stop by her side.

"Well, Miss Brownley, you are about to get your first experience at true country life."

"What do you mean?"

"While we've debated your deep and abiding concerns we've managed to mire the cart in about six inches of mud." He shouted back at her as the thunder sounded again. "We're going to have to walk from here."

"Walk?" She tried to gauge the distance they still had to cover between here and Grandmother's. Was it farther to the cottage or back towards the Pruitt's house? Her calculations were a bit daunting either way.

"Yes, walk. Not a stroll about the Common to show off your new parasol. Or a quick mince past the shops on Milk Street." Jake loosened the mare from its harness, his movements abrupt and graceless, filled with simmering anger. "A means of getting from one place to another, the way ordinary people do. Unless you'd like to give riding old Bessie here a try?"

Lenore eyed the wet mare's broad back. Bessie was not the most cooperative animal she'd ever met. She had a feeling Jake wasn't seriously offering the animal as a mode of transportation anyway.

"No, thank you." She managed her most polite tone.

"All right, then." He turned the mare loose and slapped her rump. "Get on home, Bessie." With a grunt of protest the horse disappeared into the rainy gloom.

"Come on then." He held up his arms to her. And for a moment she felt quite like Bessie. Just another beast for him to see to before he could get on about the business of getting himself in out of the rain.

"No, thank you." She tried to get out of the cart on her own. She slid and would have landed face down in the mud, but for Jake's restraining arms. He righted her, placing her squarely on her feet and shook his head, his jaw tighter than she'd ever seen it. Her straw bonnet had fallen off her head and rain dripped through the tangle of her hair as she looked up at him.

"You can't go about playing at life, Lenore Brownley. You cannot treat these girls as if they were dolls you can pick up and fling away on a whim." For a moment he sounded like the friend she remembered.

He reached up and wiped a sodden lock from her cheek with his wet fingers. "Life is real and pungent. It's full of pain and death and uncertainty. And sometimes its so damn dirty you don't think it will ever come clean."

Something dark and painful glittered in his eyes. "You can't waltz in and out of people's lives with a sunny smile and nice manners and expect everything to fall neatly into place. Life seldom works out according to plan. You may have run away from Boston, but you cannot run from yourself. You cannot hide from your problems by taking on other people's troubles. You cannot fix others until you fix yourself."

His hands lingered on her wet sleeves, warming her through the chill dampness. Almost like her first night in Maine. His voice was poignant, sincere. The part of her that had responded to him that night recognized the painful truth behind his warning. He damned himself for the same sin. "Is that what makes you so angry, Jake? Because you have been doing the same thing?"

He dropped his hands and turned to head down

the lane. "Let's get moving before you catch your death and Sylvia lays the blame at my feet."

Fury roiled through her at his refusal to answer her, at his unalterable determination to treat her like a child and ignore any real exchange between them. It was on the tip of her tongue to shout at him that she'd rather drown than go anywhere with him, when she realized just how infantile the declaration would sound. And wouldn't that just underscore his entire point? The thought burned, leaving her unable to either quell the anger inside or adequately argue her point. She tightened her lips and tugged her bonnet back into place, sending a small cascade over her ears, water that had collected in its depths.

They trudged upward out of the mud of the lane. She slipped several times and would have gone down if Jake hadn't caught her each time. They'd gone over a mile in the steady rain when suddenly the very heavens seemed to open up around them. Sheets of rain drove toward them, over them and past, only to circle back around and come at them again.

"How much farther?" She could barely see.

"About a mile." He took her arm to steady her as the rain lashed them. "We need to find a place to stay out of the storm."

"I can make it." She turned back in the direction she hoped would lead to the cottage.

"Nora." He grabbed her arm and turned her against his chest, sheltering her from the worst of the wind and water. "We're too near the cliffs. With the rain and the dark, we should stop."

For a moment she was tempted to give in to his concern and frustration, to yield to the man who called her Nora despite all her attempts to remind him her name was Lenore. But the sting of his earlier condemnations still burned.

"I'm not about to stay out here with you any longer than I have to." She told him with enough ferocity to ease some of the pain burning inside her.

His lips tightened again and he shook his head. "Let's go."

They trudged on in mutual silence, broken only by the splattering rain and wind, keeping a pace that left her breathless and bespoke his renewed anger. She'd be cursed if she would give him the satisfaction of asking him to slow his steps in deference to her wobbly legs and sodden gown. She could only wonder what Amelia and Tori would make of her report of this night's disaster.

Ten

"I see a light up ahead. We're almost there."

A sound somewhere between a grunt and a sigh was the only reply from Jake's traveling companion.

By the time Sylvia's porch came into sight he could not believe Lenore was still on her feet let alone keeping pace with him.

She had grit, that much he had to give her, city chit or not. Her sodden skirt and petticoats must have added half again her own weight. Her bedraggled bonnet draped down her back and her braided hair dripped steadily. She clutched her shawl with rigid determination in one hand and raised her skirts as she slogged on and on through the mud, only grudgingly accepting his assistance when she slipped from time to time.

The rain had lightened to a fine mist, making the lamp in the kitchen window shine in a beckoning star pattern as they emerged from the woods. He had never seen such a welcome sight.

Kate must be worried sick. She'd give him a tongue lashing for sure for keeping Lenore out on a night like this. With no sign of Bessie in the yard, he could only assume the mare at least had the good sense to wait the storm out in some shelter. He should have insisted, but Nora made him so angry. Irrationally so. What was it she had done to deserve so much of his ire heaped on her slender shoulders? Shoulders that had marched through the night against everything the elements had thrown against them just to prove to him that she could.

He was soaked through himself, chilled to the bone and still angry to his core. Angry at Lenore for challenging him at every turn; angry that Sylvia had deliberately inserted her granddaughter into the heart of a matter that both he and Devin had decided would best be handled discreetly, and angry at himself for betraying enough of his inner turmoil to give Nora an edge as she poked her way innocently toward the true source of his ire, himself and his own inadequacies.

He hated to admit that side by side with his anger was growing an unsettling admiration for Lenore Brownley as well. She'd handled the citizens of Somerset who passed through his clinic door with grace and kindness. She'd transformed the drab interior and made it a welcoming, soothing place to rest. And she'd stayed right with him like a real assistant when they'd been called to the accident at the mill. No missish ways or hysterics, just calm, capable support.

She threw him completely off balance. One minute she was the little girl he remembered with such fondness, the next she was a temptress plying her wiles. She had neglected her grandmother for years, then wanted to sit in judgment. She was spoiled beyond knowing and yet she'd been determined to march right into Mrs. Hawkins kitchen and upbraid the woman for the conditions of the mill girls' clothing. She was insidious, invading every corner of his life, his thoughts, even his dreams.

She stomped up the steps behind him and kicked off her mud-caked half-boots. She dropped her bonnet and shawl in a heap before entering the kitchen door he held open. After sweeping by him with barely a glance or the ghost of gratitude, she stood in the midst of a puddle forming around her on the brick floor as she struggled to pull her gloves off one finger at a time. Kate would not be happy about the mess, but here was a far better place to create one than dripping in Sylvia's front parlor.

"Whew." He shut the door behind them and turned to rummage in the ample kitchen drawers, retrieving a couple of thick towels. He handed one to her as he wiped his own face then shrugged out of his jacket. A shiver wracked him and he strode over to the stove to add more coal to the embers and make the room even cozier.

Lenore buried her face with a thankful sigh in the soft dry linen. The kitchen was rife with the smells of savory beef, baked potatoes, and stewed vegetables. Jake's stomach rumbled, loudly. He hadn't even realized he was hungry.

"Here's a note from Kate." He read the scrap of paper quickly. "She says she hopes we had sense to stay out of the rain and has gone to bed with a pot of tea. If we need anything, we should knock."

Lenore was using the towel on her hair which was loosened from the braid. It cascaded like a silk curtain over her shoulder as she leaned to one side. She glanced at him for a moment, nodded, then continued drying her hair. Was it exhaustion or anger that still held her mute? Probably a combination of them both.

The puddle of water around her was still growing as water seeped from her mud-splattered skirt. His conscience tugged. Sylvia had asked him to look after her. Some job he was doing.

"Can we call a truce, Nora? Just for tonight." He stepped toward her. "Pretend the past week has not happened and this is just another grand adventure from your summer visits of old."

She looked at him for a long minute, her face pale in the lamplight, her amber eyes glittering. Finally, she cleared her throat and nodded.

"All right, but don't think I won't bring things up again," she croaked. A shiver shook her shoulders spilling her hair around her. He had to stop himself from reaching out to stroke it back from her cheeks. She was cold, exhausted, and most likely hungry as well. Concern that she might suffer some other, more serious, effects from their little stroll through the countryside snuffed out the blaze of desire that had flared so unexpectedly and ferociously.

"First things, first, Miss Brownley. Get out of that sopping mess and we'll get some food into you." Jake's tone was civil and distant at one and the same time. Almost Jake again. Yet not quite. Lenore's weariness must have made her imagine the spark of something else in his eyes just now.

"I beg your pardon?" Had he just asked her to *undress*? Here, in the kitchen? Perhaps she hadn't imagined that spark.

Then she realized he had transformed into Doctor Jake. Just as she might pick up and discard a pair of gloves, he'd turned from anger to friendly appeal to dispassion. She had become one of his patients.

"It's warm enough in here now, and you women wear enough undergarments and petticoats to protect you from a dozen prying eyes." He was busy loosening his collar and unbuttoning his waistcoat. "Besides, I'm a doctor. You have nothing I haven't already seen."

"Well, you haven't seen me—" she cut off her protest when she realized he was teasing her.

"Just take off the layers that are wet." His genuine smile warmed her on the inside even as she shook her head.

"I'm sure you have ballgowns that are more revealing, but I imagine Kate wouldn't mind you borrowing one of her shawls on the pegs over there for modesty's sake." He gestured toward the door behind her then shrugged out of his waistcoat as if to show her how easy it could be.

"I'm perfectly all right I can assure you, Doctor Warren. But thank you for your concern just the same."

"You are probably right, Miss Brownley." He bowed ever so slightly to underscore his exaggerated politeness. "But I am the doctor here and you will listen to me or I will go straight up and knock on Kate's door. That should have you confined to your room with nothing but hot possets to drink for the remainder of the week."

He offered her a toothy smile, assuring her the idea had far more merit in his estimation than it could possibly have in hers.

"What? And miss the ice-cream social?" She feigned shock this time. "I understand it's the event of the season."

"If you want ice cream later, take off that gown." He tossed the threat over his shoulder as he turned to rummage in the cabinets, withdrawing a bottle of whiskey and two glass tumblers. The sight of his broad back clad only in a clinging layer of wet linen tightened her chest. It was definitely getting warmer in here. He splashed a healthy portion of amber liquid into each glass.

Her stomach rumbled in protest at the thought of

hot possets instead of the savory roast Kate had kept
warm for them. She knew enough about Jake as
both a friend and doctor to know he did not make
idle threats. She licked her lips. Modesty or appetite,
it appeared she could satisfy only one.

"Very well, I will take off my blouse and skirt.
Only. And only because the idea of slogging through
Kate's clean house in muddy clothes is wholly un-
appealing."

She lifted her cold fingers to undo the buttons
and then realized she was even further at his mercy.
The blouse she wore buttoned down the back. She'd
needed Kate's help this morning to finish the buttons at the top and now . . . well . . . there was only
Jake.

He turned back toward her with a glass in each
hand and frowned heavily at the sight of her.

"Lenore, your clothes?"

"I . . . I need help."

"Do you indeed?" He arched a brow upward at
her admission and knocked back the contents of his
glass before handing her the other one. "Drink that,
it will warm you up."

She took the glass and frowned deeply at the contents. Papa had never even let her near his whiskey,
let alone taste any. She was allowed an occasional
glass of sherry at home and only one glass of wine or
champagne when she was a guest elsewhere. The
very idea that she was holding a glass of a forbidden,
manly liquor was scandalous. And very unladylike.
And somewhat thrilling, to be thoroughly honest
with herself.

Jake moved closer.

What would Mama think?

"But—"

He grasped her shoulders dipped his head until he was nose to nose with her. For a moment she thought he was going to kiss her again. And she very much hoped he would despite the argument they had mired themselves in before the rain.

"Drink." He enunciated very clearly. "At this point, it's medicinal."

Old habits kicked in. His tone so closely resembled Papa's, she didn't even think.

"Yes, sir." The agreement tumbled from her lips then she aped his manner and tossed back the contents of the glass. Liquid fire stole her breath. She sputtered and choked. Tears filled her eyes as the whiskey burned a path clear through her. "Medicinal? That's closer to poison."

Jake shook his head and took the glass from her fingers. "I said drink it, not toss it back like a sailor newly come to port."

He spun her around to gain access to the pesky buttons on her blouse. Pure heat continued to spiral a pathway down her throat and swirl like hot coals into her belly as her breath whooshed out of her. She gasped for air.

"Oh, my."

"Exactly."

Jake started undoing her blouse, his warm fingers barely brushing her chilled skin button by button. The breath the whiskey had stolen was now locked somewhere in the middle of her rib cage. Warmth seemed to be everywhere at once. In the air, pulsing in her stomach, radiating out to the tips of her fingers, flowing down her spine in the wake of Jake Warren's progress.

She sighed, feeling all at once just as warm and relaxed as a girl could ever wish to feel. A hint of Jake's scent, citrus and sage, twined in the air with the smells of wet cloth and a good dinner. She was enjoying the contact of Jake's fingers against her far more than she should have.

Then his hands were on her shoulders and he was peeling off saturated fabric as it clung to her arms. She reached for the fastening at her waistband and her skirt whooshed to the floor in a slap of wet fabric, leaving her in her corset, chemise and mud-rimmed petticoats. Mama would be shocked into apoplexy, but Mama was in Boston and the warmth flowing through Lenore's limbs right now made her all the more grateful for the distance.

"No wonder the men who linger with cigars over their spirits always laugh and joke with such a convivial air." She surprised herself by speaking her thoughts aloud. "Convivial is such a nice word. We can be convivial tonight."

Between the whiskey and being scandalously clad—or un-clad—in a gentleman's presence, the knots inside her, tied and retied over the years until she was no longer certain where they had originally started, loosened.

Freedom. What a lovely feeling. She drew a deep breath and let it out on a long sigh.

She reached toward her abandoned glass. "Jake, I'd like—"

"I don't think so." He whisked the glass out of her reach, disapproval heavy in his tone. "You need food in your belly, not more liquor. That was for medicinal purposes only."

She turned to face him and placed her hands squarely on her hips.

"*I,*" she told him with all the emphasis she could

muster despite the mellow whiskey-inspired warmth in her middle. "Am *not* your patient."

"Indeed, not." His dark eyes perused her from head to foot. "And perhaps that's just as well. Take off a couple more of those petticoats or you'll undo whatever warmth we've achieved with the spirits and the fire."

She had never imagined standing in a darkened kitchen with Jake Warren while he methodically ordered her to strip. The thought sparked a giggle, leaving her suddenly mindful of her dampened linen chemise with the scooped neckline and the long wet petticoats that still swathed her from waist to ankle. She shimmied out of two layers and felt decidedly less clammy.

"You should take off your own shirt." She straightened her shoulders, managing to draw his gaze back to her face. "It's almost as wet as mine, at least around the collar. I'm sure Kate wouldn't mind you borrowing one of her shawls—for modesty's sake."

She would not allow him to intimidate her with her own state of dishabille. The heady glow of the whiskey's first warmth was beginning to wane, replaced by the heat of his gaze on her. She reached for his buttons and began to undo them one by one, her fingers barely brushing his skin. She was shocked by her boldness. One of his eyebrows edged up, but he didn't protest and he didn't stop her. Instead, he undid his cufflinks and by the time she reached the point where his shirt was tucked into his pants he just tugged the garment off over his head.

Her pulse hammered in her throat. With the exception of the occasional sweaty laborer passed on the street she'd never seen any man in this state of undress except in classical paintings or marble

statues. Never seen taut muscles or a broad chest
that tapered to a lean, flat waist sculpted in living
flesh. Jake was beautiful.

"Now we are even, Miss Brownley. If we are discovered in this state I suppose I shall be obliged to
ask you to marry me. I suggest we sit down. Supper
is what we both need. Then we should seek our
beds."

Food sounded too tempting despite the distractions. She took her seat at the table as Jake passed
her one of the plates he retrieved from the oven. He
sat down next to her and they ate in almost companionable silence for a few moments. The roast was
every bit as good as she anticipated. No one could
make a better meal than Kate Butler, and somehow,
coming in out of the rain to this savory feast made
the trudge through the mud nearly worthwhile.

Even if she did have curmudgeonly Doctor Warren to deal with along the way.

Her gaze wandered his profile once again. He was
relaxed now, enjoying his dinner as though he'd
never been so frozen, so transformed as when he
first left the Pruitt's doorway both nights she'd accompanied him there. As sick as Job was, she could
not figure out what set Jake into a morose mood
after visiting the elderly couple. He was so fond of
them. Something more, something deeper must be
bothering him.

What was he'd said that night? *I'm a sham. They act
as if I have done something—done anything—that made
a difference in their illness or recovery.*

In the rain, in the mud, and in a black temper he
had avoided all questions tonight.

Did she dare ask him more now?

After watching him deal so tenderly with Lizzie,

after standing beside him at the clinic, watching him work with each new problem that walked in the door; after seeing the difference he made not only for the ailments, but with the people themselves—his self-loathing comments from her first night made even less sense now than they had then.

I'm a sham.

He was an understanding and concerned doctor. *The only thing I know is how little I know. How hollow I am.*

She'd known just what he meant that night, known it to her bones, even though what she'd known was based on her experiences moving in her social circle and discovering how vacant that life was. Could that really be how Jake felt about his skills as a doctor, the real good she'd witnessed him doing? Because he couldn't save this man he cared so much about?

She'd allowed her shock over Grandmother Worth and Jacob Warren, her anger over a Jake's method of protecting them, keep her locked into old selfish patterns of treating his problems as if they were none of her concern. What kind of friend was she?

After her promise to alter her ways and search for a new horizon, she'd fallen neatly into the old patterns used through the years in dealing with her own father's dark moods and often incomprehensible behavior. The realization poured ice water through her veins and stiffened her spine. So much for her intentions to change.

She studied Jake's profile in the lamplight as he concentrated on cleaning his plate. And made her decision. Old habits would have to be a help as well as a hindrance. Perhaps years of experience had developed not only bad habits but a certain protective shell as well. After all, wasn't she Papa's darling? She had developed a certain talent in dealing with her sire's unpredictable temperament in order to earn and keep that title.

At least she hoped so.

She took a breath.

"Don't." His gaze met hers before she could even begin to form the words.

Her mouth closed with an audible snap. She stared at him for a moment in silence. "Don't what?"

"Don't begin the whole process all over again, Nora. I meant what I said."

"You didn't say much of anything." She reminded him.

"I've said all I intend to on the subject. Remember, we called a truce."

She blew out a breath and addressed the last bit of potato swimming in gravy on her plate.

"Jake—"

"No."

"You don't even know what I'm going to say." She slammed her knife and fork down on the table in an unladylike show of temper. "For all you know, I was going to ask if there were any more vegetables."

He turned fully to face her and she could feel the tension vibrating in him just below the surface. "I could see your mind at work, tumbling through the evening's, the day's, events, working up the nerve to continue where you left off earlier."

"You are not yourself when you leave the Pruitt's, Jake. You are so close to them, perhaps you don't see it that way. But you change and I can't believe it is all connected to them. I want to understand. I want to help."

"How I feel about my patients is my business." His

tone lashed at her even as his features seemed to harden into his own protective mask. "You are hardly qualified to offer help about something you will never know—things you should never know. My life is not fodder for your capricious curiosity. You don't know me any better than you know yourself. Clean your own wounds before you make any more attempts to salve mine."

"Just what is that supposed to mean?" The question jumped out of her despite her earlier bravado about being able to handle Jake's prickly temperament because of Papa's humors. The keen knowledge that he was all too right in his assessment stung her to the core.

"You've supposedly come here to figure out what to do with yourself, have you not? Sylvia as good as told me that much."

She nodded, shifting uncomfortably in her seat as she caught a glimpse of what it felt like to have your life held up for inspection, even in a the company of one in a dimly lit kitchen.

"You're hardly in a position to question anyone about their life, their choices, until you have settled your own."

His gaze pinioned her, glittering in the dark. The muscles stretching across his chest to his shoulders were taut with tension. "You cannot waltz here from your high-society life and overset everyone because you are bored by having everything most women want handed to you on a silver platter. You cannot play with people as if they are rag dolls you can pick up and lay down at whim."

"But that's not—"

"Not what? Not what you are doing playing Lady Bountiful for the week? Or is the role of investigator you are exploring, asking questions that are none of your business? For which you cannot possibly get answers? Are you not playacting at what *is* my life?"

Tears hovered as his barbs struck home. Where was that protective shell when she needed it? The weariness of the long day must be making her more vulnerable than she liked. She would not cry. She would not. "Do you really think I am engaged in an elaborate charade or are you using this attack to avoid looking at yourself from my eyes? I am just trying to be your friend."

Her statement dangled between them for a minute as they both took long breaths.

"Then be my friend," he answered her at last. His tone was flat, but some of the anger had dimmed in his eyes. He sat back in his chair. "But recognize that there are some things that are private. Things I don't want to talk about. Can't you just leave them be?"

"No."

He groaned, the sound an intriguing mixture of humor, anger, and disgust. "You're as bad as Sylvia."

She smiled. "Why, Doctor Warren, I do believe that's one of the nicest things you have ever said to me."

"It wasn't meant as a compliment."

"That is fine as well." She met his gaze across the table.

Eleven

Determination etched Lenore's face. Jake might have needled her about playacting, but there was no mistaking her sincerity in her claim of friendship just now.

Lamplight caressed the dips and hollows of her body, highlighting the enticing curves and shadows that had tormented him through the entire meal. So much for his bravado about being a doctor and seeing it all before. Sitting across the table from a scantily clad and all too attractive female was not a normal occurrence for most doctors. He doubted the whole situation was good for the digestion and it certainly had not been good for his concentration or he would have been able to ignore her long ago.

Now she had decided to heighten the tension already seething between them by sticking her pretty little nose in places and concerns where it did not belong.

She took a deep breath and exhaled. Was she really unconscious of the way the light played on her collar bones as her chest rose and fell?

"So let me get this right. I am not to worry about the Hawkins girls or any one other than myself. I should stop interfering with your clinic work or asking you questions that make you uncomfortable.

How exactly is that a change from my parents view of me and how I should behave?"

"Nora—"

She held up her hand to halt him. "Let me finish. You're right. I came here to try to discover if there was more to me than the empty-headed socialite they wanted me to be. *I* wanted to be. To see if I was more like my sister and my grandmother. And you know what? I am. Or, at least I could be, if you and everyone else would give me a chance. If you would let me help."

She was so sincere, so earnest, a part of him wanted to yield. To heap his confusion on her beckoning shoulders and release some of his turmoil over everything he could not do, everything that was expected of him. But she was so young, so seemingly guileless, and he was a doctor, the one others turned to when things went awry: calm in the face of chaos, assured under pressure, consoling in the face of grief. The one expected to have all the answers, not the questions.

When he tried to broach his troubled thoughts with his mentor, Dr. Michaels had brushed his concerns aside, suggesting he consider finding a wife. Someone to help him separate his profession from the rest of life. Someone to share the joys of living, and to help mitigate the sorrows.

And here was Lenore.

Blatantly offering at least the latter, and innocently displaying the former with her cascade of blonde hair caressing her bared arms and neck. The soft brush of her fingers undoing his shirt a few minutes ago still burned his skin. He had no desire to delve into his dark secrets when he looked across at her. He remembered all too vividly the kisses they had shared, how she felt in his arms, and how his hands itched to hold her to him, skin to skin. Mouth to mouth. To blot out everything else, all the discord, all his failures, by losing himself in her.

"I don't think so." He shook his head, unwilling to stand this particular torment a moment longer.

He almost laughed, she looked so stunned by his refusal to engage her further. If only she were dressed. If only he were. Part of him wanted to satisfy her every curiosity and whim. The other part wanted to satisfy them both in an entirely different and completely inappropriate manner.

He should have insisted she go right upstairs and then brought her a tray once she was changed and settled, completely covered, in bed. Although right now the thought of Lenore in bed brought an entirely different set of images roaring to life.

"Goodnight, Nora."

He gathered up his plate and silverware and pushed his chair back. Placing his dishes in the basin, he prayed she would just let his dismissal stand without argument. He moved to quit the room only to find her blocking the doorway with her all too enticing form and a look that dashed his faint hope to get away. One scant petticoat and stays over pantalettes and a chemise were not the type of thing a woman should wear if she intended to keep a man's attention on a discussion, even if they were her only dry clothing. Especially if she placed herself bodily in his path. He was a doctor, dammit, not a saint.

Lenore straightened her spine as he approached, an unfortunate movement that thrust her round, and all too womanly breasts more fully against the top of her corset. His mouth went dry at the sight.

Did she have any idea what she was doing to him? Did he really want an answer to that question?

"Why are you running away from simple questions?" The glitter in her amber gaze did not bode well for either of them.

"Your questions are far from simple, Nora. This is neither the time nor the place to be having this discussion. Let's both get a good night's sleep. Things will look different in the broad light of day. You'll see that most of what has you so overset is merely the storm and the time of night."

"Running away is not an answer, Jake."

"Then what are you doing here in Maine?"

"What are you afraid of, Jake?"

She refused to rise to the bait, to be diverted. He had to admire her tenacity. The soft scent of warm honeysuckle crossed the small distance between them. He realized he was staring at her lips, if only to avoid the rise and fall of her chest, the advance and retreat of her breasts with only a chemise for covering.

I'm afraid I'll make love to you until neither one of us can move. He bit the words back.

He closed the distance between them to tower over her, hoping his physical presence would move her. It didn't.

"Stop this, Lenore, stop playing with something you don't understand."

She tipped her head back in an effort to maintain eye contact. Her hair slid, draping her shoulders and her neck with a wall of a golden, watered silk. Was she truly this naive? But what would be the gain for her if she were not? He ached to touch her, to brush the hair back from her neck, to bury his face in its softness.

He needed to get out of here.

"How can I understand if no one explains things to me?"

Her soft question slipped beneath his guard to pierce him neatly in his solar plexus. How could he tell her what he could not explain to himself? How could he reveal the failures he had been living with for too long? Pain and anger warred inside him, heightened by the sight of that determined little chin jutting up at him, still waiting his answer.

He stepped closer still, watching her eyes widen as the space between them dwindled.

"What would you like me to explain, my dear?" He reached out and traced the lacy edge of her chemise with one finger. Her skin was so soft. The ache inside him tightened still further. He traced a dangerous pathway along her collar bone, sweeping her hair out of his path.

Her mouth parted on an *o* of surprise at his touch and her breathing quickened as he stroked her. But she did not step away.

Hot stabs of desire tore through his gut. What was it she had been trying to pry from him? He traced the line of her chemise from her shoulder and then lower to the middle of her chest. Her gaze stayed locked with his, luminous amber. The tips of her teeth grazed the edge of her lips. She was still quite obviously not willing to back down, even from this nonverbal challenge.

So be it.

He would increase the stakes.

"Shall I explain why it is that young ladies should only test the patience of a man so far?" He toyed with the wilted white ribbon at the top of her chemise.

"Shall I explain what it does to a man when a woman puts herself bodily in his way?"

The ribbon came undone beneath his fingers and the chemise gapped open on a sigh, slipping from her shoulders. Still, she held her ground in the doorway.

Newly-bared flesh glistened in the lamplight as the tops of her breasts came into view. Desire tightened painfully inside him. The knowledge there was little between them except a few damp scraps of fabric burned in his brain.

He was keenly aware of Sylvia and Jacob's absence from the cottage. And that Kate would sleep soundly in her quarters through any sound they might create in her kitchen. Heaven save him from the temptation the determined Miss Lenore Brownley was presenting him with. Heaven save them both, but he knew the wishes were hollow before they even formed.

He traced a slow trail over Lenore's soft flesh. Her breath was warm on the back of his hand as she dipped her head and followed his progress.

He lifted her chin so she was looking square into his eyes. Her eyes shone with curiosity, her lips were parted as if anticipating the kiss they both knew was coming.

"Shall I tell you what it does to a man to touch you like this? What it makes me want?"

"Jake." His name fell, husky and soft, from her lips. Her gaze never wavered from his.

"Shall I tell you what I intend to do about it?"

He dipped his finger low into the vee, reveling in the warm valley between her breasts and the breathless gasp he wrested from her in the process.

"Oh. . . ." Barely a sound, and definitely not a protest.

He slid one arm around her slender waist and pulled her closer, eliminating any final space between them. He forgot what lesson he had been trying to teach her. "Or should I just show you?"

"Oh, yes." She breathed her acquiescence just as he covered her mouth with his.

The brush of their lips was hot and sweet with yearning. Passion roiled through him in hot waves. He wanted her more than he had ever wanted any woman. Wanted to take her, here and now in the confines of the darkened kitchen and damn the consequences. Wanted to ignore the pain she had scraped raw with her questions and challenges. Wanted to lose himself in making love to her until neither one of them could so much as move, let alone think or feel.

He deepened the kiss, parting her mouth beneath the pressure of his own. She moaned as he laved her tongue with his, tasting the sweet untried desires she was just discovering. She slid her hands over his bare skin, his arms, his chest and around his neck.

He stroked her tongue, tasting her willingness and losing any control he might have laid claim to. She tasted so good, felt so good. As though he had been waiting a lifetime to hold her. He released her lips to nuzzle a pathway toward the bared shoulder that had been driving him wild. He kissed the hollow of her shoulder, drowning in the soft skin-warmed scent of honeysuckle that clung to her and beckoned him with each breath.

Her breasts pressed against his chest, full and resilient and all too tempting. He wanted to taste every inch of her. It no longer mattered what had started them down this path or whether her willingness was sparked by whiskey or desire. He needed to touch her, needed to hold her, needed to make love to her. And she wanted him, too, even if she wasn't truly certain what that meant.

But he did know. And the knowledge ripped into him.

He bent and scooped her into his arms. Carrying her the few short steps to the table, he set her down at the edge. One wilted petticoat drifted about her in a lacy white cloud. Her bared breasts peaked out of her chemise above her stays. She was the picture of innocence and sin perched atop Kate Butler's kitchen table. She was irresistible.

He pulled her closer and she parted her legs, sliding them around his waist. His hardened desire nestled against her softness. He groaned to be so temptingly, intimately close to her. She was a fire in his blood.

"Nora." He looped a finger in the laces of her corset. "I want to see all of you."

She nodded, her eyes wide and luminous as her gaze held his. He absorbed that innocent gaze as he loosened the ties and her stays sprang apart. She took a deep breath which opened the gap in her chemise even wider. Slowly, building the anticipation for them both he lowered the straps of her chemise from her shoulders. First one side, then the other. Lower, and then lower still. Slowly baring inch by lovely inch of her body until the chemise lay puddled at her waist.

She was beautiful. Her pale white skin flushed a delicate pink as he admired her. Her breasts were high and full and perfectly shaped, crowned with tight pink nipples that begged for his mouth. He reached out and brushed the palms of his hands over her stomach, and then higher to cup and gently weigh the fullness of her breasts.

"Jake." Breathless and soft.

He dipped his head to comply with the unknowing demand behind his name, catching one tight sweet nipple in his mouth. She gasped at the contact.

"Oh." She shuddered in his arms and clung to his shoulders, shivering. He laved the taut peak with his tongue back and forth, as she moaned and threaded her fingers through his hair cradling his head to her breast.

He caught her other breast in his hand, soft and resilient against his palm. Her other tight nipple begged attention and he trapped it with his fingers, testing and teasing.

"Jake, Jake—" Breathless confusion and delight tinged his name as she repeated it over and over again. Each time heightened the fire blazing in his blood and the ache growing in his groin.

Her fingers dug into his skin as she held him closer. He wanted to take her now. But he wanted her to want it just as much as he did. He switched his hungry mouth from one breast to the other, suckling her as he fingered the tight, wet bud he had just released.

She groaned and squirmed atop the table, pushing herself unconsciously against his rigid ache. He felt ready to burst, but he held back, knowing she needed more time.

He slid his hands beneath her wilted petticoat and found the top of her pantalettes. His fingers made short work of the ribbon there as well, loosening the fabric until it drooped about her hips.

She gasped and stiffened in his arms as his fingers slipped beneath the fine white fabric and he touched her where no other man had dared. Springy curls met his caress and he probed lower between her parted thighs, seeking and then finding exactly what he wanted.

She was dewy and wet with desire, her flesh slippery and ready for him. He released the nipple to kiss her deeply as he stroked his fingers over her slick folds. She shuddered in his arms as he touched her. And then as he found the slick nubbin of flesh she gasped into his mouth and broke free of the kiss.

"Ah, oh, Jake." Confusion and need warred in the gaze she locked with his.

His blood thundered in his ears and each pulse of his heart throbbed in the erection he longed to bury deep inside her. But he stroked her, holding her gaze and watching the confusion turn to wonder as he taught her what passion truly was.

Each stroke of Jake's finger, so deeply intimate against her drove a bolt of desire through Lenore's very soul. She shuddered and moaned as the pressure inside built higher and higher, stoked by the rhythm of his expert touch. She could do naught but cling to his shoulders as the ache inside her grew and grew and the touch of his fingers drove her closer and closer to some edge she couldn't see.

She could only feel the power and the wonder.

And then it came rushing toward her in a wave of pleasure so strong it brought tears to her eyes. But that was not the end. Wave upon wave of pleasure broke over her again and again and she could only cry out Jake's name in a husky voice she barely recognized as her own as she clung to him.

When at last the tumult had stopped there was only the sound of their mingled breathing and the echoes of her pleasure in the stillness of the darkened kitchen. She rested with her head against his chest where she could feel the strong beat of his heart thudding against her ear.

"I had no idea. . . ." She let the comment trail off, unsure exactly what she was trying to say. Exactly what she should say. Mama's instructions on etiquette had never covered any intimacies, such delights as the ones Jake was sharing with her here in the darkened kitchen.

"You are a passionate woman, Nora Brownley. And that was only the beginning." He spoke in a tone of aching gentleness. He tipped her chin up and kissed her, his lips hot against her own.

"I'm going to make love to you." He whispered against her ear, the hot whoosh of his breath against her neck spiraling a thrill through her stomach and beyond. Oh, how she wanted him to. All her questions were forgotten in a sensual haze.

"Jake, I—"

"Is every thing all right down there?" Kate Butler's voice rang down the backstairs. "Jake? I've been keeping an ear out for ye to come in once the storm abated."

Lenore panicked. Suppose Kate was heading down those stairs even now. What would she think if she discovered her charge practically naked in Jake's arms? He was swollen and bulging against her parted thighs. There would be no mistaking what was just about to take place. Just as he declared, he was going to make love to her. Kate would be beside herself. Grandmother would send her home in disgrace.

She struggled to get out of his arms. And he held her tighter to still her movements.

"She can't find us like this," she whispered.

"She won't." He returned in the same low tone even as he turned his head toward the stairwell.

"We're fine, Kate." His voice held none of the fiery desire that had scorched her only a moment ago. She blessed him for that. "I'm sorry our coming in disturbed you."

Lenore could almost picture Kate puzzling through his answer and deciding if she still needed to come downstairs. *Please don't come down, Kate, please.* The half formed prayer played through her head.

"Miss Nora?" Kate's tone held just a hint of skepticism.

A hot wave washed Lenore's face and neck and she could only imagine what she had sounded like only moments before as she had cried out her pleasure over and over again. She had lost all control and been anything but quiet. Did Kate have any idea what had woken her?

Lenore cleared her throat and struggled for calm. "I'm fine. I'll be up in a moment."

"I'm glad ye're home safe, dearling, though I knew Jake would let no harm come to ye. Yer grandmother would never forgive me if I let anything happen to ye whilst she was gone."

"I'm sorry to have worried you, Kate," she called toward the stairwell. After a moment they could hear the distant sounds of Kate's footsteps retreating away from the stairs.

Lenore looked up at Jake and found the passion banked but still glittering in his eyes. Their gazes held for a timeless moment. Then he stroked a finger over her lips and sighed.

"Nora, I'm so—"

"No." She placed her own fingers against his mouth, halting him before he could say something that would make their entire evening seem sordid and dirty. No apologies. "Please don't say it. Please. Just tell me goodnight, Jake."

"Nora." He lifted one of her hands and pressed a kiss into her palm. The gesture twisted her heart. "I meant what I said." He helped her get down off the kitchen table.

And she knew he didn't mean the apology he had attempted. The same hot thrill spiraled through her once more. She pulled her rumpled chemise back into place and retrieved the rest of her damp clothes. She'd pause long enough in the front foyer to let Kate think she had undressed there, away from Jake.

She walked to the doorway before turning back toward him.

"I always take you at your word, Doctor Warren." She told him. He stood where she had left him. Firelight flickered along the planes and angles of his chest. He was the very image of manhood, virile, strong, and vigorous.

"Goodnight, Nora." The words followed her like a caress as she moved into the darkened stairwell and left him behind.

Jake watched Lenore disappear into the darkness as a stone solid ache grew in his groin. The scent of skin-warmed honeysuckle hung in the air and on his skin. He could still taste her passionate cries against his lips. Still feel the quivering of her body against his own. Still wanted her more than he wanted his next breath.

He raked a hand through his hair and sighed. "It's going to be a very long night."

And he would have every single moment of it to contemplate his loss of control and the very real trouble he'd almost brought to Miss Lenore Eugenia Brownley's young life. Right up until the moment he heard the note of concern in Kate Butler's Irish voice, he had fully intended to make hot sweet love to Lenore.

Over and over again.

He glanced back the broad wooden surface of the kitchen table. He had never considered himself a cad. Not even when he contemplated his lack of skill and knowledge when it came to being a doctor. But here in Sylvia Worth's kitchen he had almost taken her granddaughter atop the kitchen table, treating her like a twenty-four cent bawd.

A bawd.

The thought ached, though not anywhere near as much as the physical pain of lust unfulfilled. Perhaps that was his penance. He started clearing the remnants of the supper Kate had left them. The least he could do is clean that up. There was little he could do at the moment about the destruction he had almost wrought.

The soft murmur of voices filtered down from overhead as Lenore no doubt ran through their evening for Kate and explained what had become of her gown. A wry smile twisted his lips. He didn't have to be present to know she would not be filling Kate in on the details of the last hour.

He had never been in a position with any woman where he lost complete control. Not until tonight. Not until Lenore. Who would have expected little Lenore Brownley to be his undoing? Little Lenore who followed him around and generally made a pest of herself to the point that he had wondered if she would ever leave him alone.

He chuckled in spite of himself.

If he had little Lenore still here in his arms he'd have been wishing anything but that she go away and leave him be.

If not for Kate's timely interruption . . .

He could still feel Lenore's slippery soft wet heat. Still taste her mouth beneath his. . . .

"Enough." He groaned and adjusted the fit of his trousers once again. Loose though they were they didn't leave much room for a large and aching erection. His mind was more than ready to wander the pathways of what was and what might have been. He didn't need that added to the pain of the moment.

He turned his thoughts back to the questions that had prompted the entire episode.

The Hawkins girls and Job and Martha Pruitt.

Now, there were two subjects to cool a man's ardor. The former presented a disturbing mystery and the latter had him questioning the man he was, the doctor he was, and whether he could ever be of any real help to anyone.

The conversations he'd had with Sylvia over the years cycled back through his memory. Despite what he had told her, it had been Sylvia who had been the driving force behind him going to school and completing his medical training. Sylvia who had backed him. Sylvia who had encouraged him. Sylvia who had been unwilling to allow him to quit when he wasn't sure he could go any further.

Even now, with the situation brewing at the Pruitt's, she was the first one to tell him he was doing what he needed to do. Job Pruitt was dying a slow death, and that Jake could do nothing to stop the process. No matter what kind of anguish he saw in the depths of Martha Pruitt's eyes or the pain-racked understanding in Job's, nothing could be done.

What kind of doctor was he when he could not treat the suffering of the people who needed him most?

He pumped water into the sink and put the used plates and utensils in. Then he grabbed the chunk of soap that was Kate's special blend.

A sham. A fraud. An imposter.

That's truly what he was. Truly what most physicians were. With luck and years of practice they might be able to ease the common aches or recognize unusual symptoms. But for the most part there was no healing art, only chance and pure dumb luck involved in most recoveries. Luck and time effected more cures than he did. Doctor Michaels had as much as confirmed his belief once he arrived home with the ink barely dry on his medical degree from Harvard.

Oh sure, in the beginning he had purchased his piece of the dream. Spent his soul on the belief that physicians knew how to heal the sick and mend the broken. He had hoped. He had believed. And he had Sylvia's tremendous strength of will to back him in even in times of most doubt. But after going through the schooling and then the apprenticeship and now his own practice he knew better.

And how had he repaid her, by nearly seducing her granddaughter here in her very kitchen. He snorted.

Most of his patients were truly no better off now in this modern age than they had been in the days of stone knives and bear skins. Medical knowledge.

The term was completely misleading. Unchanged by decades, centuries even, of posturing.

He sighed as he rinsed the last plate and set it on a tea towel to drain. The whole subject was a very painful one for him. And very personal.

The thought brought him up short.

How ironic.

In his attempts to keep Lenore from questioning him about a subject he considered too intimate, too personal, he became far more intimate with her than if he had just answered her.

He laughed then. Really threw back his head and laughed. The rich and righteous paradox of their whole evening was something he had definitely deserved. Maybe it was time to stop running from her.

Maybe it was time to stop running from himself.

He sighed and turned down the lamps until they puffed out, leaving the kitchen in complete darkness.

He walked into the foyer and took the stairs as quietly as he could. He hoped Lenore had already fallen asleep. He hoped she didn't despise him in the morning, in spite of the fact that she had refused his apology tonight.

He reached the upper floor and stood for a moment shrouded in darkness contemplating the closed door to Lenore Brownley's bedroom. For a moment the temptation to just go into that room and take up exactly where they had left off tormented him with rich fancies of her in his arms and the sounds of her passion.

"Goodnight, Nora." He repeated the only words she had requested from him downstairs. Then with a true exercise of will he turned himself away from her bedroom door and sought his own lonely chamber down the adjoining hall.

He didn't need to make any more mistakes than he had already made, either in his life or in this one night.

He sighed and closed the door behind him.

It was going to be a very long night.

Twelve

"A very long night indeed. . . ." Jake's low, husky words trailed off as his footsteps padded away from Lenore's room.

A painful mix of wild relief and disappointment tore through her as a shudder racked the length of her body. Too much had happened with the last hour or so. Too much had happened in the past few weeks. Too much that was real and ripe and explosive. And to think, she'd thought she might lack activities and interests once she arrived in Maine.

She caught herself clenching and unclenching her toes and grimaced as her heartbeat thumped far too rapidly in her ears. Her mind whirled.

What had made him stop before her door? And which Jake had stood in the silent and darkened hallway? Jake, her friend? The Jake who stood in judgment ready to upbraid? Or Jake, the man who had almost become her lover save for Kate's timely intervention?

She bit her lip. What had he been thinking of doing? Would he have knocked and tried a stumbling apology again? Would he have given her a cold and condemning lecture? Or would he have taken her in his arms and fulfilled the promise of passion that had blazed so searingly to life between them in her grandmother's kitchen?

The questions sent a repeated shudder through her, and then another, followed by hot and piercing spirals of the wayward longing and desire he had unleashed in her such a short time ago. Each remembered thrill brought on its heels twinges of doubt and confusion. Each touch and kiss they had shared felt branded not only on her skin, but on her very soul.

If he'd come to claim her, would she have had the moral fortitude to send him away?

How prim and proper she sounded, even in her own thoughts. Wouldn't Mama be proud of her darling daughter? The wild abandon Jake had unleashed, the waves of pleasure and passion he'd evoked put paid to that notion.

An edge of hysteria traced her spine like the tip of a cold finger. Who was she? Was she really ready to throw away the only things she knew for a night of passion? To surrender, to allow herself to be swept away without caring for the consequences?

She tried to imagine Jake, tousled and raw and all too tempting, standing in her bedroom doorway as he had stood pressed so intimately against her in the kitchen. The image made her mouth go dry. She groaned and buried her hot face in the cool depths of her pillow, but that welcome respite didn't grant her absolution from the things she wanted and couldn't bring herself to voice.

Scandalous. Her breath held as an invisible band tightened about her chest. The word emblazoned itself in bright red letters against the inside of her eyelids.

. . . *We will seize our destinies.* Somehow she doubted she was following the intent behind that bold claim when the only thing she wanted to seize right now was Jake Warren. She could still feel the velvet hardness of his muscled shoulders under her fingertips, still ached for his lips tracing the column of her throat, still smell his scent on her skin.

Scandalous indeed.

She could only hope Amelia and Tori were dealing with the consequences of that foolish pledge better than she was. Freedom and independence had led her into some foolish choices. No, that wasn't quite right, but certainly the total abandon with which she had responded to Jake's taunting had not been her intention when she began her questions. She'd truly wanted to help.

She left Boston not only to fulfill her promise, but also to avoid the scandal broth brewing behind Jonathan Lawrence's business dealings and his abrupt departure for overseas destinations unknown. What tremendous irony to have flung herself headlong into something far more outrageous and shocking than she had ever even thought possible back in Boston at the fastidious hem of her mother's determination and the forced respectability of her father's ambitions.

She could think of more than a few members of the much vaunted Brookline Daughters of Grace who would get a great deal of pleasure detailing and re-detailing the abundant nuances of her entire visit to Maine, ending with great relish with her fall from grace in the arms of a country doctor.

At one time, she would have been one of the chief tormentors of any wayward miss who had accepted so much as a kiss from a man not her husband or fiancé. But not even in their wildest fits of fantasy had any of her set discussed, let alone imagined, being ready to surrender themselves completely to a man on the scrubbed surface of a lamp-lit kitchen table and regretting the interruption that had both saved their innocence and left them aching for what might-have-been.

"Oh, dear heaven." Put bluntly, even in her mind, the whole episode sounded so sordid she winced. But it hadn't been quite that way, had it?

An image of the glittering passion in Jake's eyes and the tight pleasure of his touch made her shift restlessly against the sheets. If she were truly innocent, shouldn't she have run from the hoydenish tendencies that had surged to the fore when he held her in his arms and kissed her? The tender torment and untamable emotions he had released from some unknown center of her streaked through her again. Where had her all too proper upbringing been then?

She shivered. For a woman who had only weeks before prided herself on her ability to get through any social situation with equanimity, she was sadly out of her element.

Surely the poised and confident Miss Lenore Brownley from Boston, the darling of the social scene, her family's angel was not the same woman lying in this bed. She shifted against the cool cotton sheets again, her skin hot and aching for Jake's touch and the feel of his body pressed to her own.

For . . .

Oh, she wasn't sure what else she wanted. Heat poured over her cheeks in wave after scalding wave. Every inch of her felt scorched from their encounter. Every blessed inch.

Her decidedly unladylike and frustrated sigh blew across the broad expanse of polished oak floor to echo back to her.

She couldn't forget the look in his eyes, the dark look of pain and anger that flamed to life right be-

fore he started to touch her. When she had blocked
his path, standing between him and the escape he
sought from her questions about the Hawkins girls
and his attitude over the Job Pruitt's illness.

With a gasp Lenore sat straight up in the bed.

You don't know what you are playing with.

The challenge rang through her mind in Jake's
solid timbre. Isn't that what he had said just before
that dangerous glint came into his eyes? Just before
he had traced his finger across the lacy edge of her
chemise?

She worried her lip with her teeth and flung back
the coverlet, no longer able to remain in the bed.
The cool wood beneath her feet was a shock to her
heated system as she paced the spacious confines of
her bedroom.

Just before Jake touched her, igniting molten heat
between them, he had threatened her, and all but
begged her to drop the subject and leave him be.
He'd closed the distance between them and she had
no longer been able to concentrate on anything beyond the way he made her feel, and how desperately
she wanted to touch him in return.

Fresh heat stung her cheeks as anger rose to swirl
rapidly into the emotions she already battled. He
had deliberately used his body, and hers, to distract
them both from a subject that was obviously even
more raw than she suspected.

His fingers loosening the tie on her chemise, his
lips claiming hers, his tongue. . . . A more effective
distraction she couldn't imagine.

What dark secret lurked deep inside Doctor Jake
Warren to make him willing to seduce her beneath
her grandmother's very nose rather than answer a
few simple questions? Rather than face his demons?

Somehow, in corners of her heart she'd never felt before tonight she knew what had passed between them in the kitchen was more than a physical blotting out of those demons. He had wanted her. He had needed her. Not any woman. Her. And he still did.

The tumult still whirling inside her died down to a more manageable level as she debated the notion that she must have been very close to the truth if he had resorted to such a desperate evasion. Perhaps she could piece the truth out for herself.

His dark humor after visiting the Pruitts was indisputable.

And she knew Jake cared for Job and Martha. He had known them his entire life. Job hired him to tend his lobster pots and Martha had always baked extra pies and cookies to send home with him since Jake's mother had died when he was barely more than a babe. He sounded concerned whenever she heard him speaking to Martha. So what lay behind his complete reversal of behavior when he walked out their door?

"It just doesn't make sense."

Nothing made sense. Neither his actions, his reactions, nor her own. The jumble of her feelings for Jake Warren—desire, dismay, the need to dig deep inside his soul and see all of him. What was the cause, what would be the outcome?

Oh, what she wouldn't give to have Maggie here to pour out her troubled heart to. Or Grandmother. Surely they would have some wisdom to offer, some advice.

A gentle breeze blew the curtains away from the window, lifting them high and then gently dropping them back into place. The sensations Jake had brought to life still hummed on inside her and suddenly all she could think about was opening the door to Grandmother's room her first night and discovering she already had a visitor.

Grandmother, who had always spoken her mind and meant what she said. Grandmother, who had always seemed the essence of independence. Grandmother, who had never made any secret of her intention not to marry again, had taken a lover. And not only that, she was off with him right now to shop for her trousseau so they could be wed in a few weeks time.

Talk about seizing destiny. Did passion lie at the center of this seemingly precipitous change of heart for her grandmother? No, it was more. It was Maggie's runaway visit last summer that spurred their Grandmother's current plans, her determination to sieve and savor what happiness she could from life.

I hid my feelings for Jacob in order to protect myself and in the process cost us both countless moments of happiness.

Maggie had somehow helped Grandmother discover that truth.

When I saw all Margaret was willing to risk—all she was willing to surrender and still not consider it a loss—I knew I had lived most of my life as a coward. Faced with her example, how could I do less?

Her sister's behavior of running away to Maine with a man who had made no secret that he was heading to California once he had delivered her to Grandmother, had been truly scandalous, truly risky, especially when compared with the teachings and reenforcements of Alberta and William Brownley. Yet, Maggie made her choice with her whole heart. And in the end, Devin had chosen her as well.

Grandmother was choosing the same path and, if

anything, the choice appeared to have made her stronger in the process. Stronger and more alive, as though each moment of her life were something precious, something to be lived to the fullest.

The pinched precision of her mother's world paled in comparison to the shining happiness in Maggie and Grandmother's. They might be mother and daughter by blood, but in spirit and personality they were strangers.

She traced a finger on the misty window pane, absorbed in the possibilities facing her in her own future. The oddly humbled sensation that had swamped her when Grandmother first shared her confidences returned again twofold. She was finally beginning to understand, if only just a little bit.

When Devin brought Margaret to me he planned to continue on to California. She was willing to pay a terrible price, to sacrifice her heart in order to have what little bit of time he had to give her. To share one moment of happiness even if that was all they'd ever have.

She was still angry with Jake, but not for distracting her from her questions. Not any longer. The strong feelings between them would have been there whether she goaded him to reveal his secrets or not.

She retraced her steps and climbed into the welcoming depths of the big four poster. Whatever else might come between her and Jake, she was even more determined to get the answer to her questions. All her questions.

Even if she did have to play with fire to get them.

High, bright sunlight streaked the floorboards before Nora so much as opened her eyes. And even then it was grudgingly. The persistent tapping on her bedroom door sounded again.

"Miss Lenore, are ye all right? It's late on a fine morning for ye to still be a-bed." Kate Butler's determined call preceded the door cracking open.

"If that Jake Warren's done anything to keep ye there, I'll box his ears."

"I'm awake, Kate." Nora struggled to sit up, rubbing her eyes.

"Well it's about time ye answered me." Kate bustled into the room with a tray of chocolate, fragrant biscuits, and dark blackberry jam. Kate must have been worried, breakfast upstairs was nearly unheard of in Sylvia Worth's cottage.

Instead of approaching the bed straight away, Kate placed the tray on the oak bureau and turned to examine Nora with a skeptical eye. Nora's stomach rumbled a protest.

"Ye're not usually one to sleep the day away." The diminutive housekeeper picked up the bundle of wet clothes Nora had dropped when she entered her room last night. "These are soaked through, just as I feared. And after yer late hours last night."

Kate turned and fixed a keen eye on Nora. "I was afraid you were feeling not quite the thing and let ye be for a spell. I've been up the stairs a half dozen times to check on ye since Jake left. Now I find he rushed ye home in the rain after all, just because he had to leave at first light for Kittery."

Jake left at first light. . . . Nora feigned a much wider yawn than was necessary. Was she grateful or disappointed she would not have to face him while the intimacy they had shared was still raw? She deliberately scrubbed her cheeks with the palms of her hands, pretending she needed the brisk contact to help her fully awaken. Kate's reference to the previous evening had her cheeks heating too much to go unnoticed. She didn't want to have to explain any of what had gone on in the kitchen last night.

"I'm fine, Kate." She offered a sleepy smile which needed no pretense to produce. Between the long walk in the rain, the lateness of their supper and tossing and turning most of the rest of the night, Nora felt like she barely slept.

"Indeed?" Kate tilted her head to one side and continued her skeptical appraisal.

"Of course," Nora nodded, trying both to meet and not meet Kate's gaze at one and the same time. It was a difficult feat, especially after the limited sleep she'd had, but she was afraid her wits were not quite up to fending off a determined effort by the older woman to discover the reasons for her exhaustion.

"Is that for me, I hope?" She motioned toward the tray, her stomach rumbling a second time.

"That it is." Kate finally turned from her perusal and picked up the tray. "I hope ye have a better appetite than that Jake. He grabbed a biscuit and bolted from the house, mumbling something about Bessie and looking as if he hadn't slept in a week or more."

"Really?" Nora buried her face gratefully in the mug of chocolate Kate handed her. The fact that Jake hadn't slept well either was almost more revitalizing than the chocolate's sweet warmth. "This is delicious, Kate."

"It always was one of yer favorites. Yers and Miss Maggie's. Between the two of ye it's a wonder ye didn't eat the entire county out of chocolate." Kate chuckled at the memory as she made her way around the room, straightening and tidying as she went.

"As if you'd let that happen." With a little food in her belly, Nora began to relax. Surely only she and Jake would ever know how scandalously she had behaved, how they had both behaved last night, she corrected herself.

"Are ye quite certain ye're none the worse for yer trek in the rain last night?" The question came again with vestiges of concern still etched in it from the previous evening. Kate's gaze met hers in the reflection over from the oval mirror in the corner. "I caught sight of yer mud-caked boots and ruined bonnet on the porch. And it looked so fetching on ye."

"I looked anything but fetching by the time we got home last night." Another half-lie to add to her tally. The glowing approval in Jake's eyes as he bared her skin in the lamplight had assured her otherwise.

"I'm sorry we woke you coming in so late. Jake and I had a small disagreement. But after getting the wagon stuck in the mud and slogging our way home in the rain I suppose it was inevitable that there would be some . . . tension at the end of the day."

Now *there* was an understatement if ever there was one.

"I knew there was something in the air." Triumph rippled through the housekeeper's tone and put a speculative sparkle back in her eyes as she jumped on Nora's evasion. Nora was just grateful she was no longer the object of Kate's keen vigilance.

"Young Jake's been prickly as a pine cone of late. All jumbled up, especially since he and his da moved in here. Ye spent the better part of two days with him in his clinic, did ye gain any insight into what ails the lad?"

Nora shook her head, able to finally meet Kate's eye with an truly honest answer. "Not really."

"Well we can spend the rest of the day discussing the oddness of most men's humors in general and Jake Warren's in particular if we like. Now that I know what it is that had my senses jangling." Kate breathed out a relieved sigh. "You youngsters were always having yer disagreements, but ye always made up. In fact, I often thought that Jake provoked you just so he could see you blush or stop you from the list of questions you used to plague him with."

Ahhh, so part of Jake's drive to distract her from the questions she posed last night was rooted in old habits. Interesting.

"Still, in the end," Kate continued. "Like as not, it was you who had the final say."

"Really?" She'd forgotten, but the reminder bolstered her determination.

"Indeed." Kate nodded for emphasis and gathered the wet bundle of clothes once again. She headed for the door with a misty smile on her face.

"Bring that downstairs when ye're up and dressed." It was her turn to gesture toward the tray. "We've plenty of time still before we're to leave and meet up with the others."

"Leave?"

"Aye."

"Where are we going?"

"Lass, have ye forgotten?" Kate paused with hand on the doorknob. "Today we pick berries. Tomorrow we set up tables and decorate the pavilion in the Common. The ice-cream social's only two days away. This year the money raised is going to benefit yer clinic."

Oh, good heavens, the ice-cream social.

If there was anything she felt less like doing, Nora couldn't put a name to it. At least it was still two days away. And a part of her glowed over the fact that Kate had referred to it as her clinic. She'd grown quite fond of the place, despite her fears when Grandmother had asked her to work there.

She pushed from the bed's warm confines with a feeling of regret. She didn't feel up to socializing with anyone today. In fact there was nothing she would like better than to stay right here in her room.

"You're right, Kate, I did forget. Will Jake be joining us?"

"Oh, my no. Mayhap ye'd best stay in bed the day after all." A furrowed line of worry creased Kate's forehead for a moment as she raised an eyebrow and fixed Nora with a frown. "Have ye forgotten he's to spend the night in Kittery? Doctor Michael's new apprentice is just in and Jake's going to take him about to meet the locals for a few days."

A few *days*. The thought dismayed Nora far more than she cared to admit to herself. What about the Hawkins girls? What about forcing Jake to root out the cause of this problem he was trying to wrestle with on his own? What about the newfound intimacy they had shared?

Kate took a step back to the bed. "He took young Daniel and a couple of horses to try to retrieve the wagon from where ye both had ta leave it last night. Why, just the thought of having abandoned it to the weather seemed to set his jaw tight."

"I'm sure." Nora managed the answer, all too easily picturing Jake's tight jaw and knowing the wagon's predicament was the least of their evening's escapades which might have set him in a rush to leave.

Nora had the sneaking suspicion Jake Warren was relieved he would have to face none of these questions for the foreseeable future while she was stuck berry picking and decorating for a social with nothing else to think about.

"And I suppose this means he'll miss the social?" she asked, surprised she spoke aloud.

"A doctor's schedule is never quite his own, now, is it? Still, he's promised to be back in time for Sunday services," Kate soothed. "And to help with the cranking the ice cream that's to begin right after."

Nora just could not get around how neatly Jake had managed to evade her, to evade her very real concerns, once more. Well, in his absence there was little she could do about his morose attitude, but she could at least work on her other project. The faces of little Lizzie and her friends swam up in her thoughts and clamored for their share of attention.

Kate leaned in and peered straight at Nora. "Ye are definitely flushed, Miss Nora. I think ye'd better stay here rather than venture out to pick strawberries this day."

"Will we be going anywhere near the Hawkins place on our expedition today?"

"Aye. The best field is just the other side of their hill." Kate looked as if her nerves had begun to jangle again.

"Then I wouldn't miss this trip for the world. I'm sure all I need is a good dose of fresh air and sunshine." She smiled her most winning smile at the Irish woman. "I do have a letter I need to start, so I can sit up here for a bit and rest. Then I'll come down and work on getting the mud off my boots."

"And what exactly to you plan to do over at the Hawkins place?" Kate was not diverted in the least.

"Trudy Hawkins is not one who goes in for much unexpected socialization."

"I just wanted to call on one of the girls who was injured at the mill yesterday and see how she is faring."

"Well, I don't know about that. I distinctly remember Devin warning Miss Maggie to steer clear of her and that no-good husband of hers not a month or so before they left on their trip."

That revelation further piqued Nora's curiosity. "I wonder why. What do you know about them?"

Kate shook her head. "Neither one of you Brownley girls backs down once ye've set yer minds on something, do ye? All I know is that they keep to themselves and she seems to keep those girls they house well enough. It's a pity the little mites don't get much beyond the basics there. Still, it's better than a life on the streets, I do suppose."

"But you said that Mr. Hawkins was no good."

Kate sniffed. "He doesn't do much beyond tend his few animals and skulk about the town. Lately he's taken a fancy to yer grandmother's goddaughter, the Widow Johnson. Calls on her quite regular, so I'm told. Although what she sees in that ne'er-do-well farmer I cannot fathom"

Nora had a hard time picturing Deirdre Johnson entertaining someone Kate considered a ne'er-do-well, let alone a married farmer. Flirting with a handsome professional man like Jake she understood all too well, especially now that she had tasted passion on his lips.

"But enough gossip. If yer sure ye feel up to it, I suppose a little fresh air on a fine day will not hurt ye. Write yer letter and I'll go finish scrubbing my kitchen table. . . ."

Nora felt the heat spreading across her cheeks

once more at the reference to the kitchen table. She wasn't sure she'd ever look at that piece of furniture the same way again. She scrambled from the bed.

"I won't be long she said as she moved to the basin on the far side of the bed, her back to Kate.

"As you like." The small Irish woman was already whisking out the door. "But if ye still have a mind to call at the Hawkins place, provided there's time, ye'll do so with me by yer side or not at all."

With that declaration, the door snapped shut and her capable tread and jaunty hum retreated down the hall.

Nora splashed water on her cheeks and toweled herself dry before moving to the writing desk by the windows. Salt tinged the breeze, promising a fine day indeed for berry picking. A corner of her heart tugged, wishing Jake were going to be leading the expedition as he had when they were young.

Well, he might have slipped away for a day or two, but she would concentrate on him when he returned. Right now she had a letter to write to Tori. She had so much to tell her friend, and only a small portion could she actually put in a letter.

"So I'll start with what I can tell her." She sat at the desk and opened the inkwell.

She'd outline the problems with the occupants of Hawkins House. Tori could ask her father for advice about the girls who graduated and disappeared.

Thirteen

"I think this one is finished." Nora called Kate over as Gerald Phillips gave the handle a final crank.

"We'll see about that." Kate loosened the lid and dipped her spoon into the depths of the container. The hum of voices and clatter of other teams of volunteers taking their turns at cranking the ice cream filled the warm summer air.

"Ahhh, yes." Kate grinned her satisfaction at the taste and consistency after first giving Gerald a spoonful and looked at Nora, "That last dollop of sugar and cup of berries ye added made all the difference. See what ye think yerself."

Kate offered her a small bite on another spoon dug from her apron pocket.

"Good," Nora proclaimed, but then she'd thought it tasted fine five minutes earlier when Kate the taskmistress had shaken her head and insisted on additional sugar and fruit to make the frozen concoction perfect.

Kate nodded. "That makes six strawberry and eleven plain vanilla. That should keep them satisfied for a bit."

"What, no chocolate?" Lenore teased as she licked the rich sweet cream and strawberry blend from her lips.

"I tried my best last year. I've yet to manage getting

it to blend right with the cold cream. It either ends up in streaks or chips." Kate shook her head after signaling for Gerald to take this pail to the ice house to join the others awaiting the beginning of the ice-cream social. At a nickel a dish, they should make enough to keep the clinic in supplies for at least a month.

"Actually little chips of chocolate mixed in with regular vanilla sounds good." Nora had started out teasing, but now she was wondering. "What if you mixed it with the cream the way you do for hot chocolate, then churn the whole mixture?"

"I never thought of that, Miss Lenore. Aren't ye the clever one." Kate's face lit for a second then she spotted something not to her liking and she was off across the grass wagging her finger. "Not there. Put the sweets on the table in the pavilion. We using that area where ye are for games and races and such."

Nora flexed her cramped fingers. Cranking ice cream was hard work. At least if you wanted to make enough to feed the whole town. The green watered taffeta gown she'd chosen to wear today was not exactly light enough for such labor either.

She wished for a moment she could be like one of the fishermen on the Somerset docks and just wipe the perspiration from her brow with the bell sleeves of her gown. She had already used the handkerchief she kept tucked in her waistband. She hoped she could spare the extra one tucked in her sleeve for emergencies.

She shaded her eyes and looked around the small sunlit field in the heart of Somerset, ringed in a half circle by the church and rectory and flanked by a row of homes belonging to cotton mill and Worth Lumber's foremen and their families. The pavilion was festooned with gaily colored ribbons fluttering in the breeze. Children darted everywhere as if the festivities had already begun.

In fact, the social aspects had indeed been well underway since the parishioner had spilled onto the green after services. Neighbors gossiped as they worked, mothers supervised their gamboling children as best they could, and the men lent an occasional hand in setting up the games or turning the cranks for the ice cream they would all enjoy while they had the day away from their ususal labors.

A particularly piercing giggle spilled across the grass, making Nora wince.

Having failed to entice Jake to her house for luncheon, Deirdre Johnson had decided to volunteer her services to assist with the final preparations for the ice-cream social. She'd claimed Jake in the church foyer and as far as Nora could tell had made no move to relinquish his attention ever since.

And Jake seemed more than willing to remain in her thrall. He'd avoided any opportunity to continue the discussion started the other night by avoiding Nora altogether. He'd returned from Kittery at first light, driven her with Kate to Somerset in the dogcart and barely directed more than a word or two her way in the process.

Looking toward the table where Jake and Deirdre were working, Nora tried to stifle the rising tide of jealousy. She tried and failed miserably.

"Why, Doctor Warren," the sultry widow was gushing. "You are too witty for the likes of me. I might have lived in San Francisco for a time, but at heart I've always been just a simple girl from the country."

There was nothing simple or country about Widow Johnson. From the chipstraw sun bonnet perched at the top of her meticulous coiffure to the radiant blue of her gown that nipped in her narrow waist and clung in all the right places, Deirdre had obviously dressed with the greatest care to set off her dark hair and flawless complexion.

Nora tried to tear her gaze away, but found herself worrying at her lip and wondering if Jake had ever enjoyed the distractions of the widow's lush appeal in any way approaching the shattering intimacy he'd shared with her the other night. She did not like the pictures forming in her mind. Not one bit.

Gerald approached, looking as glum as she felt at the moment. "What's the matter, Gerald? You haven't looked very happy all afternoon. I can look for another assistant if you've something else you'd like to do. I think they are going to start the games soon."

"I'd as soon stay here with you, Miss Brownley. I don't feel much like fun today." The teenager informed her as he tugged on his suspenders. "Callie slipped me a note in church. Mr. Hawkins is sending her away tomorrow night."

"I'm sorry to hear that." She struggled to keep her alarm out of her expression.

Would the tall, self-possessed girl disappear like her predecessors? Under Kate's watchful eye the other day she hadn't made much headway with Mrs. Hawkins beyond a grudging agreement that she would stop buying the girls clothing in bulk and let them go to the general store and pick out their own clothes and shoes from the catalogs. Made to fit, of course and at the added expense of the Brookline Daughters of Grace. Or Sylvia Worth if need be; it had been Grandmother who encouraged her involvement after all.

But she hadn't been able to budge Mrs. Hawkins's

pronouncement that she would not have her routine overset for something as frivolous as an ice-cream social. She only had so much time to teach the girls how respectable homes were run, after all. Besides, the hatchet-faced woman had sniffed, they did not have the funds sufficient to provide such luxuries.

"These girls are lucky to have a roof over their heads and a place to learn how to behave like decent folks," she'd insisted.

"Callie seems like a nice girl." Nora offered what comfort she could to the young girl's equally youthful swain.

Gerald nodded. "It's not fair. She don't want to leave."

"She doesn't." Nora corrected as another brittle giggle from Deirdre was joined by Jake's rich rumble.

At least some people were having a good time. Mrs. Hawkins had left the back pew with her charges immediately after the final bells had pealed. Nora remembered Lizzie's wistful expression when she'd mentioned the upcoming treat.

Sunday's our day to learn how to keep a respectable home. We come straight home from service and Sunday school and spend the rest of the day cleaning the house from top to bottom.

Her answer had so neatly dovetailed with Mrs. Hawkins's later dictate Nora couldn't help wondering if the girls were drilled in all the things they were not allowed to have because of their unfortunate status. It was not as if they had asked to be orphans. What kind of woman begrudged an occasional treat to a child?

Her eyes were drawn to the sight of the Widow Johnson being escorted to a bench by the town's very solicitous doctor. Nora was quite certain she was not going to be able to stand an entire afternoon catching such moments in progress. But how was she going to avoid them without appearing to be either rude or jealous?

The possibility of a respite dangled. A possibility that would benefit more than just herself if she handled things correctly. Perhaps she was growing to like charity work. Tori and Maggie would be so proud.

"Gerald," she said. "Go ask your mother if you could help me run a small errand for an hour or so. Then tell Kate I am going to buy an entire container straight from the ice house. You decide which flavor you think the Hawkins girls would like. I think you and I will go pay them a call."

Gerald's eyes lit with enthusiasm. "Yes, M'am. I'll be back before you know it."

He jammed his cap on his head and raced away.

"Could I join you on your little jaunt?"

The smooth masculine voice behind her, so close to her ear nearly made Nora jump. She turned to look up into Richard Moore's quietly knowing smile. He had his gaze fixed in the same direction as she had. The bench currently occupied by Jake and his sister.

"I just thought the girls might enjoy a treat. Wouldn't you rather spend the afternoon with your neighbors and the men who work for you?" Although he had always been unfailingly polite to her, and he certainly was solicitous of his sister's welfare, there was something about Richard's mantle of familiarity Nora found disconcerting.

"I believe Deirdre can represent our family adequately for a brief span of time. She has always been able to hold her own in any company."

He pulled his eyes away from her and focused his full regard on Nora. "Besides, I thought I'd inquire after the little girl who was injured the other day. Laurie, I believe."

"Lizzie." Nora supplied.

"Ah, yes. That's right." He offered her his arm. "See, I shall need you to keep me straight. And as I am the girls' employer, my entreaty may hold some sway in getting Mrs. Hawkins to deviate from her routine long enough for the girls to actually enjoy the treat you intend to offer them."

His argument had merit. And when he smiled, Nora decided Richard Moore could be quite charming. Especially as his sister leaned closer to Jake, surely giving him a better view of the ample charms threatening to spill from her neckline.

She took his arm and the crossed the Common to meet up with Gerald and the bucket of frozen delight they were going to deliver to Hawkins House whether Mrs. Hawkins liked it or not.

"Give Mr. Moore and Miss Brownley your thanks for the treat they brought to you, girls," Trudy Hawkins frowned at the rows of contented children arranged on benches at her long kitchen table.

A chorus of gratitude sounded from their smiling faces.

"Thank you, Sir. Miss." Little Lizzie spoke from the corner where she sat with her foot propped up.

"You're more than welcome," Nora assured the child even as Mrs. Hawkins gave her the full attention of her baleful stare. At least her husband had not joined them. Even the mention of him had seemed to freeze the room.

"Now you've all had enough time off from your chores." Mrs. Hawkins rose from her seat. "You mustn't dawdle."

Reluctant agreement issued from the children.

"Callie, you may clear the table with the assistance of your young friend there." Mrs. Hawkins obviously included Gerald in her expectations. "Pray wash the pail Miss Brownley brought the ice cream in first so she may be on her way without delay."

Her blatant effort to get them on their way stunned Nora. Her mother was known for her high-handed manner, but this treatment of guests, guests who came bearing gifts, was going too far.

Richard caught her eye across the table and she nearly burst into giggles as he raised and wiggled both his eyebrows with a merry twinkle in his eyes. She frowned at him to make him stop, especially as the girls closest to her also noticed his antics. One hid her smile behind her fingers, the other covered a fit of laughter with a very unnatural-sounding coughing spell.

Callie and Gerald sprang to their feet and began to gather the bowls and spoons with a loud clatter. They disappeared into the wash room with their booty. Perhaps Mrs. Hawkins was not so hard-boiled as she appeared. Setting them to this particular chore would at least afford them an opportunity to say their good-byes with a semblance of privacy.

The last of the girls scattered as Mrs. Hawkins delegated them tasks leaving only Lizzie in the kitchen.

"Are you at least excused from chores due to your injury?" Richard asked.

The girl shook her head, her dark hair, freed from its single braid, rippled over her shoulders.

"I've been polishing Mrs. Hawkins silver set these past two days."

"Idle hands are the devil's tools." Mrs. Hawkins pronounced as she returned to the kitchen bearing the now clean and dry bucket. She really was in a hurry for them to leave. Nora was still digesting the news that Mrs. Hawkins possessed a set of silver. From the sparse furnishing of the farmhouse, she never would have guessed that Mrs. Hawkins enjoyed some of the finer things in life.

"I know what you must be thinking, Miss Brownley. But I have that silver so the girls can learn how to care for it, since most of them are destined for a life of service. You might thank me one day when you admire the sheen on one of your friend's tea sets." Trudy Hawkins frowned at Nora. "You've had your turn at playing Lady Bountiful, now perhaps you'll leave us in peace." Mrs. Hawkins's small store of patience was definitely used up.

"There's no need to take on so with Miss Brownley," said Richard, rising to her defense. "As I explained, it was my idea that brought us here."

"So you said." Mrs. Hawkins did not look as if she believed anything he said.

"It's all right, Richard." Nora wanted a chance to hear the other woman out. What kind of life must she have led to leave her so bitter? What would she teach the girls in her care? "Go on, Mrs. Hawkins."

"Life is harsh for folks not born with more than they know what to do with. I've only got so much time to get these girls ready to meet whatever is thrown at them once they leave my doors. Their lives are likely to be harsh days of toil and trouble. There'll be little time for treats and such, and I'll not waste what time I have mollycoddling them. They need to be prepared."

"There's no call to upbraid us for something most people would consider a kindness," Richard protested.

"I understand what you are saying, Mrs. Hawkins," said Nora. And surprisingly she did. Nora rose from her seat and reached for the ice cream pail. "But I think you are also wrong not to give your charges a chance to see that life is more than toil and turmoil. That there is music and laughter and . . . and . . . ice cream to make the days bearable for us all. To balance the rest, even if just for a moment."

A tiny spark of awareness had sprung to life within Nora, not only in relation to the Hawkins Home for Wayward Girls and its manager, but for Jake and his dark humors. She needed a brisk walk back to town to put it all into place in her thoughts, but she just might have struck on the heart of Jake's problem: he had no balance.

"I know you think I am interfering in your business, Mrs. Hawkins." She used her mama's most imperious tones. "But I can assure you, as one of the members of the group that helps support you and these girls, that I have every intention of continuing to encourage you to do better by your charges. You may begin by making sure that Callie remains in your care for the foreseeable future."

Mrs. Hawkins face was beet red. She looked ready to have a fit. Richard was looking at her with intense admiration. It was time for them to leave while they still could manage to do so with dignity.

"Gerald," Nora called. "You'll see Callie again. It is time for us to go."

Instead of going by way of the main road, Richard

led them on the return to Somerset up through the meadow on the path that she and Jake had taken to bring Lizzie home after her accident at the mill. She supressed a shiver, feeling almost as if the Hawkins House had malevolent eyes marking their progress away. How did the girls fare living there everyday?

After assuring himself of her promise that Callie would not be sent off to parts unknown for the time being, Gerald had grabbed the empty ice-cream bucket and raced ahead to return to the social and tell his mother the good news. He was disappearing into the woods at the top of the hill when Richard stopped and looked intently at Nora.

"I must tell you how much I admire the way you stood up to that old termagent, Lenore."

How strangely formal his use of her first name sounded to her, when not so many days ago she had demanded Jake drop his use of the more familiar Nora. Richard's eyes glittered in the sunlit meadow and he smiled at her from beneath his mustache warmly enough, but there was something cold and harsh lingering in the depths of his gaze that unsettled her.

"Nonsense." She looked down at the path to escape his eyes.

"No, really." He hooked his finger under her chin and raised her face. "There are not many girls of your station willing to champion the cause of those less fortunate."

She shook her head in denial. For some reason she did not want to reveal to this man the depths of her concern about the eventual fate of the girls who passed through Hawkins House.

"If I am their champion, they are in dire straits indeed. I am merely showing an interest, at my grandmother's request." She tugged at Richard's arm with the hand she had rested there as they climbed the hill. "I think we'd better continue back. Kate most likely has a list of things she could use my help with."

"Very well. But a young lady such as yourself should not be working so hard, especially for so little appreciation from the beneficiaries of her efforts."

A year ago, a month ago, she would have been thrilled to be walking on the arm of a handsome gentleman who obviously admired and respected her. And for more than the way she tied the bow on her bonnet or glided over the dance floor. Today, she just longed to get back to the Common and try to puzzle through the flash of insight she had about Jake's puzzling reaction to Job Pruitt's lingering illness.

They continued up the hill in silence until they reached the shaded rim surrounding the trees that separated the mill from the far side of Somerset.

"Let us take a breath here in the coolness," Richard halted again.

She nodded and gently pulled her arm free from his to step away a pace and fan herself with her hand. The ice cream, followed by a climb in the sun had left her more than a little thirsty.

"I will be glad to return to the pavilion," she said. "I am quite parched."

"I am, too." Richard moved closer, almost looming over her.

She stepped back again toward the rim of trees, only her foot struck a wayward root and she nearly fell. Richard caught both her elbows and righted her, pulling her to within inches of his chest.

"Careful," he husked. "I have you."

He's going to kiss me. Her mind froze.

For several heartbeats they stood as they were, both breathing in and out in a rapid tattoo.

"I meant what I said, down below." His hands on her arms tightened and he pulled her slightly closer. "I admire you, Lenore. I appreciate all you have to offer."

He bent his mouth over hers and leaned in for the kiss she had feared he would claim. The brush of his mustache on her lips galvanized her. She jerked her head away. "No!"

Another set of hands grasped her arms and pulled her from Richard's embrace straight into a wall of warm, solid muscle.

"You heard the lady, Dick." Jake's voice growled in her ear. She had never been so grateful. "She's not interested in your appreciation."

"What are you doing up here, Jake? Aren't you the beneficiary of today's festivities?" Richard did not look ready to surrender just yet.

Jake pulled Nora slightly to the side and behind him. "As a matter of fact I was looking for you. A very delighted Gerry Phillips sent me this way. Your sister suffered one of her spells."

"Deirdre!" Concern tinged Richard's voice. "When? What happened?"

The transformation in Richard was remarkable. One minute he was nearly a cad. The next he oozed frantic compassion. "Where is my sister?"

"I took her home and gave her a dose of laudanum. Her maid is with her, but she is asking for you."

"Thank you, Jake. I'm sorry if I frightened you, Lenore. I'll leave you here with Jake."

With that, Dick was heading down the path

through the woods and off to seek his sister. The re-
sults of the consultation on Deirdre Johnson's case
Jake had held yesterday with Dr. Michaels and Dr.
Myers, his new apprentice, did not bode well for her
recovery. But now was not the time to dwell on that.
He would call on the siblings later in the week for a
frank talk. Right now he was more interested in
Nora, who was trembling by his side.

"What were you thinking to go off with a man unchaperoned like that?" he snapped and immediately
wished he'd held his annoyance, his agitation about
her, at bay.

"I didn't go off alone. I went with Gerald and
Richard joined us. We took ice cream to the Hawkins
girls."

Her own annoyance surged to the forefront as she
drew herself away from him and turned to face him
with an angry light snapping in her amber gaze.

She looked so lovely in her green gown trimmed
with deeper green edging. Almost as lovely as she
had looked robed in little save the passion he
evoked in her. For the past two days he'd done nothing but think about her the last time they'd been
together, when they'd been alone and twined in
each others arms. He had barely been able to tear
his eyes off her the entire morning in church and
later as they labored to get the social underway. Distracted by Deirdre for only a moment, he searched
the village green only to be told by Kate that she'd
gone to the one place he'd warned her not to go.

And with someone he did not quite trust. The
sight of her twisting away from Dick Moore's kiss was
burned into his soul.

"So, now you see what comes of such behavior."
She frowned at him. "Nothing happened."

"Only because I intervened. You might at least thank me."

She was quiet for a moment. Too quiet, as she looked up at him. "You're right. Thank you."

He did not quite trust her too-quick surrender.

"What was I thinking of being alone with a man who admits he admires me?" she continued as she stepped close enough to him that her breasts nearly grazed his lapels. The scent of honeysuckle and Nora twined around him.

"What was I thinking spending the afternoon with a man who actually admitted liking my company? A man who knows how to have a conversation and who wanted to kiss me not to shut me up and not to make me leave him be, but because he likes me." The tip of her tongue peeked out from between her teeth as she glared up at him. Her breath was hot on his collar.

He reached for her. "I like you just fine, Nora."

But he was going to kiss her sure enough to shut her up. Lord, but she did like to talk.

His lips grazed hers and she opened her mouth with a gasp. Instead of pulling away, of retreating, as she had done in Dick Moore's arms, she flowed into him. He pulled her tight against him and suckled her lips like a hungry man, running his tongue over the outer edges of her lips as her fingers dug into his shoulders.

Suddenly, she tore her mouth away. He looked deep into her gaze as a thousand questions sparkled in the air around them and for a moment the bright possibilities of life, of living, beckoned.

"There's a commotion by the pavilion." She gestured with her chin over his shoulder.

He turned to see young Dan Butler scrambling

down from the seat of the Worth Lumber wagon.
Jake rested his forehead against Lenore's and took
a shuddering breath. He'd been ready to pick up exactly where they had left off the other night, and
from the looks of her, she had too.

"Later," he breathed. "Later I—we—"

"We'll talk later; right now, someone may be hurt.
Someone may need you. We'd better go see."

Had she always been this wise? He'd have to ask her.
Later.

"Come on, we'll have to run." He grabbed her arm
and set off at an even pace, one she could match even
in her Sunday slippers. His heart sank when he realized young Daniel was waving frantically in their
direction, waving at them.

He met them at the edge of the Common.

"Mrs. Pruitt sent me, Doctor Jake."

A gasp went through the crowd that had gathered
behind the lad.

"It's Job," young Dan explained unnecessarily. She
said you should come at once. I drove here as fast as
I could."

Fourteen

"She said you needed to come now, Dr. Jake."

Fear etched young Daniel's voice and furrowed his youthful brow despite his straight spine and clear gaze. Dread streaked through Nora in the span of a single heartbeat.

Whatever Jake had been about to say before Daniel's arrival hung suspended for the tiniest moment as though the very world held its breath. And then Jake's hands tightened hard at her shoulders as if he were trying to grasp the invisible burden he had just received. The pain of his grip on her was nothing beside the stark look of anguish in his eyes.

Her heart twisted and the fright vibrating through her tightened a notch.

"Nora?" He spoke her name, with an abrupt gruffness layered with a plea that pierced her.

Her gaze locked with his, recognizing that he needed someone to go with him. That he wanted her to go with him. He needed her support at this moment more he had ever needed anything before in his life, whether he admitted it to himself or not. There was no time for explanation or doubt.

"Yes." She nodded her agreement, her understanding, for emphasis.

He needed her. That was enough. That was everything.

"Come on, then." He pulled her closer, unconcerned with the people gathered around them, probably staring. They did not matter. Nothing mattered at the moment, nothing but the crisis looming on the horizon and his overwhelming dread of it.

The hard kiss he pressed to her lips was anything but romantic. It was the empty chasm inside him reaching out to her, trying to fill itself with something other than what was to come.

He released his grip long enough to take solid hold of her hand and then they were racing side by side for the Worth Lumber wagon as young Daniel ran behind them. They climbed up into the wagon and were rumbling along almost before she was seated. Jake leaned forward, his face a mask, frozen by the same tension and foreboding she had tried so desperately to get him to explain.

Finally, she thought she understood what it was that caused him to wall himself in whenever he left his old family friends' house. This was the moment he'd been dreading. This was the moment he'd been trying so hard to deny, the moment when the limitations of Job's mortality and Jake's medical skills failed for the final time.

Job was dying and Jake was helpless to stop him.

Nora's heart squeezed as she eyed his profile and could almost feel waves of bitter pain and self-loathing for the impending failure writhing inside him as they jolted along at breakneck speed.

All those times she had watched him care for his patients and marveled at his abilities to understand them so completely flew through her thoughts like the trees they were passing.

She swallowed hard as tears blurred her vision. Here was the dark side to the compassion that enabled him to be such a fine doctor. Here was the price he paid for the talents bestowed upon him.

Oh, Jake.

"Ya! Ya!" Jake urged the horses to a faster pace as though he could outrun whatever demons plagued him and by some miracle conquer the undefeatable illness that even now ate its way to the end of Job Pruitt's life. As if he could hold back death by his presence at Job's bedside and shield Martha from her inevitable loss one more time.

Nora dared a look back to find Daniel on his knees in the wagon bed, clinging for dear life to the side. Tears streaked his face, making pale tracks down his dirt-smudged cheeks. Here too, this boy's sorrow, his fear was not for himself but for the people he'd known his whole life.

She pulled her handkerchief out of her sleeve and held it out to him. He accepted it with a nod, struggling so hard to be stoic, despite his age.

The ache inside her tightened still further. Everyone loved the Pruitts. So many people would miss Job. It was a wonder. Surely he knew, perhaps it gave him some peace to know that the whole community would rally around to support and comfort Martha.

How many of her friends, her parents' friends, back in Boston could make such a claim?

She herself barely even remembered the passing of Amelia Lawrence's father, save for her friend remarking that her mourning clothes had quite set off her pale complexion and dark locks.

They topped a rise and the Pruitt homestead came into view. The same neat little house, the garden, the barn, yet it seemed etched in stark relief, black and grey and white against a colorless sky.

She must have made some sound as she pressed

her hand to her mouth because Jake transferred the reins to one hand and gripped her other hand with his. He squeezed, but said nothing, not even meeting the gaze she turned toward him.

She longed to fling herself into his arms, to guard him from what was coming as though she could use her very body to shield him from Job's impending death and from the inevitability of things even a doctor had no control over. But she knew she could not. All she could do was stand beside him and provide whatever support he would allow her to give.

He released her hand almost as quickly as he had taken it as they flew past the barns, reached the house, and brought the wagon to a skidding and shuddering stop. The horses quivered, their backs covered with sweat and their chests heaving.

"Tend the horses." Jake tossed the order over his shoulder as he jumped from the wagon. His strides were quick and even as he rounded the side and lifted Lenore bodily to her feet.

"I'll take good care of them, I promise." Daniel's answer came in the same clear tone.

Jake met the boy's gaze for a moment and then nodded. "I know. You're a good lad. Your father would be proud."

"So would yours, Doctor Jake," young Daniel answered.

Nora had forgotten that he was handling so many tasks on his own while his father accompanied Jake's father and her grandmother to Portland. She had forgotten, but even in the depths of his anxiety, Jake had not. How could he ever think he was not good enough to be a doctor? Not compassionate?

He took Nora's hand in his again. His grip was so tight it was as if he were wringing the blood from it.

The lines and angles of his body seemed etched in tension as they headed for the door. This was the first time they had come to the house that Martha Pruitt had not been standing in the kitchen door like a welcoming beacon.

Despite her worries for Job as his health grew worse and worse, the habits of a lifetime had always sent her to greet her guests with a warm smile. Her absence now only underscored the fearsome reality of their arrival.

No, no.

The need to vent her denial grew inside Nora, but she swallowed the words back. Her repudiation of the inevitable was nothing compared to the woman inside who was losing her husband, or the man beside her who was losing more than a friend and a patient entrusted to his care.

He was losing a tiny bit of himself.

Jake pushed open the door, his grip on Nora's hand tightened further as the door swung inward. The house looked empty. No one stirred in its depths. Nora could feel the tension squeezing through Jake as he pulled her along behind him and they entered the kitchen.

She glanced up at his face.

Where there had been pain and doubt on the ride over, she saw instead a relaxed countenance. His lips were not pressed in a grim line and the furrows had left his brow. Instead, she read confidence and calm assurance in the set of his face and the squaring of his shoulders.

Jake the man might be suffering the torments of the damned at losing Job, but Dr. Jake was ready to offer the comfort and compassion his patient and his family would need. Only the intense pressure of his hand on hers signaled just how hard he struggled to maintain this posture.

Nora shivered as they approached the doorway to the bedroom Martha and Job Pruitt had shared for the past fifty years in sickness and in health. She had never been present at a death before. Never. But that didn't dull her certainty. Death was in the house. She could feel its choking darkness just as surely as she could feel the numbing grip of Jake's fingers.

The bedroom door swung inward.

Martha sat on the edge of the bed. Her face was set in a gentle, encouraging smile, even as she glanced over at the door.

Job lay wasted and pale against the pillows. Dark circles lined his closed eyes. Deep creases cut into his cheeks and the sides of his mouth. His lips were parted and his head was thrown back. His chest moved in slow, uneven breaths.

Nora's stomach clenched and a cold shiver traced her spine. There was a sharp scent of earth and embers in the air. The smell of death—ashes to ashes, dust to dust.

"Hello, Martha." Kindness ached through Jake's tone.

Martha glanced up at them again, dry-eyed and resolute.

"He knew." She spoke in a soft tone that barely broke the silence as she continued to stroke her fingers over the back of her husband's hand.

"He knew this morning. He was up before the sun, just like he always was. His voice was so clear, stronger than I've heard it in so very long. He was Job again. My Job, without a hint of pain. It was so good to hear him, to see his smile."

Jake at last released his grip of Nora's hand and walked over to the bed. He put his hand on Martha's shoulder with gentle understanding.

"He told me he would be going soon. He said he loved me, that he'd loved me from the first moment we met at the ice-cream social. I was ten and he was twelve. We talked all day and said everything we needed to say. He wanted you to know he thought you were the finest doctor this county had seen in a long, long while." She smiled up at Jake, her lips quivering at the edges, even as the fingers of her other hand sought her husband's and held them ever so gently.

"You remember, Jake. How he used to say that all the time?"

"Yes, Martha. I remember." Jake's tone was husky and low.

"He asked me to open the windows wide, so he could smell the earth and feel the breeze on his face. He asked me to sit right here beside him and talk to him awhile and he told me not to be afraid. So that's what I've been doing."

"You've done a fine job, Martha. A fine job." Jake assured her as tears clogged Nora's throat and began to trickle down her cheeks.

Jake bent and touched Job's still cheeks and then listened to his chest. Each breath the man took seemed to come slower and slower. As though he was journeying from a far, far distance to take each one.

"Job was right, Martha. He is going." Jake offered his confirmation in the gentlest tone Nora had ever heard him use.

"Yes." Martha's gaze didn't stray from her husband's beloved face. "I shall miss you, Job Pruitt." She spoke in a tone filled with pain and hope and loss. "I shall miss you every single day of my life for as long as I live. And I shall love you every minute just like I always have. Go with God, my sweetheart. We will meet on the other side."

As though his wife's words had released him from the struggle to live, a single sigh shivered out of Job's body. And then he drew breath no more.

"Oh, Job." A sob tore from Martha and she laid her head on her husband's still chest. Her hands stroked his arms, his fingers, his cheeks as she released her sorrow.

Tears streamed hot tracks over Nora's cheeks as she moved forward unable to remain apart from Martha's grief. Although they had known Job Pruitt's time was limited and there was little anyone could do, the grief was too fresh and agonizing, sweeping aside any rationale.

Lenore stroked the grieving woman's back, matching the rhythm Martha set with her loving touches to her husband. Jake's gaze met Lenore's in helpless witness to a life so finally gone. There was nothing either of them could do ease the pain for this woman.

They stood that way for some unknown span of time, listening to the sounds of Martha's sorrow and missing Job for his many kindnesses and the patient wisdom with which he had spoken his sage advice. Minutes or perhaps hours passed by. Nora couldn't truly say. It felt like time had somehow dislocated itself, as though they existed in a place lost to death and sadness and the normal accounting just didn't apply.

Eventually Martha exhausted the first spate of her grief and sat up, blowing out a long shuddering breath and swabbing her tear-streaked face with her apron.

Jake looked from Martha to Job and back. "I'll send Young Daniel for the rector. They will come and take—"

"No." Martha pressed a gentle kiss to her husband's hand before pushing to her feet. She managed a watery smile as she faced the concern tightening in Jake's face. He took a step toward her and opened his mouth, but she held a hand to stop him.

"No, Jake Warren, I have taken no further leave of my senses than I have at any other time in my life. I know my husband is dead. And I know I must release him to the care of others who will prepare him for his eternal rest. But I have lived with my Job for all these years. We have spent every night together whether in sadness or in joy. I will spend this one last night with him. I need to . . . watch over him."

Her words struck a strange chord in Nora. To watch over him. She understood how much Martha needed to do this.

"Martha—" Jake tried again.

Martha put a hand on his arm, stilling his protest. "It's the right thing to do, Doctor. I cannot explain it any better. I just know it's right. The price of life, of living, is pain. Love mitigates the price and makes the living, however long or brief, worthwhile. Saying good-bye is something I must do in my own time and in my own way."

Jake searched her gaze with his for a moment while Nora held her breath and waited for his agreement.

"Very well, Martha." Jake nodded and Nora sighed in relief. "You know best."

"And that's what makes him such a good doctor."

Martha told Nora, smiling, but just a ghost of her normal self. "He knows what his patients need."

"Yes." Nora nodded, her throat too tight from the conflicted blend of emotions tearing through her.

Martha patted her cheek as their gazes locked. Through Martha's eyes Nora saw a recognition and understanding of all that lay unspoken between herself and Jake, of all the world had to offer them and that they had to offer each other, if only they dared.

"Take him home now, dear. Help him to understand. And love him for all he's worth."

Nora could do little more than nod to her directive. Here in the Pruitt bedroom filled with pain and memories and a lifetime of love, it did not seem like a strange thing for Martha to have said.

"Martha, is there anyone you would like us to fetch for you?"

"No, dear. I'll be fine. Send the rector in the morning."

"I will." Jake nodded.

Jake's hand sought Nora's as he offered Martha a parting hug and left her alone with her dead husband. Looking back, Nora was struck with Martha's words. It seemed so right for her to stay and watch over her husband. As soon as they left the bedroom, Jake's jaw tightened, cast in solid iron forged by Job's death. His fingers were stiff against her own as he drew her through the house.

Outside, the sun was sliding lower in the sky and the blend of blue and deep purple shadows was tracing its way across the landscape. Where before there had been no color, now it was everywhere. Blue, purple, orange, burnt sienna, colors that were almost too bright to take in, stunning in the wake of the pain that had just ripped through them.

A fresh salt-tinged breeze whipped up from the sea, drying the tears still damp on Nora's cheeks and ruffling Jake's hair. She glanced up at him, longing to comfort him, to make him tell her what he was feeling before he locked it away deep inside him to fester and churn. She was certain, down to the depths of her soul, that he needed to tell her all of it. To pour it all out no matter how dark and painful. It could not be good for him as a doctor, as a man, to hold in the terrible anguish she could see written on his features.

As they stood in silence, the sound of the dogcart rattling closer filtered through the numbness that was setting in. Kate Butler pulled up, driven by Young Daniel. Nora blew out a sigh of relief. How the lad had known to go and fetch her was but one of the mysteries that made the boy so good as a messenger. He must have run all the way back to town to fetch Kate, leaving them the wagon if they needed it.

Kate took one look at Jake and Nora's faces and leapt from the cart with far more agility than Nora would have expected, bless her big Irish heart.

"Ye did yer best." She told Jake with no preamble. "Where is Martha?"

"Inside with Job." Jake answered in a deadened tone.

Kate nodded, her expression unsurprised. "I thought as much. Martha Pruitt is an ancient soul. She will need to stand watch over her husband one last time. Will ye be all right if I stay the night with her?"

"Oh, I don't think she wants—"

"Don't worry about what she says, Miss Nora. I'll sit in her kitchen and keep the kettle on for tea when she's ready. She will need me here."

"I'm sure you know her better than I do."

"Yer grandmother and I discussed this likelihood before she left on her trip." Kate dropped her voice as she dabbed at the tears on Nora's cheeks with a sideways glance at Jake's stoney features. "I'll tend Martha, and ye tend our lad here. Go on home, the two of ye." The housekeeper spoke louder now. "There's some chicken in the cold cellar. See that he eats something. I will see ye tomorrow."

With that, Kate Butler disappeared into the Pruitt home and firmly shut the door behind her.

"Jake—"

"She knows what she is doing."

"You'd best get home to your mother, Daniel. It will be dark soon." He nodded to the boy. "You take the dog cart home tonight, we'll trade in the morning."

"Thanks, Doctor Jake." The boy scrambled back up onto the seat. "Are you sure you don't want me to take the wagon? The cart will be easier to handle along the cliffs in the dark."

"Exactly my point, Dan. You're a good lad. Your dad, and Job, would be proud of how you handled yourself today." Jake's voice broke a little as he said Job's name, but he had switched back into being a doctor for the moment, giving the boy just the right note of encouragement.

Young Daniel nodded. "I'll see you in the morning, then."

As Daniel drove off, Jake grabbed Nora by the waist and lifted her into the Worth Lumber wagon as though she weighed nothing at all. He jumped into the wagon beside her and flicked the reins, turning the horse back toward her Grandmother's.

Nora wanted to weep. There was so much pain and anger in the man beside her. And there was nothing she could do to help him, especially if he would not talk to her about it. And she could tell just from looking at him that he had no wish whatsoever to speak with her about anything.

Not now. Perhaps not ever.

She bit her lip and let the tears flow in silence as they rattled along the road they had taken in anger and rain just a few nights before. It did not take long before her grandmother's cottage rose before them. Jake directed the wagon toward the barn, pulling the horses to a halt inside.

She waited until he had lifted her to the ground. "Jake—"

"There is nothing to discuss, Nora." But the look he turned her way was filled with pain. Pain for Job and for Martha, pain because he could do nothing to stop the man's death. He shrugged out of his jacket and set to work settling the horses.

"Jake, Kate was right. There was nothing more you could have done."

"And that's the whole point, isn't it?" He bit the words out over his shoulder as he kept his attention on unharnessing the horses and readying their stalls. "There is nothing I could have done. There never is."

"Jake."

"I don't want to hear it."

"What?"

He turned to face her, his face a tight mask of furious pain. "Whatever urge you have to try and make me feel better about all of this. There is no feeling better. *There is none.*"

He flexed his fingers, gripping and ungripping his fists in his agitation. "I am a doctor. A physician. My charge is to heal the sick and mend the injured.

If I cannot do that then it is all pretense. I might as well tour the countryside selling snake oil and chariot beads to any fool ignorant enough to offer me money."

He flung a piece of harness as far back in the barn as his strength would allow. It rattled, loose and broken, against the barn wall before thudding to the ground to disappear amidst the thick piles of clean hay.

"I'm a charlatan," he said in disgust. "I am nothing."

His words hung in the dusk permeating the barn. Tufts of hay loose in the breeze drifted past. Everything in her rebelled at the condemnation he heaped on himself and the pain festering inside him where it could not heal.

She crossed to his side and placed a hand on his shoulder. He flinched at the contact and raked a hand through his hair, but did not move away. The smell of leather and hay barely registered on her senses as they stood in silence for several heartbeats.

The gaze he finally turned toward her was almost as dead and lost as Job Pruitt's. "I don't know why I've allowed myself to carry on with this as long as I have. It's time to call it a day. Go to bed, Nora. You don't need to stand here and listen to my ego, my failings."

But she did. She stayed put feeling helpless and inadequate and knowing he needed her far more than he wanted to admit. He ignored her, continuing to dismantle the harnesses then dumping a bucket of oats and mash into the feeding trough for the horses.

"Why did you take me with you?"

"What?" He stopped what he was doing to give her a baleful stare.

"Why did you take me with you when Young Daniel came for you?"

His eyes widened and then narrowed. "Go to bed, Nora. My reasoning, my problems aren't really any of your concern anyway. You'll go back to your parents soon enough and your life will be the tidy, polished, and superficial thing it was before you came here."

He was trying to hurt her, she could see it in the dark look in his eyes. He wanted to make her run away so he could avoid talking to her about the very things he needed to say. Did he really think her so shallow she would run from him? After all they had been through together?

There might have been a time when she would have. When her very proper sensibilities would have sent her steaming from his presence if he so much as lifted an eyebrow in a critical manner. But that Lenore Brownley seemed a pale forlorn creature of the past.

So much the better.

"Maybe that's not what I want." She told him softly.

"No?" He lifted his eyebrow as he turned his gaze to hers. "Indeed, then what is it you want?"

She took the tiniest step closer to him. "I want a real life."

"What?"

"Real life."

He snorted angry disbelief and gripped her shoulders, pressing her backward until the barn wall brought her up short. The rough-hewn timbers scratched into her back through the watered taffeta of her dress.

"You may not know much about what you want in life, Lenore Eugenia Brownley. And you may have come here looking for answers. But if there is one thing you do *not* want, it's real life."

He towered over her, dark and angry and hurting so much she could feel the pain pouring from him in hot waves. A tiny rational portion of her warned her to stop now before she pushed him too far. But the rest of her told her this was the only way to break through to him. The only way to heal. The only way to help.

She swallowed, straightened her spine and held his gaze. "Why?"

A tight growl came from his throat as his hands transferred from her shoulders to cheeks, cupping her face and lifting her face up to meet his as he closed the distance between them, pressing his body to hers. Nora's heartbeat quickened in a queer mix of fear and desire.

"Because reality is not pretty." He spoke in a low tone that cut deep into her heart. "It isn't stylish dinner parties and lacy dresses in the latest fashion."

His breath was hot against her cheeks, his fingers traced her jawline without gentleness and arched into her hair. "It's dirty and painful and bloody. And filled with sorrow. It's hard and it's frustrating, and takes the kind of grit and determination that melds peoples souls together."

She licked her lips and dared to answer him. "Like Job and Martha Pruitt?"

"Yes." His gaze searched hers. "Exactly like that. Their life wasn't pretty, but you couldn't get more real than that."

Nora slid her hands over his trim waistcoat and around his waist, watching as his features tightened.

"She told me to take you home and love you for all you are worth." Her words spilled into the sudden silence between them and echoed across the dimly lit barn.

The price of life, of living, is pain. Love mitigates the price and makes the living, however long or brief, worthwhile. That's what she'd said.

"Did she? Well I'm not worth much right now."

"You are to Martha. You are to any number of people." She slid her hands up his back and arched herself against him. "You are to me."

"Martha was grief stricken." He reminded her in a deadened tone even as she saw something flare alight in the depths of his gaze.

"Yes. But she is also is a very, very smart woman." She stopped a hair's breadth from his mouth. "I seem to have been surrounded with very smart women from the moment I arrived in Maine."

He groaned as she reached up on her tiptoe. "This is not a romance, Nora. If you do not get out of here now, your life may get a whole lot more real than you are truly ready to face."

Again, a veiled threat. She could feel the vibration humming through him. His pain and his need sizzled through him, calling out to her.

In that moment Nora understood something that left men wondering the world over, how any woman ever knew how and when and why to do what they needed most. How to help even in the face of turmoil. Deep inside her, she knew what to do to help Jake Warren. She would do exactly as Martha had directed and as Grandmother had said when trying to explain her feelings for Jacob.

Nora smiled up into Jake's dark and turbulent gaze and stepped directly into the storm.

"Kiss me, Jake, and let me show you all you're worth. Let me love you for all your worth."

Fifteen

Kiss me, Jake, . . . let me love you for all you're worth.

Jake's breath locked in his chest. Nora's words rang through his skull, tearing into his already tormented soul to reach deep inside him and breach barriers he'd once thought impenetrable. Temptation battered the ragged remnants of his control.

Her eyes glowed even in the near darkness of the barn, smoked amber and promises. He had the distinct and unsettling feeling she could see clear through him. That she understood all the pain and uncertainty raging inside him. And that she wanted him anyway.

But that wasn't possible, was it?

Did it matter?

She could not possibly understand what she was offering him. Apparently, the lesson he'd attempted to teach them both only a few nights ago had gone for naught.

Proper young misses did not suggest such things. Only Nora could blend boldness and innocence into such an intoxicating, tempting mixture.

Remembering her indignation as she pulled free from Dick Moore's arms this afternoon, he knew she was an innocent. That her offer was meant for him alone. That she would be his alone. Awe and pride hammered through him.

He peered at her hard in the remnants of light left to them. The sweet honeysuckle scent of her beckoned. Her lips called for his caress. Her arms twined around him, demanding his embrace. Her gaze offered solace from the torment inside him. Her mouth, her body, would more than blot out the pain of his failure, fill the emptiness for at least this night. But he knew that if he took her up on her outrageous offer, one night would not be enough.

He should let her go, send her into the house and find what comfort he could at the bottom of a whiskey barrel. She couldn't really mean what her actions, her words suggested. He ground his teeth together and fought for mastery of his own desires. She was not a woman to be used and set aside. And he had already taken far too many advantages of Sylvia Worth's younger granddaughter. For a timeless moment he teetered on the edge of the beckoning precipice, unable to let go, unable to damn them both.

"Jake." Her breath caressed his lips while her fingers burned against the skin at the nape of his neck, making his decision for him. He wanted her far too much. He had never made any claims to being a saint.

And the demons riding his soul demanded a sacrifice.

He covered her lips with his own, the contact rough and needy and anything but gentle. She moaned into his mouth as she opened to him, accepting his assault without complaint, meeting him more than half-way as their tongues slid together, hot and hungry. Her body melded to his. Her breasts were full and high and round against his chest. He wanted to take her, here, now, in the hay against the barn wall. To shed their clothes and find solace in the physical release of thrusting himself into her soft young body, over and over. The images burned hot trails across his mind.

Hell and be damned to the consequences.

He pushed her back against the wall and found the buttons of her bodice. One by one they popped open as he tugged at them with impatient fingers. His mouth continued to savage hers and her hands gripped his shoulders for support. Let her stop him now if she truly did not wish to give him what she offered, for he could do nothing to stop himself.

The top of her gown gaped open and he pulled the bodice from her skirt and slid it down her arms before tossing the garment aside to leave her in the frilly confines of her chemise and satin-covered stays.

He released her lips for a moment. She was so incredibly beautiful. Her breath came rapidly, thrusting the pale fullness of her breasts in enticing display. Too readily the image of her, limp and responsive, in the kitchen sprang to mind, complete with all the things he'd wanted from her. He had stopped himself then. Shown a restraint that seemed a pale and pitiful thing beside the need raging inside him now.

With his palms, he traced her shoulders, her bared arms, and boldly cupped her breasts. She moaned and her head fell back as her breasts filled his hands. He fondled her through the thin veil of her chemise, she was round and soft and oh, so tempting.

Her nipples were tight points jutting against his palms. He teased her, gently pinching and twisting. Wringing yet another sigh from her to reach inside him and scour his heart. He wanted her as he had never wanted any woman, as he had never needed anything in his life.

Touching her was not enough and the thin fabric of her chemise was a barrier not to be tolerated. He pulled at the lacings of her corset and it released with a sigh to slide over her hips and to the floor.

Next, he grasped a handful of her flimsy chemise in each fist and with a quick motion tore it from her body. She gasped and her gaze went wide, plumbing his own as he bared her so precipitously. She knew what he wanted from her. He could read it in the bitter-sweet mingling of desire and fear in the depths of her smoked amber eyes.

He paused for a fraction of a moment, his breath coming harsh in his throat. Her breasts begged for his touch, his kiss, but he held back a moment longer. Let her stop him or there would be no turning back. The thought pulsed through his brain, a half-hearted request, a broken prayer.

Her own breathing came ragged and uneven as she held his gaze. His heartbeat thudded in his ears as he waited and then she straightened her shoulders ever so slightly. She had made her own decision. And he was incapable of questioning it now.

So be it. A growl of pure male satisfaction was the only answer he could give her over the white-hot desire flaming inside him.

Her breasts glowed in the soft fading light inside the barn. Her skin tempting and flushed a soft pink. He gripped her waist and bent to hungrily apply his mouth to her soft resilient flesh, pressing a series of hot kisses to her softness. She was fresh and succulent and so alive, the perfect balm for the darkness writhing in his soul.

He circled her breast with kisses and flicked her tight nipple with his tongue. She groaned his name and threaded her fingers through his hair, tugging him closer. He teased her a moment longer and sucked her nipple deep into his mouth, laving it with his tongue, tormenting it with his teeth as she moaned and cupped the back of his head. Then he transferred his attentions to the other taut nipple, teasing her, tasting her, as she moaned and held him to her.

Her responsiveness would surely burn him to cinders and land him in hell a good deal faster than he'd thought. But it didn't matter. He needed her. He would have her. There were no more questions.

He gripped the fastenings to her skirt, loosened it and heard it sigh to the floor. Her petticoats followed in short order, until she stood clad in only silky pantalettes and her own beauty.

He stood back from her again. Their breathing rapid and loud, mingled in the air scented with hay and sorrow and skin-warmed honeysuckle. Yes, this would blot out the pain. She would blot out the pain and the death, the anguish that came each time.

She would give him the only relief, the only forgetfulness, he was likely to get.

"You are beautiful. Let your hair down, I want to see it as it flows around you," he told her, meaning every word. She complied, pulling the pins free and shaking her head to loose a golden silk waterfall.

"More than beautiful."

"Thank you." Soft and husky, innocent seduction.

He gritted his teeth as her answer pierced him and drew blood somewhere deep inside him. Ever the well-bred young lady, she would no doubt stop to thank him for ridding her of her virginity by the time he was through with her. That cynical thought alone should have been enough to stop him, to make him recover some sense of the man he'd thought himself to be. But nothing mattered but the need driving him and the promise of relief beckoning in her eyes.

He pulled her back into his arms and covered her mouth with his, drinking greedily from her softness as he tasted her lips, her tongue and the wellspring of understanding so deep inside her. He played his hands over the velvet softness of her back.

Then he kissed a pathway downward, laving her neck, suckling her breasts and then moving lower still. He knelt before her in the hay and ran his hands up over her legs from ankle to calf to thigh to the plump rounded firmness of her buttocks.

He pressed a kiss against her belly and then lower where he could feel the heat of her feminine softness through the silky fabric. Her hands trembled cool and soft at his shoulders. He nudged her thighs apart and pressed his mouth to the juncture of her thighs. She was hot and wet. Her hands fluttered at his shoulders and gripped him hard as he kissed her there, massaging her with his lips, nipping her intimately. He cupped her buttocks and tilted her toward him, opening her more fully to his kiss.

"Jake. Oh, Jake." She gasped his name, breathless and needy. And then that was no longer enough. He released his grip of her long enough to undo the fastening and slide this last protective covering to the ground.

He rolled her stockings down too, first one and then the other, enjoying the softness of her thighs, the firmness of her calves, until she was naked before him. Beautiful. Sensual. A feast. His for the taking.

His.

A rush of possessive desire dizzied him and he nudged her pale thighs apart to press his mouth to her virginal softness. He suckled the nubbin of flesh between her thighs. She gasped and moaned, clutching him as he tasted her desire, flicking her with his tongue over and over and over while his own need swelled to bursting within him.

"Jake. I can't. Oh—" Not a denial, a plea.

She moaned deeper, the sound throaty and compelling as shockwaves rippled over her body and she convulsed against him, trembling as he carried her over the brink. As the last waves died away she sank into his arms as though she could stand no longer. Her legs slid to either side of his. She was naked, replete, and lovelier than he had ever seen her. He wanted her more than ever.

"I don't know what to say." She told him in a breathless voice tinged with wonder and dawning sensuality. It was the most erotic mixture he had ever heard.

"Then say nothing." He coaxed her mouth to his and kissed her. Softly. Completely, as he soothed his hands over her back. God, how he wanted her.

He drew her backward with him into the hay and then rolled her beneath him, never breaking the molten heat of their kiss. She sighed as he nestled the rigid length of his arousal between her thighs. He would go mad if he didn't take her now. He released her mouth and pushed upright long enough to tear the shirt and pants from his body.

"Oh Jake." Her eyes had gone wide again at the sight of him.

He forced himself to stand still for a moment as her gaze traveled the length of him before coming to rest on the hard and pulsing span of his erection.

Letting her peruse his body took more control than he'd ever imagined he possessed.

She sat up and reached out to him, her fingers closing over his shaft. He sucked in his breath at her tentative touch, her daring gesture, so cool and soft.

He groaned as she traced its length. Innocently erotic. Boldly naive. He would die. Right here. Right now. With her fingers gripping him.

"Make love to me."

Her request forced his eyes open and he met her gaze. She was unsure, he could read her thoughts so clearly they hurt. But she would not back away from him. He knew that as if she had spoken a vow aloud. Everything in him writhed. He would have her. He had to. He would damn himself with the act. What kind of man took a virginal young girl to salve his own pain? With every ounce of honor he'd ever possessed he struggled to take control of his own passions.

"Go now, Lenore." He hissed the words through gritted teeth. "Before it is too late."

Her fingers slid into his and she tugged him back into the hay beside her, pressing him onto his back. Her fingers slid over his lips and then she replaced them with her mouth, kissing him with soft sweetness.

"Make love to me," she whispered again. "Make us both forget."

He groaned, unable to resist her plea as she pressed the soft fullness of her breasts to his chest and kissed him. He locked an arm about her waist and pulled her fully atop him. Her legs slid, silken and soft, to either side of his as she returned his kiss with all the new found passion inside her.

She was so close. The damp heat of her arousal so close to his own. And as he kissed her she brushed against him. Slick and wet and soft. Twin moans mingled in the air. Shocking and visceral. Her gaze met his and she slid back against him. The slick folds of her eased over the thick head of his arousal, caressing him.

"Oh, God. Nora."

"Yes." A simple agreement. "Oh, Jake, that feels good."

He couldn't move from the spot. And she repeated her movement, easing the tip of him inside her body and then out again as though she had been born with the knowledge of exactly how to drive a man out of his mind. In and out. Her movements experimental, hesitant, torturous.

Her face was alight with desire and pleasure and he couldn't stop her. Then further, she pushed herself onto his rigid length, taking him more fully into her. Meeting the barrier of her virginity. His groan and hers, ripped the air around them.

"Jake . . . I want . . ." She licked her lips. "I want."

She would tear him apart with the expression her face. So achingly lovely, so sensual, so honest.

He pushed upward, piercing the barrier, melding his body with hers, lodging himself deeply inside her. He caught her gasp of pain against his lips and then kissed her, slowly, deeply, trying to tell her without words how he felt. Her pain was his. If he could take it for her he would.

"Nora, I'm sorry." He whispered the words against her mouth.

"Love me." She answered, ripping his heart from his chest.

And then he could do nothing but comply with her request. He moved inside her, watching her face as the friction of their bodies rippled through her.

Passion tightened her features as the pain passed and the moan she emitted echoed through his soul.

"Oh, oh!" She straightened atop him and leaned her head back, spilling soft silken hair over his thighs as he cupped her hips and rocked her against him. Slow, sweet friction. Back and forth. In and out.

She was so perfect.

Her breasts swayed a sensuous rhythm with each stroke. Wet slick, velvety heat caressed him and the desire riding him demanded satisfaction.

He pulled her down to meet his kiss. Long. Slow. Complete. A matching rhythm to the tempo of their lovemaking. His hand captured her breast and he caressed her hardened nipple. Each slow stroke was torture and pleasure. Heaven and hell rolled into one. He needed each one.

He turned her beneath him in the hay, placing her atop the heap of their discarded clothing. Her golden hair fanned her head to mix with the hay. Her hips cradled his own. And he sank deeper still into her soft heat.

Her legs wrapped his waist and he stayed that way for the span of several heartbeats. She was so soft and beautiful beneath him.

"Nora." He moved inside her, watching her face.

Her eyes slitted and she arched against him.

"You are mine now," he told her.

"Yes."

"Mine." He repeated, savoring the taste on his tongue as he slid in and out of her.

"Yes, oh . . . Jake."

He gripped her tighter, closer, and sank into a kiss that joined their mouths, mating them fully as he increased the tempo of his body. Each thrust branded her as his. Each thrust blazed such pure pleasure throughout his body he knew he would never let her go.

He groaned into her mouth and pushed faster, harder. She clutched him closer and echoed his desire as she matched his movements, measure for measure.

He drove himself into her again and again, lost to an ageless rhythm that demanded all from him. A slave to the blinding white-hot pleasure building higher and rippling the length of his body, she clutched him and cried out her own pleasure beneath him.

And he spilled himself deep inside her, trembling and unable to tell which of them had needed this more.

For a timeless stretch he was lost in the hazy aftermath. Their bodies still joined, damp skin to damp skin. Their breathing gradually slowing as their hearts pounded together.

Then he pushed up onto his elbows to view her in the stillness of the darkened barn. She looked wellloved. A woman. She was definitely no longer little Nora Brownley who had dogged his heels so many years ago.

Who would have known?

"Oh my." She smiled up at him.

"Indeed." He smiled back, tenderness wrapping around his heart.

"I had no idea." She told him in that honest, appealing way that tore him in two. "There really are no words."

He chuckled, amazed that she had made him laugh. Surely on her back in the hay was not what she had dreamed of when she had considered surrendering her virginity and yet there was no regret in the gaze she shared with him. Only wonder.

She was amazed. And she amazed him.

He could stay right here, locked in an embrace, making love to her over and over again for the rest of his life. But reality would intrude on their little oasis all too soon. It was time for a discussion.

He took a breath. "Nora—"

She placed her fingers over his mouth. "Not now, Jake. Later."

How she had known what he intended to say, he didn't know. But she had put a stop to his good intentions once again.

He leaned down and kissed her.

Softly. Gently.

Trying to tell her all the things she wouldn't let him say, and that she had offered him something he'd given up hope of finding. Something he would have gladly traded his soul for. Balm for a spirit torn to pieces by death. How could he ever explain that? Did she already know?

He hugged her closer. It felt so good just to hold her in his arms and kiss her. To trace her tongue with his own and taste the stirring of new passion as he did so.

She twined her arms around his neck and sighed into his mouth, returning each kiss. Desire swelled easily, lengthening and thickening the hot flesh still buried inside her as he increased the pressure of his kisses, sipping her newly-awakened passion, drunk on the wine of her innocent sensuality.

She moaned into his mouth as he filled her and then she arched against him, asking him wordlessly to begin the same sweet friction they had enjoyed such as short time before.

She was right. All the things they needed to talk about could wait until later. Right now the need burning quickly to fever pitch inside them both overrode any other consideration. She wanted him to make love to her again. He was more than willing to comply.

He tried to go slower. To kiss her in languidly sweet torment and build her pleasure to higher and higher heights. But the fire between them came fast and furious, like lightning sweeping a summer sky, rippling through both of them. Hot, sweet friction, ageless rhythm. Their cries mingled together in the darkening barn as he gave them both up to the sound and fury, the sweet sensation of loving her.

And the knowledge that he could never let her go.

He awoke some time later. Lenore lay curled against his side, naked and lovely, kissed by the bright moonlight filtering through the barn. Looking at her tightened his throat and caused his eyes to burn. She had given him something more than the sweet gift of her virginity. She had freed him from the worst of his demons. She had freed him from the vacant landscape of his failures. At the moment all he could do was stare at her, his heart full to bursting with emotions he'd never thought to lay claim to.

He loved her.

The thought startled a smile to his lips and spread an odd warmth throughout his body. He loved the perfect little princess, Lenore Eugenia Brownley, the one destined to be society's darling. The woman curled in such sensual and innocent disarray at his side.

He pressed a soft kiss to her brow.

She sighed, draped one slender soft limb across him and slept on. Tenderness ached through him.

He could not stay here in the hay with her like some stable boy laying his first woman. She needed a proper bed with sheets and blankets and comfort.

Morning would come soon enough and he'd been a doctor long enough to know that loving her twice would leave her sore in places she'd been unaware of before. He have to see what he could do to alleviate that. With all the care his years in medicine had taught him he pushed to his feet and scooped her into his arms. Her arm draped his shoulders and she sighed against his neck.

"Where are we going, Doctor Warren?"

He chuckled again, unable to justify the formal use of his name with her naked form pressed to his chest.

"To bed, my fine young woman." He told her, trying for a proper doctorly manner and failing miserably as his newfound feelings for her husked his voice.

"Indeed." She lifted her head from his shoulder and sought his gaze with hers. "And what do we intend to do when we get there?"

There was a wicked little gleam in the depth of her smoked amber eyes, a gleam he was all too aware he had put there in the first place. She was a sensual woman, his beloved Nora. She would no doubt lead him a merry dance across the years, one he would be happy to perform as long as it kept her by his side.

"Sleep," he told her without preamble even as his body responded all too readily to that teasing little glint.

"Oh." She sighed in disappointment and bit her lip before looking back at him again. "Are you sure?"

"Quite sure." He forced the words out as he crossed

the space between the barn and the house. Moonlight caressed the dips and hollows of her shapely body, glistening over her skin. She was so beautiful he ached with it. He longed to taste every inch of her and to feel the arch of her body to his as he pulsed deep inside her again.

She sighed once more and rested her head back against his shoulder. "All right then. We'll sleep."

Damnation.

He'd never realized the torment of wanting a woman who wanted you right back.

It was going to be another very long night.

Sixteen

Dull gray light streamed the windows in conjunction with soft, pattering rain.

A day meant for sleeping.

Nora felt snug and warm despite the inclement weather. She was tempted to remain in the bed, enveloped in warmth until someone dared to come and retrieve her. She hadn't felt this decadent since she had arrived in Maine.

She sighed, blissful and content in a new and deeper way that she ever remembered feeling. She could happily stay in this bed forever.

And then the events of the previous evening rushed back to her. She had fallen asleep. Naked. In the barn. Fallen asleep there after making wild passionate love, not once, but twice with Jake. Now she was in her own bed in her grandmother's house.

But she was not alone.

Jake Warren lay warm and solid beside her. Undeniable evidence that she had not merely dreamed their encounter in the barn. Heat flooded upward to scald her cheeks and increase the wild pounding of her heart.

Along with the memories of their lovemaking in the barn, came the painful knowledge of Job Pruitt's death and the grief it engendered for everyone who cared for him. She had loved Jake exactly as Martha had asked of her. She had gotten him through the first brutal crush of loss. But what of Martha? What of Kate?

What now?

She nearly jumped out of her skin when Jake's fingers brushed her forehead in a casual caress. He slipped his hand under the mass of her hair and nuzzled the side of her neck with his lips. Somehow it was even more scaldingly scandalous to know that he was not only in her bed with her, as naked as she, but he was awake and fully cognizant of her presence beside him.

His hands caught her shoulders and he turned her to face him. Skin to skin she rubbed against him as she turned. The feeling was exhilarating, and horrifying, all at once.

She was a woman now. He had claimed her as his and she had claimed him. Nothing else seemed to matter as the sensations they had created flowed through her as she gazed into the face of her lover.

Her lover.

The musky scent of their lovemaking twined with Jake's clean sage and citrus scent and a hint of the hay they had used with such wild abandon. She took in a deep breath and let it out slowly as she faced him full of wonder. Full of questions.

Her cheeks burned as his hazel gaze bored into hers.

"Nora, are you all right?" Gentleness edged his question and dipped his words in concern as he brushed her cheek with his fingers. He traced her jawline as though she were made of the finest crystal.

What could she say?

She had never been in such a situation before and nothing in her repertoire of polite responses to dinner party questions prepared her for what to say to one's lover the morning after she had surrendered her all to him.

And then demanded more.

So she did the only thing that seemed natural. She closed her eyes and kissed him full on the mouth. He groaned at her touch and pulled her toward him. Naked flesh met naked flesh, soft breast to hard chest, muscled thigh against slender hip. The heat raging through her changed in an instant to desire.

His rigid length pulsed against her belly. So hard and yet, silky smooth at the same time. He stroked her skin, skimming his fingers over her waist and down her leg over and over as he met the passionate demands of her mouth.

The fire raged low in her center, in the place only he had touched. Only he would ever touch. A fire stoked by the rhythm of his lips on hers, his tongue against hers, and the intense love she felt for this man.

She was more than ready for him as he turned her beneath him. As though they had been made precisely for this purpose, their bodies fit together and his full, hot flesh slid into her. She groaned as she accepted his length deep within her. It felt so good. So right, to be in his arms. To have him buried deep inside her. To not be able to tell where she began and he ended.

"Nora, look at me. I want to see your eyes as I love you."

So simple a request and yet the entreaty burned through her and sent hedonistic spirals echoing in its wake.

She opened her eyes and slid her legs up around his waist, arching herself against him as he pressed himself deeper.

"Yes, that's it." He pulled out ever so slightly and then pushed himself ever deeper into her body. Pulling her up and pushing down inside her core.

And all the while he kept his eyes locked on hers, feasting on her.

She moaned her pleasure, her encouragement and still held his gaze. His own tight with desire as the flames between them flared higher and hotter than ever.

"Oh, Jake." Her fingers gripped his arms pulling herself closer to him.

"Nora." He ran his fingers through her hair and moved ever so slowly. Tortuously. In. Out. In. Building the sweet pressure inside.

"So good. So beautiful. You are everything I want, Nora. Everything I need."

She clung to his shoulders, needing every sweet inch of him. He bent and pressed soft, drugging kisses to her lips, their breath mingling even as the friction building between them picked up a tempo of its own.

Hotter. Higher. Swift and powerful. As their gazes locked once more, pleasure rocketed through her. She cried out his name over and over as her body shivered, wracked with the joy he gave her and he found his own release.

In the aftermath, their breathing echoed loud in the bedroom. And then below, outside, there was another sound. The distant rattle of harness and the sounds of doors opening and closing.

Tension gathered throughout the length of Jake's body as it pressed so intimately to hers.

"Grandmother." Nora clutched him closer as a ribbon of fear streaked through her.

"Earlier than I expected." He dropped a quick kiss

to her lips. "Don't worry. Take your time getting dressed. I'll delay them downstairs."

"What about our clothes, the barn last night?" Worry crowded in, despite the knowledge that what had happened between them she would never regret.

"I covered them with hay before I carried you inside. Just in case."

She blessed his foresight on both counts. Suppose they had still been twined naked together in the barn when Grandmother and Jacob arrived home?

He jumped from the beneath the covers to stand strong and naked before her. She sighed, admiring his manly physique, despite the circumstances.

He bent to retrieve the shirt she vaguely remembered him wrapping around her before carrying her in last night. She giggled.

"And just what do you find so amusing, in your view, my lady?" he whispered with humor.

"I never saw that scar before. The one from the shooting accident."

His finger grazed the puckered scar high on his left buttock. "I still don't think that was an accident. I think your sister aimed for me on purpose because I had been teasing her about her aim."

Nora still remembered the shock and agony she had felt when she thought Maggie had killed Jake when she shot him. She'd cried buckets that day. She supposed she'd loved him even then. The memory might be amusing now, but at the time she had been horrified.

He straightened and twinkled at her. "Once Devin heard the story, he locked his pistol away where she can't get it."

Nora wished they could have stayed in the bed for the full day. Laughing and talking and loving another to their hearts' content. The sound of trunks hitting the porch put paid to that idea.

He crossed to the door with hardly a sound and paused for a moment as though judging the whereabouts of the people downstairs, then he winked and blew her a kiss before disappearing out the door.

No matter how badly she wished to linger in the bed and pretend she didn't have to face anything more worrisome than the passionate demands Jake might have of her, Lenore forced herself to face the present situation. They needed to present themselves, fully dressed, in short order.

She scooted from the bed and struggled to ignore the after echoes of pleasure still rippling through her body as she found fresh pantalettes and petticoats and struggled into a day dress before stopping in front of the mirror to make some attempts with her hair.

"Dear heaven."

The sight that greeted her almost sent her scampering back to the bed to hide beneath the covers and stay that way. Her eyes were wide and startled, her hair wild, and her lips puffy and kiss-bruised. She looked well-loved. A true hoyden, not at all the decorous young woman her grandmother had left in Jake's keeping only a few short days ago.

There was no help for it now.

With rapid movements she brushed her wild mane of hair into submission and twisted it into the quickest and best chignon she had ever achieved. Then she splashed cool water over her face until her eyes sparkled and her cheeks held a fresh-scrubbed appearance that would have pleased her mother no end. There was nothing she could do to eliminate the slight puffiness still evident in her lips. But she would have to do.

Struggling for the aplomb she had always admired in her friend Amelia she swept from the bedroom and down the stairs to face her grandmother's return.

"—excellent trip, my boy. I'm sure Sylvia will have a great deal of information to share with Devin and Maggie when they return." Jacob's voice trailed toward her as Lenore reached the bottom of the steps. They were in the parlor. So much the better.

"Indeed." Grandmother sounded unruffled. "Now, where is my granddaughter?"

"She should join us in a moment, Sylvia." Jake sounded calm and easy going. For a moment Nora was tempted to leave him in charge of their two elders and make good her retreat. *Coward*, a distant corner of her mind railed. She straightened her spine and forced her feet forward before Grandmother could issue a reproof for his use of her Christian name.

"I'm right here, Grandmother." She fixed a smile of greeting on her face as the three occupants turned toward her. Her mind all but screamed her guilt as she avoided Jake's gaze and willed herself not to think about the touch of his lips, his body pressed to hers.

Grandmother's gaze traveled her length and back again in quick review. One brow twitched and Nora sensed questions gathering behind the pleasant smile her grandmother favored her with. She swallowed the lump of tension that swelled in her throat and pressed a kiss to her elder's cheek.

"I'm so happy you're home," she said as honestly as she could.

"As am I, my dear." Grandmother patted her shoulder. "I am always happiest beneath my own roof and well Jacob knows it. But where is Kate? It is so unlike her not to greet us."

Nora blew out a sigh and her gaze sought Jake's before flickering quickly away. "Kate stayed with Martha Pruitt last night—"

"Job passed on yesterday." Jake offered at the same time.

"Ah." Grandmother sat farther back in her chair as Jacob came to her side and rested his hands on her shoulders. Her fingers sought his in silent communion. "We knew it was only a matter of time."

Her gaze included them both and Nora forced herself to hold still and not turn away from her grandmother's all too perceptive eyes. What was she thinking? Had it occurred to her that the two of them had been on their own for the evening?

"The rector?"

"Will be stopping by to help with the arrangements today." Jake answered.

"They had a long life together and much happiness." Grandmother sighed. "Jake, help your father with the trunks, if you please. Lenore, come and sit beside me."

Nora joined her grandmother on the settee, ignoring the tender parts of her that had never been tender before as she sat and the men left the room.

"Jake has never taken the death of a patient well. It is not in him. He wants to heal every ill and mend every break. It is one of the traits that makes him such a fine doctor and yet it is to his detriment at the same time."

"Yes, Grandmother."

"Then you are aware of his feelings of failure and self-condemnation? How was he last night?"

Deep concern laced the question with more than

appeared on the surface. The urge to run flickered through Nora once again. She settled her fingers more firmly together in her lap and swallowed.

"Did he at least sleep?"

All night with me in his arms.

"Yes, Grandmother. As well as could be under the circumstances."

Silence held for the span of several heartbeats and then her grandmother's cool fingers covered her own. "Lenore, loving a man, any man, is not an easy path, and not a path to be chosen lightly. Be sure it is truly what you wish."

Tears burned at the back of Nora's eyes all too readily. Her grandmother had known so easily. Despite their attempts to look unchanged, presentable. She should have known there was very little that escaped Grandmother's sharp gaze and keen insight.

Heat poured over Nora's cheeks and her throat tightened. Instead of offering her any censure or lecturing her on proper behavior, her only concern was her granddaughter's well-being.

"I am trying, Grandmother." The words came husky as she met her grandmother's gaze.

"That is all I can ask." Grandmother patted her hands and then released her with a slight sigh.

Her words still echoed in Nora's thoughts as she stood in the clinic a day later, pondering the meaning of them and all that had happened between herself and Jake in such a short time. They'd had little time to themselves once Grandmother and Jacob had returned, what with Job Pruitt's impending funeral.

Even now, she had come to Somerset on her own

to open the clinic and settle the supplies needed for the day, while Jake met with Doctor Michaels.

She finished sorting and arranging the files Jake would need for the coming clinic visits and draped her apron on the back of a chair. The small span of time they might have between his arrival from Kittery and seeing his first patient would be the first they had spent alone since Grandmother and Jacob had returned.

Her nervousness grew with each passing moment. What would they say to one another? What did he think of her? She completed a third circuit of the empty clinic and could stand the emptiness of the office and her own beleaguered thoughts no longer.

The post should have arrived by now. And if she hurried she had enough time to go and retrieve it. Perhaps the report they awaited of the missing girls would be there and it would offer them something to talk of other than the intimacy they shared and the questions about the future it couldn't help but engender.

The short walk to the general store took only a few minutes and she was rewarded with a huge pile of journals and correspondence. One envelope stood out thicker than the rest. The postmark startled her heart to a faster beat.

"Thank you." She managed a warm smile for the elderly gentleman who owned the store and acted as postmaster.

"The one you wanted?" He returned her smile.

"Yes, yes, I think so. Do you mind?" She gestured to a small bench.

"Go right ahead, Miss Brownley. Make yourself ta home."

"Thank you." She sank down onto the bench and

settled the pile beside her before tearing into the thick envelope. She pulled out the contents. Sheet after sheet of vellum, filled with information, she tilted her head to catch the light spilling in the broad windows behind her and began to drink it in.

There was no employment agency by the name supplied by Mr. Hawkins, neither in Halifax nor any port along the eastern seaboard of both Canada and the United States. The girls who had left Somerset on the mail packet had vanished for parts and places unknown.

Her stomach clenched with each new paragraph and she forced herself to read on despite the dawning horror growing inside her. This was indeed just the information Jake and Devin and Maggie had been looking for. Yet the evidence before her chilled her and started a twist of nausea deep in her stomach. This was not a small paragraph of horror buried deep in the local paper, something Papa might mention at dinner or Mama might deplore with a raised and skeptical eyebrow over tea. This was real and all too close.

She knew the girls at the mill. Little Lizzie and Callie, who had been destined to leave Somerset today. Thank goodness she had spoken so sharply to Mrs. Hawkins on Sunday and put a stop to that plan.

Despite her initial reluctance to be involved, she knew these Hawkins girls and her heart ached for the ones who had disappeared. *Most likely sold to an underground market,* the report concluded. A *market. Sold.* As the country teetered on the verge of war over this very issue, how could such a thing be happening right under the very noses of the good citizens of Somerset? The idea was stunning in and of itself.

How this had come about, how many girls were lost was hard to tell. To think of the future they were being sold into, like animals, led unprotesting and trusting to the slaughter. Who was to blame? Who was accountable?

Tears burned the backs of her eyes just as she became aware of a presence beside her.

"Hullo, Nora . . . Lenore." The dulcet tones and floral perfume of Deirdre Johnson filtered into Lenore's upset.

She all but gritted her teeth, years of training coming to the fore to stop such an unseemly display despite the dismay roiling inside her. If there was one thing she didn't need at this particular moment it was the uninhibited intrusion and pointy-spiked conversation of Deirdre, complete with her glossy black curls and vivacious coloring.

"Hello, Deirdre," she managed the greeting in return, even as her mind continued to whirl with the information she had just learned. Who could be behind such deeds and how could they be stopped?

Deirdre's dark eyes perused the envelope in her Lenore's hands and the thick sheets of vellum, clutched awkwardly to her breast, and then trailed to the items piled carefully beside her on the bench.

"My dear, you have come to retrieve the post for Doctor Warren. How charmingly domestic of you." Deirdre managed to sound anything but charmed despite the warmth oozing in her tone. "But truly it was unnecessary. I have been assisting Jake for weeks with this little task, as you well know. And of course, reading another's mail in broad daylight, why, I am surprised anyone, even you, would do such a thing. Here let me help you get those pieces back in the envelope where they belong."

Deirdre's slender fingers clutched at the vellum. Nora's breath locked in her throat and for a moment she felt almost as though she were being attacked here in the relative safety of the Somerset General Store. The idea was stunning. Her stomach churned still further as a cold shiver of fear streaked up her back despite the warm sunlight mantling her shoulders and the conspicuous presence of the post master.

"Are you quite all right, Miss Brownely?" The elder gentleman leaned over the counter, his face scrutinizing hers.

She struggled to pull herself back under control as Deirdre's fingers gripped the vellum and pulled it from Nora's unresisting grasp.

"Yes, yes I'm fine, thank you. I don't know what came over me." She managed the words as she watched Deirdre deftly tuck the betraying contents back into the envelope.

As much as she hated to admit it, Deirdre was right. She shouldn't have opened it without Jake's consent and most certainly not here in public. The entire contents of the report needed to be considered before they could act on it.

She blew out a long breath and stood.

She needed to get back to the clinic. Jake would arrive any time now and he would need at least a few moments to consider what they had in their hands before he was inundated with patients and his medical worries of the day.

There would be no time to discuss anything personal between them and perhaps that was for the best. She didn't truly feel up to facing the consequences of what they'd done.

"Thank you, Deirdre." She moved to take the

envelope from the widow's hands and Deirdre side-
stepped her with a light laugh.

"My dear, you are not yourself today, are you?"
Those laughing dark eyes perused Nora's with the
sharp intent of a hawk. And then the long delicate
fingers waved toward the pile of correspondence
sliding in haphazard disarray toward the edge of the
bench Nora had just vacated.

"Oh, dear." Nora rescued it before the entire pile
rained onto the floor of the general store.

"Come along then, Lenore. Goodbye, Mr. Tucker."
Deirdre's overly sweet voice grated along Nora's nerve
endings as the widow preceded her out the door,
calling to her like a wayward child.

"Yes, thank you." She managed hurriedly out the
door behind Deirdre, uncomfortably aware that the
one piece of correspondence Jake most needed to
see was not in her possession.

"Deirdre, Deirdre." For a moment she thought the
widow intended to leave her behind as she quickly
navigated her way to the end of the walkway. But then
Deirdre stopped and turned to smile her wide vivacious smile, those unfathomable dark eyes sparkling
in the sunlight like pieces of polished ebony.

"Come along, dear. Did you think I would leave
you?" She laughed, the sound not entirely pleasant.
"Of course not, what rubbish. Nora, darling, you do
need to get hold of yourself. You are behaving in a
most peculiar manner."

She reached out and took Nora's arm, almost like
her brother had the other day. "I can't think what
Aunt Sylvia would have to say or what impression
you might leave on our dear Doctor Warren, or poor
Mr. Tucker. Why, he was almost overcome with his
concern for you. Did you notice?"

"I, well, yes." Nora stumbled through her answer. Deirdre Johnson had the knack for making her feel more awkward and unpresentable than she had ever felt in her life.

All she wanted was to retrieve the envelope from Deirdre's grasp and excuse herself from the other woman's company. Unease cloaked her. "Thank you, Deirdre. Now if you could just give me the envelope."

"Oh, this?" Deirdre looked down at the envelope she clutched, her eyes wide and uncertain as though she hadn't even been aware she had it. Then she laughed again. The sound was wild and slightly off key. Nora winced, her nerves rubbed raw by the entire encounter. She must be even more disturbed by what she had read than she had realized because everything about Deirdre made her want scream.

"Certainly, certainly." Deirdre agreed even as she moved off again at the same rapid pace that had taken her out of the general store. Nora had no choice but to follow her. Perhaps Deirdre was just determined to play her part in delivering the post to Jake. After all she had been performing the task regularly for the past few months.

Nora hurried after her, trying to tell herself such was the case and still the unsettled churning in her stomach. But Deirdre turned off to the right down a path that led directly out of town and away from the clinic.

"Deirdre? Where are you going?" Nora called after her. The unsettled feeling in her stomach grew stronger. Where on earth was Deirdre going and why? The dark look in the widow's eyes and the off-key laughter played through her mind again as Nora ran to the corner, unwilling to lose sight of the other woman for any length of time.

"Deirdre?" She reached the corner and the woman was no where in sight. The unease she felt increased ten-fold. She felt as if menacing eyes were taking her measure. A menace beyond Deirdre's capriciousness.

For a moment she was tempted to run to the clinic and ask Jake to find the intimidating widow and deal with the situation that had gotten so strangely out of hand so quickly. But it had been Nora's choice to go and get his post for him, and her clumsiness that had allowed the all too important information to leave her grasp.

What on earth could Deirdre be playing at?

"Deirdre?" She stepped off the walkway and took a few steps into the shadow of the buildings on either side of the path. "Deirdre?"

"I'm right here." Husky tones shivered over the back of Lenore's neck as Deirdre's hands covered her eyes. The widow stood behind her all too close. Goose flesh pebbled Lenore's arms. The sooner she retrieved the envelope and left Deirdre Johnson behind the happier she would be.

"Deirdre, if you would just give me Jake's letter, I will be on my way." She strove for a mix of her mother's most commanding tones and her grandmother's determination.

In response, Deirdre's hands slipped from her eyes and clamped down on her shoulders in a painful vice. "You will, will you? Always the perfect little Miss Lenore. I'll have this and I'll have that," she mocked. "I don't think so, my dear. Not this time."

"Deirdre!" Nora struggled to get out of the other woman's grip. "I don't have time for games. Jake is waiting."

Deirdre's grip tightened still further and Nora gasped, "You're hurting me."

"Not yet." A husky laugh shivered over Nora's shoulders. "Not yet."

"Let me go."

"I don't think so. You have become an impediment, little Nora. And I don't have any more time to waste on you."

What on earth did that mean? A shadow detached itself from the others in the alley.

"Deirdre—"

"Ahh, there you are. I've been waiting," Deirdre purred as someone else joined them.

Pain split the side of Nora's skull, sharp and hot, and then the ground rushed up to meet her.

Seventeen

Footsteps thudded on hard wood, accompanied by the rustle of petticoats.

"What now, Mademoiselle?"

"Just help me with her and stop asking questions."

The voices trickled into Nora's thoughts like rain water, insistent, high pitched and unwelcome through the haze of pain threading her temples.

"*Oui*, Mademoiselle."

Hands tugged her and the pain thickened as a sense of movement drew her closer to consciousness. Where on earth was she? Why didn't she remember what was going on?

She tried to open her eyes. Light split her head and she groaned.

"Hurry, she is waking up, you fool. That oaf, Hawkins, did not hit her hard enough."

That was Deirdre's voice, hissing commands as her sense of motion increased.

Dear heaven, *Deirdre!*

The encounter in town and the envelope the other woman had refused to give back shot through Nora with a bolt of fear and a hot twist of nausea. She'd been abducted. That was the only explanation.

She struggled and groaned as the pain in her head blazed brighter. "Let me go."

Was that weak croak her own?

"Oh, Mademoiselle!"

"Hold her and stop acting like a ninny, Colette. I don't have time for this foolishness. He should have hit her a little harder."

"No." Nora struggled again, winning her freedom so abruptly it stunned her. She forced herself to her feet even as the room tilted around her. Her hands were bound and she couldn't get her balance.

She would have fallen if Deirdre hadn't gripped her hard. She was enveloped in the woman's cloyingly sweet perfume.

"You're not going anywhere." Deirdre's anger hissed in her ear. "You've interfered far too much in everything I'm trying to safeguard here. I have to protect my brother, I always have. I promised Mama."

"Please, I—"

That was as far as she got before a silken scarf was shoved roughly into her mouth. She gagged, but could not spit it out. Breathing was even difficult. She felt as if she might faint again at any moment. She willed herself to stay awake, to pay attention.

"That's better. I should have done that in the first place." Deirdre sounded as though she were making mental notes about how to best carry off an abduction.

Nora shuddered as fear raced along her spine.

"Madame, do you think it wise to handle her so? What will Mr. Richard say? What of the Doctor?" Deirdre's maid hovered behind her, wringing her hands. Her face was pale and her eyes wide.

"*Madame?*" Deirdre emphasized the word as her dark eyebrows arched skyward.

The maid bobbed a brief curtsey. "Your pardon, Mademoiselle." She corrected. "I meant no offense, but I am afraid."

Deirdre drew in a deep breath and blew it out slowly. Then she smoothed her hands over her hair and down along her voluptuous figure as though the very act of stroking herself were satisfying.

"There is nothing to be afraid of, Colette. This woman has caused me all the trouble she ever will. I am seeing to it that she causes no further harm. You can understand that, can't you?"

"*Oui,* Mademoiselle, but what will Mr.—"

"Don't worry about Mr. Richard and don't worry about the doctor or anyone else who pops into your head to worry about." Deirdre's tone rose as she spoke. She stopped and rubbed her temples for a moment. Colette watched her mistress and chewed her lip.

"I am in charge. You know that. I'm always in charge. It's always up to me."

"*Oui.*" Colette bobbed again and her gaze no longer met Nora's.

"Then pray, do not argue with me further." Deirdre rubbed her temples again. "Dick will more than understand when I explain everything to him. I know he will. He always has and he wouldn't want me to suffer. Not after all I've done for him."

Her voice trailed away at the end as though she were so completely lost in her own thoughts she had forgotten where she was and what she was about.

Fear trailed Nora's spine again. There was something very wrong with Deirdre Johnson. Something in her mind. And that was far more unsettling than anything else that had happened so far, which was saying something indeed.

Nora closed her eyes, blotting out the sight of Deirdre Johnson and her maid, wishing for just a moment that she could slip back into blessed un-

consciousness and wake to find herself snuggled safe
in the bed with Jake beside her.

Dear heaven, Jake. Would he have any idea what
had happened to her? Would anyone?

The thought choked a sob from her. She gagged
on the scarf again. She had never felt so helpless,
so useless, in her life. To be trussed up like a parcel
waiting to see what Deirdre would do with her.
Would she kill her outright? Keep her a prisoner
and demand a ransom from Grandmother?

But in the pit of her stomach Nora knew what
fate Deirdre had planned for her. She was going
to disappear like the girls in Jake's report. Like the
Hawkins girls. She was going to be sold and no one
would have any idea where to look for her because,
for the second time, the information was just going
to disappear.

Why had she given in to impulse and stopped to
read the report there in public? Why had she let her
curiosity get the better of her instead of waiting to
read it at the clinic, to hand it to Jake and let him
handle it as he had asked her?

So much for being able to take care of herself and
being able to make it through life on her own. The
faces of her family swam through her head. Mama.
Papa. Maggie. Grandmother. Jake.

Tears burned hot on her cheeks.

"Mademoiselle, she is crying."

The soft sympathy in Colette's tone brought her
back to herself. She caught back the rising hysteria of
her own self-pity and fought to bring herself under
control. Losing herself would not help the situation.

"I don't care if she is crying." Deirdre said in a
tone that questioned Colette's sanity in even pointing the fact out. "Let her bawl. I need my drops."

She stalked from the room, slamming the door behind her.

Colette stared at the door for a moment and then turned back to Nora.

"I am sorry, Mademoiselle. She is not herself when she is like this." The maid shook her head sadly and cast another glance at the door.

She knelt at Nora's side and touched the scarf muffling Lenore's mouth. "I will remove this, but you must remain silent or she will know and . . . that would not be so good. You understand?"

The maid's dark gaze met hers and Nora nodded, willing to agree to anything in order to have the use of her mouth again. To truly breathe again.

"Bon." After darting another quick glance at the closed door, the maid tugged the wet silk out of Nora's mouth.

Nora drew a deep breath. She longed to beg Colette to release her, but sensed whatever bonds held the maid to her mistress would not be easily broken. Even by the dark dealings Deirdre engaged in.

She prayed she had not already reached the boundaries of what Colette might be willing to do to help her.

"Thank you." She croaked out the words and then swallowed trying to moisten her mouth. "I will be as quiet as I can. Do you have any idea why I am here?"

The maid shook her head. "No, but it does not matter. She will do as she wishes. As she says, she always has."

That sounded almost like a pronouncement of death. Nora swallowed again and forced herself to keep panic at bay.

"What do you mean?"

"Mademoiselle Brownley, my mistress has been

through many . . . trials . . . in her life. They have wrought some . . . distress . . . in her. You see that, no?"

Nora managed a nod, seeing far more than she wanted to see.

"That is why we come here. To what is familiar to her. It is Mr. Richard's idea of what will make her happy and keep her . . . settled."

"Sometimes we think it is working." She glanced toward the door yet again and sighed. "And others we do not."

"But—"

Colette shook her head again. "That is all I can tell you, Mademoiselle. I cannot explain her to you. I cannot explain her to myself. But she has always been good to me even when there was no one else."

"Will you come back?"

Colette stood and shrugged. Nora realized she couldn't face the prospect of the maid's retreat. She still didn't know where she was or what was happening.

"Please, where am I?"

"You are in our home." Colette answered simply as she reached for the doorknob. "Rest now. When Mr. Richard comes, things will change."

With that she swept out the door without a backward glance and Nora was left with nothing but her own rising fears. She blew out several deep breaths and struggled for calm. Deirdre had abducted her in the clear light of day in the middle of town. Surely someone had seen them. Surely.

The darkened confines of the small pathway between the two buildings where Deirdre had gone with the envelope played through Nora's mind. She shuddered, feeling again the hot pain as Deirdre hit her and the rush of the ground coming up to meet her. How long had she been lost to the world? She tried to gauge the time from the late sun shining in the windows. Afternoon? But how late? Surely Jake would have arrived at the clinic by now? Would anyone be able to tell him she had gone for the post? Would he go and look for her? Or would he be too caught up in his preparations for his patients?

Jake glanced at the clock for the fourth time in the past twenty minutes. Each time had been just a bit more unsettling than the last.

Where was Nora?

It was unlike her to not be in the clinic on time. And she had come to town early. She had gotten his files and supplies ready. And then she had disappeared. Wherever she was, he didn't like it. He had the troublesome feeling that something was wrong. But what?

He realized he was pacing like a caged animal and forced himself to stop. Nora was resilient and capable. More than likely she was visiting someone in town. She had become so much a part of his life here. He smiled at the thought, no longer able to picture his life without her. And that was the frustration.

She had come to the clinic early. He had managed to get here earlier than expected. He wanted to talk with her. It would have been their first time alone since Sylvia and his father returned from their trip to Portland.

He needed to see her, to hold her. He needed to tell her all the things that had been pent up inside him for the past few days. All the things he had realized and he hoped she would have realized as well.

"Nora, where are you?"

The door opened behind him and he blew out a breath of relief. "I'm so glad you're here."

The greeting died away on his lips as he turned to face Dick Moore.

"Why, thank you." Moore nodded cordially though puzzlement knit his brows. "I'm happy to be here, though truly I didn't expect that kind of warmth in your greeting. I was looking for Deirdre, have you seen her?"

"No, I have not."

"Ah, well, then. Where is Miss Brownley today?"

"I don't know. I was expecting her when you came in just now."

"Hence, the warmth of the greeting." Moore smiled again. "I don't blame you, Doctor. She is quite charming."

"Yes." Jake wanted to throttle the man. Especially after how close he had come to manhandling her after going with her to the Hawkins's place.

Hawkins House. Could she have defied him yet again and gone there on her own?

Moore took a few steps farther into the clinic and tapped his fingers against the counter where Nora had organized Jake's files. "Are you sure you haven't seen Deirdre? I know she intended to bring you the post and to speak with you about her headaches. They've been increasing of late. I am concerned about her. And you mentioned some new information."

"Ah, I should be happy to see her, but the post is not here and I've seen neither Nora nor Deirdre in the past thirty minutes." Frustration edged his tone despite himself. "Perhaps they are together."

Moore laughed, but tension underscored the sound. "Somehow I doubt that. Deirdre is not always . . . comfortable . . . in the company of other women."

A fact Jake had already noted.

The door opened again. Again it was not Nora but a boy from the general store. "What is it, Matt?"

"Pop Tucker sent me over with this. He said Miss Nora must've dropped it when she went out after Miss Deirdre."

The envelope in the boy's hand was slightly crumpled and already torn open. The sight shifted the unease he'd been battling to a higher plane.

"Thanks, Matt." He accepted the envelope from the boy's fingers. "How long ago was Miss Nora there for the post?"

"Oh, I don't know, Doc. Maybe an hour ago. Maybe two."

The timing heightened his anxiety still further.

"How odd." Moore looked at the envelope. "Do you know where they went?"

"No, sir. Miss Deirdre came in and said some stuff to Miss Nora and then she laughed and they went out together."

"Together?" Moore's question seemed to have more purpose than appeared normal even given the women they both sought.

"Well yeah, Miss Deirdre left and then Miss Nora scooped up all of the post and hurried out after her. After that they borrowed my cart, but I thought they would be back here by now."

"Your cart?"

"Yes. Miss Deirdre said there was something she and Miss Nora had to fetch and then they would be back here together. I'm gonna catch hell for letting them take the cart. Pop's got deliveries for me to make."

"We'll make sure you get the cart back, son." Moore's gaze locked with Jake's and something in the man's eyes sent a wave of concern down Jake's spine.

"Thanks, Matt." Jake said again and the boy disappeared back out the door.

"What is it?" he asked as the soon as the door shut behind Matt.

"I'd suggest we go to my house. Immediately. And pray they are still there." Moore turned on his heel.

"Why?"

"Because my sister is not always herself, Doctor Warren. Surely you are aware of that. You are a medical man."

Jake gritted his teeth. If only being a doctor could make him as all-knowing and all-powerful as others seemed to think. "That doesn't mean I'm omniscient, man. What are you trying to tell me?"

Moore turned back toward him. Tension rode his face and fear sparked in his eyes. "I'm telling you Deirdre is unstable. And if she has taken Nora somewhere then it can't be good. Deirdre does not seek the company of other women. Ever."

"Surely—"

"My sister is slowly going mad, Doctor. She was diagnosed with syphilis some time ago. An occupational hazard. I brought her home to help quell some of the demons in her mind. It helped for a while, but things have gotten much, much worse of late."

His tone sent the unease inside Jake tumbling into a dark well of fear. Questions writhed inside him. If this was her diagnosis why hadn't Moore come to him in the first place? Why had he not restrained her? The symptoms were classic, and he'd only just begun to suspect following the consultation he'd mentioned from the past week.

"Let's go."

Nothing mattered at the moment but Nora. Wherever she was, she couldn't possibly know what kind of danger she might be in.

Nora tugged at the bonds holding her hands together again. Her wrists had begun to burn. She was quite sure she'd scraped them raw in her efforts to break free, but she couldn't just sit here. And wait for . . . whatever Deirdre intended to do with her.

The whole situation was ludicrous. Abducting her in the heart of Somerset in the middle of the day, trussing her up like a parcel awaiting shipment, and then leaving her here like yesterday's post.

The door opened without warning and Nora ceased her struggling as the object of her thoughts entered the room in a cloud of floral scent.

"I've decided what to do with you," Deirdre told her with far more warmth than she had spoken previously. She didn't even seem to notice the missing gag. "I'll send you off just like the other girls and you'll learn your lessons just as they did. It will truly be delicious. Then the dear Doctor will cease looking at you like a moon-struck calf."

"The other girls?" Her heart sank. It was as she feared. Deirdre was planning to send her far away where no one would know where to look.

"Of course. Well, you knew, didn't you? You read that horrid letter." Puzzlement mantled Deirdre's brow for a moment. "Where is that horrid letter? Colette? Find it and burn it, will you? The last time I burned a report the house went as well."

"The house? You burned down Jake's father's house?" Another stunning revelation. It was too much to comprehend. No wonder Deirdre needed her drops. "You almost killed them!"

Deirdre laughed. "Well, they aren't dead, are they? They are living with you. How cozy for you and your grandmother. You get to have your lovers under your roof with just the right patina of charity to make it acceptable."

How could Deirdre know? Or was she only repeating idle gossip? It hardly seemed worth worrying about right now.

"It was an accident." Deirdre was still talking about the fire at the Warren house. "I couldn't let them know my secret. I couldn't let anyone know. Besides it was Hawkins's fault. He is such an oaf."

"So Hawkins is working with you?" Did she have any idea what she was saying? Of course she did. Deirdre had told her maid it was Hawkins who had hit her in the alley. And she'd greeted him. Nora shivered, remembering the menace she'd felt near his house. Had he been watching her?

Deirdre laughed, the sound high-pitched and off-key. "Not with me, for me, silly. I'll send you off just like the other girls. That will be fun."

"For whom?"

"Well, not for you, of course. Although you may begin to like it after a time. I know I did." She smiled, her gaze distant as though she had drifted away. She ran her hands over her body again, from the full swell of her breasts and downward. "I liked it quite a bit there for a time."

Her gaze sharpened again and she leaned down toward Nora. "But to begin with you won't like it at all. All those men, pawing at you and enjoying you. And they will, you know. It won't matter if you don't like it. They will enjoy it all the more."

Nausea twisted in Nora's stomach again. "You would send me to a—"

"Brothel." Deirdre pronounced the word with visible relish. "Yes, you can say it. That's where you'll begin. Where they all begin, even me. And if you go on from there, well that's your choice."

Despite her own fears, horror rose inside Nora. Deirdre had been sending those innocent girls into a life of debauchery. A life the Hawkins House was supposed to be saving them from. How many? Oh, how many of the mill girls had been turned into whores at the hands of Deirdre Johnson?

"Hating it yourself, how could you do that to others?"

"I told you, you'll get used to it. If you play your cards right you can make a lot of money too." Deirdre smile, warm and friendly. "It's a way out. An escape they wouldn't otherwise have. I know it was for me. For Dick."

"For Richard?"

"Of course. Oh, he didn't want me to do it at first, any more than I wanted to. He used to hold me all night when I was finished and promise to make it up to me. Dear, sweet, Dickie. But he knew it had to be done. It was the only way for us to be free. To be safe. And it worked. It worked for us. It will work for them. And for you as well." She paused a moment to study Nora and tuck a few loose strands of hair back from her face. "Although I really don't care if it works for you. You have become a nuisance. I actually hope you stay a whore for the rest of your life."

She knelt down and cupped Nora's face in her hands, stroking her thumbs over Nora's cheeks very gently. "Don't fret. It won't matter for you if it happens once or a dozen or a hundred times. He won't want you afterward and that is all that counts. Maybe I'll have Dickie take you first. Yes, that would be the least I could offer him. He can break you in a little and then we'll send you on together."

"Deirdre, please—"

"Shhh, it won't matter." Deirdre brushed her fingers across Nora's lips and then downward, tugging at the buttons on her bodice to pull them open one by one.

"What are you doing?"

"Getting you ready. Dick should be back soon. I want him to enjoy the present I have for him."

"No!"

"Shh." Deirdre finished with the buttons and then undid the chemise beneath and pulled the edges apart. Cool air tightened Nora's nipples.

"That's better. Dick will like this. He has a fondness for you." She brushed her fingers lightly over Nora's breasts.

Nausea swirled hot and awful in Nora's stomach. She moaned, sickened by the situation and frightened to the core. Deirdre's low chuckle echoed through her. Then she released her and gave vent to another bought of wild laughter.

"Now you're ready. If you keep moaning like that, I think you'll do very well at your new profession my dear."

Nora shivered in revulsion, wondering if this were a familiar pattern. Her mind recoiled at the image of young Callie or Lizzie subjected to this same kind of treatment, night after night. With strangers. That was the life Deirdre had lived, the life she herself was facing.

"Yes, I'm quite certain Dickie will enjoy being the

first. Or the second, if you've already given yourself to the good doctor."

"Deirdre!"

"Dick!" Deirdre turned in a swirl of skirts.

A hot knife of fear stabbed Nora. Please, no, please, this can't be happening. Even as the thought ran through her mind she saw Jake over Richard Moore's shoulder. Her heart leapt. He pushed past Richard, doffing his jacket as he approached her. He pulled her into his arms and sheltered her within the confines of his jacket. She'd never felt so safe or so loved in her life. And he'd yet to speak so much as a word.

His hands stroked her back and found the twine binding her hands. He made short work of it, freely her to return his embrace.

"But Dick, she was for you." Deirdre wailed, sounding much like a petulant child despite the malice of her intentions.

"Oh, Deirdre."

From the safe confines of Jake's arms Nora could see Richard Moore's face. Sad and resolute, he pulled his sister into his arms. "Darling, darling Deirdre."

"I wanted her for you. For you." Deirdre had begun to cry against his shoulder. "And the doctor was for me."

"Yes, sweetheart. But we are better off together, aren't we, always?" Richard stroked his sister's back, the cadence of his words sounding as though he had repeated them many times. "We're together and it will be all right."

"Together." Deirdre repeated.

"Yes, sweetheart. Together, and I'll always take care of you."

"Always?"

"Always. Nothing will ever hurt you again. I promise."

"Oh, Dick." She hiccoughed against his shoulder and snuggled against him. Nora's heart twisted. The sight was both sad and poignant. Obviously Deirdre was quite mad and Richard knew. But Nora couldn't help the feeling that what Deirdre had told her about herself and Richard and their past was probably true.

A nightmare neither one of them had ever fully escaped.

"I'll take care of her from here, Doctor. I promise." Richard Moore's voice came thick and soft.

Jake's gaze locked with the other man's for a moment as he pulled Nora closer. He nodded.

"Let's go." He whispered as though trying not to break whatever spell Richard Moore had woven over his sister.

Nora was more than ready to comply. She retied her chemise and struggled with the buttons on her bodice, finally giving way to Jake's more capable fingers as he buttoned her back to rights. They were out the door and out of the house as quickly as her shaking limbs would allow. The sun had begun its dip toward the horizon and the cool breeze of the evening had begun.

"Jake, the girls—"

"I know." His jaw was tight. "I read the letter Deirdre must have dropped when she attacked you. And although he claims he had no idea, Moore was able to fill in the gaps."

"Oh, Jake."

"We'll be able to stop this now, Nora. Now that we know where the girls have been sent, we should be able to help them."

He shook his head and glanced up toward the

room where they'd left Deirdre and Richard. "There isn't much that can be done for Deirdre though. Not if what her brother tells me about her illness is true."

"Hawkins was in on it, too," she whispered struggling to escape the horror of what had almost happened. Of what had happened to Deirdre and the other girls.

Despite her fears of the past few hours, Nora couldn't help but feel sorrow for her. Whatever hell existed in Deirdre's mind wasn't pretty.

"Are you all right?" His fingers brushed her cheek and tipped her chin up.

"Yes." She told him, meaning it. "I was never so happy to see you as I was just now."

"Nor I, you." He told her softly. "You mean more to me than my life, Nora Brownley." He bent toward her and pressed his mouth very gently to hers. "I love you."

"That works out very well then, Doctor Warren, for I love you, too." Her heart felt big enough to encompass the world.

"Marry me, Nora."

"Why, Doctor, I thought you'd never ask."

He smiled at her then and the breeze lifted a stray lock of hair from his forehead. And Lenore knew their life would not be parties or social engagements. There would dirt and grime and real life to deal with.

And she couldn't have asked for more.

Epilogue

Nora smoothed her hands over her pale blue satin gown and tried to still her trembling fingers by running them across the gathers of her skirt. To little avail.

Today, she and Jake were to wed.

As she looked out over Grandmother's property she couldn't help thinking about how much had changed in the time she'd spent here and how much was still the same.

She took a deep breath, letting fresh air ripe with evergreen and the salty tang of the sea fill her lungs as her gaze drifted over the pine trees and brush clinging to the rough-hewn rocky bluffs surrounding the cove. Sunlight sparkled on the water in the distance. Gulls dipped and swirled over the water, riding a sea breeze that nipped her cheeks and nose with the first hints of autumn. A ripple of nervous anticipation swirled through her again and she clutched her fingers together.

They were almost ready to leave Grandmother's cottage for Somerset and the church. Soon all eyes would be on her, but the only gaze that mattered to her was Jake's. Despite assurances to the contrary she couldn't help wondering if he really understood what he was about to do.

Did he know what he was getting into?

She nibbled her lip and reached her hand up to toy with the diamond necklace Grandmother had given her and then to make sure her hair was still held in the sleek chignon she'd only had to pin a half-dozen times this morning.

"Your hair looks perfect, Nora, as always." Her sister, Maggie, joined her at the rail and slipped an arm around her waist. "You have no idea how I envy you."

Nora pulled back and looked at her sister in amazement. "What are you talking about, Maggie? You have beautiful hair. I've always wanted curls like yours."

"But yours always does exactly what you want and looks gorgeous no matter how you style it."

"And you don't have to style yours at all and it still looks lovely."

They looked at each other for another moment and burst into laughter. They'd shared a lot of laughter recently. It felt so good to have her sister back again.

"Well, that is a enchanting sound on such an important morning." Grandmother Worth stood in the doorway, resplendent in watered gray silk with burgundy piping. "You both look charming."

"Thank you, Grandmother. As do you." Maggie offered a quick curtsey and Grandmother chuckled. "My only surprise is that Mother didn't arrive to outdo us all and give her acerbic comments on the upcoming nuptials."

"Really." Grandmother's smile widened. "Well, you needn't concern yourselves on that account. The bank draft and strict travel instructions I sent Alberta two weeks ago ought to keep her happy and distant for some time. She and William should be at sea heading for Milan as we speak."

"Grandmother—"

"Oh, you didn't."

Arms around each other's waist, Lenore and Maggie dissolved into giggles again.

"I most certainly did. This should be a perfect day for all concerned." Grandmother nodded for emphasis. "I never take chances with the things I truly want. Now, Dan Butler and Kate have gone ahead of us. Devin is bringing the landaulet around so we can be off. You both need to fetch your wraps."

Sure enough Maggie's handsome husband rounded the corner of the cottage with Grandmother's traveling coach. He pulled the horses to a stop and jumped down to execute an elaborate bow. "Your carriage awaits, my ladies."

"I'll get the shawls and we'll be all set," Maggie said as she scooted past Grandmother, brushing a kiss against the older woman's cheek. "You both make exquisite brides."

Grandmother smiled after Maggie for a moment and then turned her attention to Lenore. She took a deep breath and blew it out slowly. "It is a fine day for a wedding."

"Even finer for two of them," Lenore returned.

"Indeed. So it is."

Devin busied himself with checking the harness fittings as he spoke to the horses.

"If only everyone could have such happy endings," Lenore fingered her necklace again.

"Well, I'm glad you youngsters were able to settle matters with the young ladies Mr. and Mrs. Hawkins had been so mishandling. Elmira Gallagher is as happy as a mother hen with her new charges."

Grandmother looked pensively at the cove, but
Lenore knew her gaze was focused elsewhere. She
slipped her arm around her grandmother's shoulder.

"It is a mercy her mama did not live to see poor
Deirdre's plight, I am sorry to say." Grandmother
sighed.

"You have done so much to fix things, Grandmother. To stand by her despite everything. And
think how many of the missing girls have been
found already." As pitiful as Deirdre's medical con-
dition made her, Nora was more concerned with the
recovery of the girls who might one day suffer a sim-
ilar fate if they were not found.

"I know, darling. Richard's search has been very
productive." Grandmother patted her hand. "And
I've given him the money he needed to see his sister
properly cared for. She will have every comfort avail-
able to her in the time she still has."

Grandmother turned her gaze back to Lenore.
"Now, today is not for sorrow. I merely meant to tell
you how proud I am of you. You came here searching
for your life, my dear Lenore. Have you found it?"

"Yes." The smile she gave her grandmother felt
wide enough to encompass the world itself. "Oh,
most definitely yes."

Grandmother brushed a quick kiss to her cheek,
engulfing Lenore in a soft scent of lavender. "Then
all is right with the world."

Maggie rejoined them with the shawls and a few
minutes later they were settled in the capacious seats
of the carriage and on their way. Nervous tension
tightened inside Lenore again.

"Lenore, dear, you are allowed to smile," Grandmother observed in a teasing tone as one eyebrow
arched upward. "This should be the happiest of

days. Not one for sighs and the nervous chewing of lips."

Lenore stopped immediately. "Aren't you the least bit nervous, Grandmother?"

"Nervous? Nonsense. Jitters are self-indulgent at best, and delusions at worst."

"Grandmother—"

"The time for nerves was back before you made your decision, child, not after." Grandmother's sharp tone was belied by the hand she sent questing after the correctness of her own hairstyle, until she caught Maggie's amused gaze.

Grandmother cleared her throat and settled both hands back in her lap. "If ever two gentlemen were gaining the best part of their lives it is the two we join at the church today."

Nora smiled. Grandmother was right. For the first time in her life Lenore could hold her head high with pride in her own accomplishments and not just how attractive she appeared at table. She enjoyed the work she had taken on with the girls who worked at the mill. She could not imagine ever returning to a life filled with shopping, parties and purposeless amusements. And she would never regret anything that had passed between her and Jake.

The grief he carried over not being able to help his patients enough would always be a part of him, but after he'd allowed her to see his private agony and share it with him, she'd been able to show him how much good he did despite the limitations of modern medicine. She could almost see the light that sparkled in his eyes when she looked up to find his gaze fixed on her, even from across a room. She thought of how reverently and passionately he had loved her that one night. Tasted the promise of a lifetime of such nights in his kisses ever since. She knew he loved her. He needed her.

And she needed him. She smiled again and nodded to herself.

Grandmother reached over and squeezed her hands. "We will take the happiness today offers and for all the todays ahead. There is nothing to be nervous about."

"Except tripping on the hem of your gown as you walk down the aisle," Maggie interjected with a giggle.

Grandmother raised a quelling brow. "I see Jacob has been speaking out of turn."

Lenore smiled. Her nerves had vanished and now her fingers trembled with anticipation. Love and sharing life each day would carry them through to the next.

They arrived at the church and Devin handed them down from the landaulet. He seemed to take extra care with his wife, his hands lingering on her waist and his eyes glowing as he looked at her. Lenore hoped she and Jake would be as happy in their marriage as her sister and brother-in-law were in theirs.

"Did you tell them?" Devin's deep green eyes sparkled in the sunlight.

"Not yet. This day is for them," she smiled up at her handsome Irishman.

"Well, you may as well tell us now or we'll be distracted by curiosity throughout the ceremony." Grandmother's expression held no censure.

"It's a good thing our house is going to be ready before winter . . ." Soft spots of color pinked Maggie's cheeks as she looked first at them and then up at her husband.

"Because Maggie is going to make me a father in early spring." Devin finished with pride as his hand slipped around his wife's waist and he looked deep into her eyes.

A baby?

"How wonderful." Nora gave her sister a gentle hug. "And here I thought love was making you so radiant since your return."

"It has." Maggie whispered as she accepted their grandmother's congratulations. "I am so happy you will be here, too, Nora. And not just because that means there will be a doctor living just next door."

"Everybody's waiting, Miss Nora," Callie poked her head out of the church doors and interrupted them. "Can I tell Mrs. Gallagher you're ready so she can begin playing?"

"Go ahead, child," Grandmother instructed.

The music started a moment later. Maggie walked up the steps first while Devin took Nora and Grandmother on each arm to escort them to the front of the church.

They entered and it looked as if all of Somerset had turned out for the double wedding. The Gallagher Girls, as they were now known, sat in the back looking like a pastel bouquet in their new gowns and bonnets. They turned and waved, whispering and smiling to one another. Kyle and Rachel Jenks jumped up together from their mother's lap to get a better look at the two brides. Mr. Connor snoozed quietly in a corner. Mrs. Pruitt and Kate nodded with pride from the front pew.

But the only one Nora paid any real attention to was Jake, standing tall and proud beside his father at the front of the church. His eyes were shining and a soft smile lifted one corner of his mouth. Her heart jumped and she had to remind herself to breathe. He was so handsome.

"Mine," he mouthed toward her. She smiled and mouthed the same.

Devin squeezed her hand in his arm. "Ready?" he asked.

She and Grandmother both nodded and they moved forward to meet their grooms.

Nora's hand slipped into Jake's as the rest of the world faded to a blur around them and the minister began the ceremony. She would take the happiness today offered and for all the todays ahead with no regrets.

"I love you, Nora Brownley," Jake whispered later as he bent to seal their vows before God and man.

"That's Mrs. Warren," she corrected softly and felt him smile against her lips.

Historical Romance from
Jo Ann Ferguson

__**Christmas Bride**	0-8217-6760-7	**\$4.99US/\$6.99CAN**
__**His Lady Midnight**	0-8217-6863-8	**\$4.99US/\$6.99CAN**
__**A Guardian's Angel**	0-8217-7174-4	**\$4.99US/\$6.99CAN**
__**His Unexpected Bride**	0-8217-7175-2	**\$4.99US/\$6.99CAN**
__**A Sister's Quest**	0-8217-6788-7	**\$5.50US/\$7.50CAN**
__**Moonlight on Water**	0-8217-7310-0	**\$5.99US/\$7.99CAN**

Call toll free **1-888-345-BOOK** to order by phone or use this coupon to order by mail, or order online at **www.kensingtonbooks.com**.

Name_____

Address _____

City _____State_____Zip _____

Please send me the books I have checked above.

I am enclosing $_____

Plus postage and handling* $_____

Sales Tax (in New York and Tennessee only) $_____

Total amount enclosed $_____

*Add $2.50 for the first book and $.50 for each additional book.

Send check or money order (no cash or CODs) to:

Kensington Publishing Corp., Dept. C.O., 850 Third Avenue, New York, NY 10022

Prices and numbers subject to change without notice. All orders subject to availability.

Visit our website at **www.kensingtonbooks.com**.

Put a Little Romance in Your Life With
Melanie George

__**Devil May Care**
0-8217-7008-X $5.99US/$7.99CAN

__**Handsome Devil**
0-8217-7009-8 $5.99US/$7.99CAN

__**Devil's Due**
0-8217-7010-1 $5.99US/$7.99CAN

__**The Mating Game**
0-8217-7120-5 $5.99US/$7.99CAN
